The Final Resting Place of a Butterfly

Elizabeth Redmond

Acknowledgement

No one tells you this is the hardest part to write.

Dad. I made you a promise. I know the joy you would feel to have lived to see this. Thank you for being the most wonderful father a person could be gifted.

Sean, my love. The very first person to have read this work.

The first person who said, "You have something here. You need to do this."

Your belief in me has been monumental; your love and support are humbling, and honestly, I cannot express what you mean to me. The words do not exist.

A massive, special thank you to the following beta readers and cheerleaders:

Darragh Jennings & Betsy Speer for priceless feedback. Helena and Bea, for listening to all things book-related over the years and for so much encouragement.

Thank you to my very patient editor. Thank you to friends over my life who have insisted, "you should be writing."

And most importantly, this is dedicated to Aidan and Natalie.

Everything is always for you.

Table of Contents

Prologue

A night in the middle of the Mexican Revolution.

The darkness was not of a swallowing sort but illuminating.

As with the moonlight, she could see everything in the room as if it glowed, lit from within.

She looked at the two of them piled into one bed like little hibernating animals in the embrace of warmth. Despite having splendid bedrooms of their own, they always wound up in their mother's bed. In the stillness, they looked for just a moment like the poor agrarian children of Mexico. Huddled together, limbs intertwined, asleep in a world where they did not feel the burning of their mother's eyes upon their skin.

Her breath became ever shallower as tears moved down her face and stole into her mouth; they too, were hiding.

To wake them would be cruelty.

She knew she had waited as long as she could, and this was now the moment that she had to turn away from them.

She heard the baby in the hall beginning to fuss.

Bombs went off on a not distant enough street, counting down their departure.

For a moment, she was tempted to abort every part of this plan and, throw herself on her children and beg God's mercy. Her quickening heart crawling into her throat screamed at her to beg for their forgiveness and for His - to be ready to die to be with them.

Except that she knew if she did this, she would not be the only one whose throat would be slit or whose skull would be taken off with the blast of whatever pistola would be most handy on this street on this night.

Without a word and with seemingly no oxygen in her lungs, unable to feel her legs, she turned her back on her small children, opened the door, and left them.

She left them.

Chapter 1

Manhattan, March 1912

"The timing is terribly unfortunate."

Esther clucked and handed her employer the highball glass with bicarbonate of soda.

"Now, don't add the water until you are ready for the reaction- take it with you and drink it there."

"If Ed comes looking for me-"

"I will handle the good doctor. Don't worry, I will come find you."

"This had to happen tonight."

Amanda sighed as she turned away from the back door of her kitchen.

There were so many important people, all beautifully dressed, milling about their home. She really had no time for this, she thought, exasperated.

The air was heavy with expensive perfume and easy laughter, and the gathering itself emitted a sort of white noise. The place was positively buzzing, a hive of the elite.

She hoped she had not drawn attention to herself. Esther told her this should settle her stomach, but Amanda Tappan knew by now that all too familiar feeling. She knew like her own name the sick that bubbled up simultaneously in the stomach and the throat and then sat there like a brick of bile. This first appearance of the condition, which had become a faded memory, left her disappointed.

She was hoping to skip that part this time around.

She had felt increasing dread as the night, and her stomach raged on. More than anything, she did not want any hiccups to ruin this night as it was so important to Edward, but she felt as if she'd faint if she didn't at least splash cold water on her face.

She scurried down the marbled hallways, ducking into the back hall, certain she wouldn't make it and would vomit into the large potted plant between the front foyer and the guest water closet, but she made it in and closed the door right on time.

She had managed to keep it down. The quartet playing in the lounge would surely drown out any noise she made now as she stood facing the commode. The tiles were cool upon her back as she pressed against them for a moment before lurching forward, gagging, choking, nothing coming up.

She knew one of Esther's magical remedies would help, so giving in, she added water from the sink to the bicarbonate and watched it bubble and fizz angrily in the highball glass.

Relieved to be alone, she wondered if what she was feeling was partly nerves. She was covered in a mist of cold sweat; certain she must look as sick as she felt- pale, with dark shadows under her eyes. She held her breath in an attempt to hold her dinner down. She would only have a few moments before he would notice her not playing hostess.

She gulped the salty concoction down just as a knock found the door, startling her.

"It's Esther," came the whisper through the door.

Amanda had managed to cultivate a reputation in these circles for being a wonderful hostess, even if most people did not realize how shy she truly was. She hated having to entertain strangers but was so naturally good at it that people were drawn to her.

She unlocked the door and let her housekeeper in.

"Is anyone looking for me?"

"No, no, you're fine. Dr. Tappan has had a fair amount to drink, and he is surrounded by people giving one of his speeches."

"My husband seems to have the nose of a blood hound for when I'm not in the room."

If Edward went looking for her and she was gone too long, she would hear about it. This added an urgency to her actions.

She simply did not have the energy for one of his interrogations.

"Hurry up.", she hissed at herself, contemplating the vile possibility of putting a finger down her throat.

"Give the bicarb a minute to work, Mrs. If you're ill and it's food-related, you will most certainly have it come up. I swear by it."

"It's exhausting. Edward always wants me on, like a lamp, glowing for everyone's enjoyment."

She took deep breaths, trying to settle her treacherous stomach.

"Is it your nerves again, Mrs. Are you upset?"

"No, nothing like that.", she lied.

"I feel I have finally learned how to play the game that is New York, just as we are getting ready to leave it. Oddly, I was enjoying myself tonight until this started."

She had learned to sit quietly as a church mouse at her husband's dinners for however long she could get away with it until prodded into conversation. With a small smile playing on her lips and a distant look in her eyes that said she did not want to be engaged in conversation. She often had a look that Ed called "away with the fairies" - all the while, she was listening intently to every word.

Often, she was following more than one conversation at a time, taking it all in and logging the details for consumption later. Cataloguing who the most intelligent, insufferable, or sneaky were at the table. Although she found most of her peers to be silly and Ed's pals boring, droning on only about themselves, she had to find ways to keep herself entertained at these gatherings. She did so by making mental notes that would surprise her husband when she would mention them after the fact.

"I don't know Mrs.," Esther said gently,

"I'm sure you are well bored of it, but I wish I had your society life. I can be quite shy and awkward, and you're so popular without even trying."

"Ed says it's my sweet decorum that everyone is so keen on. At a time when American women are all too eager to serve their audience a helping of their opinions, it is appreciated that I stay silent. Hence my likeability." she said, rolling her eyes.

"I don't make waves."

Young, modern, American women were changing, everyone knew. Edward and his young wife both knew that he would never allow that in his own house. Obedience was the order of the day.

Amanda had an inviting face with large eyes and a smiling,

welcoming nature. She knew Esther was right; everyone seemed fond of her everywhere she went. Even those people who could not stand Edward lit up at seeing his lovely bride. She did not enjoy attention like her social butterfly husband. Most of the time, she also did not care much for the company.

The outside air she let in opening the small bathroom window was crisp and freezing, threatening snow. It was a needed relief against her face. Her pounding heart began to slow as she took deep breaths.

"Is it snowing yet? Oh my Mrs. Tappan, you will catch your death!"

"No, it feels good." she kept inhaling with a small shiver.

Esther tried to give orders to her mistress and often Amanda listened to her, even though they were the same age. The woman of the house found it endearing.

"I think I would like to lie down in the bath for the rest of the night and count these little blue damask tiles on the wall."

"If you're that ill, Mrs. I should inform Dr. Tappan, and surely, he will understand you need your bed."

Worry crept onto the diminutive brunette's face. Common sense would say Amanda would be in the right telling her doctor husband she was unwell.

"No, I will be fine, honestly. My stomach is even quieter now after drinking that. Tonight just feels different, and I don't want to miss out, for once."

Amanda was almost enjoying herself, even though the place was packed, and the room temperature was rising. She was enjoying answering the questions about their future, perhaps because she knew this was the last time she would ever have to endure them. In a few days, they would be packed and gone. She didn't want to end up stuck in the bathroom, feeling like she was failing her obligations to Edward, who would eventually notice and become cranky in her absence. She wanted to be out among the hordes of those silly, rich folks. It was a going away party and she was enjoying bidding them goodbye.

These constant soirees were not only expected by her husband, but the top tiers of society demanded them, and you were not allowed to disappoint. People wanted an excuse to see and be seen, and whether she liked it or not, rubbing elbows was a prerequisite of her married life.

'Good riddance to this place,' she thought, taking deep and slow breaths, hoping this feeling would just pass.

Being married to Edward came with a certain amount of notoriety. He was a Harvard doctor and pioneer in the new field of cardiology. Most people in passing conversation did not realize that his work included actual surgeries on the heart, the subject of which often left others aghast to hear him discuss it.

"You mean to tell me they *cut* on the patient's heart?" more than one bewildered housewife had asked Amanda with face aghast. Amanda loved seeing their reactions nearly as much as Edward loved boasting about his work.

His father had been an obstetrician, another Harvard alum, a fact that was never far from Edward's lips. Edward was becoming a very busy, important man, and so his young wife knew chaos was all part and parcel. She tried her best always to be accommodating and accept all the extra trimmings that came with this lifestyle, for she understood how fortunate she was.

She could have been born into a life like her sweet Esther. A housekeeper, now a widow, with no children and no marital prospects. She knew Esther would love to have a family, so she said nothing about the true cause of her illness. It wouldn't matter soon, as Esther would become just another memory, fading over time.

Amanda took pride that she was a good wife, but there were times she felt a blanket of expectations, heavy on top of her. As the years passed, the expectations grew more heavy and profound. There were days when seemingly small things bothered her to the point of agitation. She would feel her heart start to run away from her, her mouth going dry while her palms became wet. She would panic every now and then in, even in simple social settings. As wonderful and well-rounded as Amanda was, this little problem of hers frustrated her husband and herself. It was becoming a regular habit, and it needed to stop, he would remind her.

"You need to learn to control yourself." He would chastise her.

Ed often would remark she was a nervous little thing, usually through a thin smile to match his equally thin moustache. Though he attempted to make it sound like an endearing statement, she knew it was another complaint. Ed had shown, he thought, great patience with her over the years for these moods, which he assumed were typical of the fairer sex; however, hers were becoming quite disruptive.

"Although, I never saw my own mother behave this way.", he had mentioned more than once.

These idiosyncrasies of his wife's personality, how she could be so capable and solid one moment, and the next she was as flimsy as a paper doll on a windy day, drove him mad. He would try to tell himself that no one was perfect, even if perfection was a worthy goal. In his mind, she would be perfect, the epitome of a woman, if only for her occasional grating nonsense. The tears and the melancholy. She tried to hide it from him. He tried to make excuses for her. Depending on his mood tonight, there could be a great fallout from her being noticed absent because he would assume she was simply up to her old nonsense again. She had never had a breakdown in front of anyone outside the household, and it was Esther who seemed to understand these moments and give solace.

"You should go," she told the housekeeper.

"I don't want a search party organized for the two of us-"

All these concerns of disappointing her husband had riled her up, and mid-sentence led her to bend over on cue and project her dinner into the porcelain bowl of their very modern and expensive toilet. The bicarbonate of soda had indeed done the trick.

Esther looked away but then handed her a cloth and rubbed her back gently.

Tears lined Amanda's eyes. Times like these were when she missed her mother the most.

The close bond she had as a small child, the warmth from her parents, was hard not to miss even many years later. She thought about her parents often. Edward insisted that she needn't dwell on the past, as it was, "your insistence on being miserable that keeps these unpleasant moments popping up."

She felt suddenly vulnerable in front of her housekeeper, sniffing and approaching the sink to clean herself. She remembered the drunken coteries of the rich parading about her home.

"Thank you, Esther, if you see the Dr. looking for me, inform him I will be out of here in a moment. That will be all." She dismissed the girl too coolly; she was afraid, but it was done.

"Yes, Mrs. You need anything, I won't be far." Esther turned swiftly on her heel and shut the door behind her.

Amanda felt a twinge of sadness as she glanced up at her pale complexion in the mirror.

"Make up your mind, girl.", she said to her reflection.

No wonder she drove Ed mad at times.

It was the undercurrent in New York, the posturing and social climbing, the gossip and conniving that she never had any interest in. She found the elite behaved as if they were in an opera or a play. The melodramatics turned her off. In this way, she was vastly different from her peers. The ladies her age seemed children to her, gossiping and immature. They took joy in almost sinister and biting behaviour. Edward explained to her that she had been forced to grow up and that was one reason she felt at odds with her peers. Forced to grow up all too soon.

She had never been so happy as a child as with her parents, having dinner and spending time together. Her mother at the piano, teaching her scales, trying to sculpt her into a musician and Amanda failing terribly.

"Tomorrow, Mozart and Chopin, but today we will continue with scales." her mother would say with a wink.

"Do not worry if you make a mistake; this is how we learn in all things and one day, your fingers will know the music better than you do, and they will fly across the keys as if they belong to another."

Amanda never shared her mother's belief in her abilities or her musical talent, but the memory of those lessons played forever in her mind, a haunting echo of a happy pocket of time.

Amanda knew her melancholy came from wishing things to be different, from an absurd desire to change the past, to have had more time with them. She knew it was not acceptable or rational to feel these things, but it was a wound she feared would never heal.

When she held her first baby in her arms, she ached for her mother to hold him too. That yearning for her parents never abated, in fact seemed only to grow more powerful as she got older. While most ladies her age wanted the finer things that she was lucky enough to call her own, she simply wanted to replicate that close and loving atmosphere of her childhood. She did not crave luxury but desperately wanted a family and time with her consistently overworked husband. A simple life, something beautiful without being overly complicated, something to savour and reminisce about in her golden years. She wanted something nice to tell her grandchildren.

This would be their third child; she thought in amazement as she rinsed her mouth with the Odol mouth rinse, tucking its brown glass bottle back into the cabinet before smoothing out her emerald, sateen dress. She felt a bit better having gotten that over with and thought perhaps she would avoid food and drink for the rest of the night. Her previous pregnancies had gone well. Arthur in 1907 found her with barely a bother on her and then Amelia in 1909 had been an easy pregnancy as well. Her figure had been maintained, and she was healthy as a horse. A thoroughbred, no doubt, Edward would insist. She wondered how different it would be this time around in another country. It already felt different physically.

She turned to the side in front of the mirror and stood up tall, adjusting her posture and enjoying the reflection, copying her movements. That reflection would be changing yet again very soon.

She sighed, not feeling much better, but knew she must get back out there. She checked her teeth, pinched her cheeks, and threw herself back out into the crowd of waiting guests.

Chapter 2

"Amanda, darling",

Mrs. Heatherington wobblily approached her, covered in so much fur she resembled a giant, drunken chinchilla. She stunk of patchouli and had lipstick on her teeth, as usual.

Amanda often had to stop from recoiling when approached by the most pompous old hag in all of Manhattan. She feared a physical reaction would come across as rude as could be, and there was no greater sin in Amanda's mind than deliberate ugliness, even towards those she found loathsome. She hoped her annoyance could not be read on her face.

"Good evening Mrs. Heather-"

"Where have you been skulking off to, my dear? I have not had a chance to talk to you about this most exciting news."

Mrs. Heatherington was always interrupting. A most obnoxious habit, sometimes it was impossible to get a word out of one's mouth before this woman had stolen it.

"I still can't believe it!" chimed Eleanor Kelly, swooping in behind her mother.

Mrs. Heatherington's newly married eighteen-year-old daughter helped herself to another glass of champagne from the circulating trays bobbing by, flashing Amanda an inebriated smile and twirling around in her gold gown as if she were a show pony. Amanda suspected she would end up a perpetual drunkard like her mother, but at least she would be a nicer one, presumably.

"Hello, and congratulations again to the new Mrs. Kelly; so lovely to see you both," Amanda smiled out of obligation.

"Wasn't it such a lovely wedding?" purred Mrs. Heatherington.

"Indeed, the finest I've seen." Amanda obliged yet again.

Mrs. Heatherington had married late in life and was obsessed with her only daughter.

After years of solitude, a frumpy and lonely librarian from a middle-class and unknown family from Connecticut had her life turned asunder after she helped an equally lonely gentleman find some books on the Civil War one rainy Tuesday. How she accomplished this magic trick, no one knew, but she managed to charm a very lonely real estate developer who was eager to have children. All the sewing circles said she snagged that poor old widower just in time.

She struggled for years to become pregnant and then, at thirty-seven, lost twin boys- still birth. So, when she gave birth to Eleanor at forty years of age- all ten massive, healthy pounds of Eleanor, they were the talk of New York. Mrs. Heatherington then discovered - she quite liked being the talk of New York.

Mr. Heatherington was fifty-two when they finally had their daughter, and when Eleanor was just toddling around, he died suddenly one morning at breakfast, leaving the two women very alone and very wealthy. Mrs. Heatherington raised her daughter to be a favourite and trusted companion, and where one was found, the other was sure to follow. With nothing better to do with their time, they perfected their favourite hobby, aside from spending the old man's money - gossip. The two were often found perched one against the other like well-dressed yet still physically mismatched bookends.

Amanda often wondered if what she felt towards the women was jealousy. To envy was a sin, but if she was honest with herself, it rang true. They got under her skin in a way that felt shameful. Her own mother surely deserved to be with her daughter.

"I mean mother, isn't it just wild- Mexico! Of all places? Why, if I wasn't so utterly frightened at the thought, I'd be fascinated!" Eleanor tinkled with phony-sounding laughter.

"Well, when Eleanor told me, I simply couldn't believe it. Why leave a successful medical practice? I asked her. I said what on earth is Dr. Tappan thinking? But then I remembered Edward's mother is from Mexico- a European, certainly?" she asked Amanda with a look of concern that seemed exaggerated.

Amanda smiled, "Yes, although I never had the pleasure of meeting her, Edward's mother was Spanish-"

"Quite right. My own great, something was Spanish as well, from Madrid. They say we are Spanish nobility, and I don't doubt it. My family, we are very European. Mexico! Mexico just seems so – foreign!"

Mrs. Heatherington was adept at stating the obvious.

"I mean, sometimes I can't believe there is any sort of real world outside of New York City. I spent an afternoon in Poughkeepsie once, and I thought I was going to die."

She widened her eyes in exasperation, but it provided a near-comedic effect with her ridiculous statement.

"I can't imagine being out in the sticks of the United States, for example, but goodness- Mexico. Why on earth would old Edward want to leave New York? Nobody ever wants to leave New York! He must be on some very lucrative contracts."

She sniffed, eyeing Amanda's face for a reaction.

Amanda put her champagne to her lips to say nothing.

Spanish nobility, my foot, she thought.

"I wonder"- interrupted Eleanor, her already bulging eyes widening to massive orbs,

"You won't be out walking around alone in the- what is it called, with the, out there in the pyramids or something, no -the Amazon rain jungle- or forest? I mean, it's not actually a forest like we have in New York; it's the jungle, right?"

"The Amazon is actually in South America, mostly in Brazil.", Amanda corrected her, smiling, ever polite.

"Oh, I thought Mexico was certainly South America?"

Eleanor blinked at Amanda, confused, but continued drinking champagne, not bothered by the answer Amanda desperately wanted to give, the correction just behind her clenched teeth.

She never understood how certain women, especially of such wealth could be so blindly misinformed about their physical world and seemingly blasé about it. They had the time and resources to learn and yet often chose simply not to bother.

Amanda had been delighted, months earlier, to find a large globe in Mrs. Heatherington's sitting room. One of the only times she ventured over to the older woman's penthouse, lured by the appeal of a game of gin rummy, Amanda had been amazed the woman-owned anything educational.

She had been disappointed to find the globe came apart- the top portion of the globe opened on hinges and had inside of it: four bottles of booze. Gin, Rum, Vodka and Whiskey are all the finest labels. Upon further inspection, there were no names or geographical information on the countries on the fake globe, and she found Australia was almost certainly painted upside down.

Based on that example alone, she reminded herself that she shouldn't have been surprised by these sorts of questions from the duo. They were, without a doubt, her least favourite of the neighbours in Hammersmith Tower. The six story Gothic building they'd lived in since after they were married was grey and forlorn from the outside, though elegant still. It had a very small elevator and an even tighter staircase. Amanda managed to become trapped with these two in some part of their building on an almost daily basis. She would not have minded them so much if they were not so intrusive, so daft, and always there. If Amanda bought a paper from Jimmy on the corner, those two appeared. If she came into the lobby with her bags of shopping, Henry the porter always jumping to her assistance, the other two were there. If she thought she had the elevator to herself and the operator, those two would end up boarding after her. One of the first apartment buildings in New York to have an elevator and Amanda was quite convinced those two must just ride up and down in it all day for fun. She would not miss these ladies at all. Mrs. Heatherington was proof of the ignorance of the elite. There were too many of those at the turn of the century in New York who refused to imagine life could have meaning or importance anywhere else. They looked down on anyone outside of Manhattan. On the contrary, Amanda knew she was the sort who imagined – relished the idea, in fact that life would be infinitely better anywhere else.

"I mean, Mrs. Tappan.",

Mrs. Heatherington continued somewhat mockingly,

"You have two small children you are taking to a whole new

country."

She shook her head and guzzled another drink.

"Mrs. Heatherington, I do understand, but the basic premise of these United States is people bringing their children to a whole new country."

"Yes, but darling, those people are fleeing war, poverty, not a fabulous life in Manhattan. And besides, we got rid of our heathens. I hear Mexico is just full of all those Indian types, not even Christians. Will you be in the city or out rurally?" the old woman asked with scepticism etched on her face.

Amanda gave in and grabbed herself yet another champagne as the tray flew by. Sobriety was no longer an option.

Eleanor Kelly was very confused.

"So, no Amazon then?" she asked before stuffing a canapé into her mouth.

"No, I won't be out walking in any jungles, certainly not alone.", Amanda began, trying to keep the frustration out of her voice.

"We will be in the capital city, as large as New York. I will have, Edward says, a much larger household staff than what we have here, and I will have chaperones, of course. Ed has plans to purchase a motor car, so I will never be without a driver and a girl, a local when I'm out and about in the city."

"A local?"

Mrs. Heatherington grinned, raising her eyebrows,

"As in – a what, one of those types- an Indian? Heathens." she crinkled her nose.

"They have real, honest to Betsy Indians!" Eleanor laughed like an obnoxious child.

"Do they speak – well do they even speak Spanish or that Aztec stuff? Oh, my heavens- what if they don't speak English? What in the world- Amanda- how will you even communicate with these people to tell them what to do? I mean, our girl speaks English and still presses the bed linens incorrectly."

"Well, I will have a translator in Edward", Amanda pointed out.

She was now scanning the smoke-filled room, hoping to see Ed over tall, coiffed heads and wave him over to come to save her. She longed to be able to do one of those whistles like the construction men in the streets, where you placed two fingers in your mouth and suddenly sounded like a train. It was a vulgar thing to witness, and it hurt her ears, but it was certainly effective. Where was Edward? She would never get away from the Heatherington women if she didn't get away soon. She knew they would monopolize her night unless she returned to the bathroom to be sick of course. Although they always seemed very fond of her, she couldn't stand the thought of being subjected to their insipid questions all night long. Perhaps if they spent more time reading the newspapers instead of dishing rumours, they would be able to locate Mexico on a map. Amanda grumbled this thought to herself, never daring to utter such a suggestion. She was floored that Eleanor knew enough to know the word "Aztec". However well-intentioned, she was not appreciative of their overly concerned tone at the family leaving. It was dramatic and implied the move was a huge mistake. Mrs. Heatherington never could mind her own business.

"However, I have been starting to learn Spanish. It shouldn't be too difficult as my mother spoke fluent French- she did teach me a good bit before she died."

"My dear, but you were only a child, and you hardly speak it now- surely you don't remember more than 'bon appetite', guffawed Mrs. Heatherington.

Amanda's face went red hot as if she had been slapped.

Amanda caught her breath at her mother's soft voice drifting into her head as if she were standing behind her, whispering into her ear.

'Je t'aime pour toujours ',

Her mother had taught her that as an infant. She could say that perfectly, but she did not feel like sharing the tender phrase with the pair of morons before her.

"I will love you forever",

said again the night she died. Murmured quietly, just an hour before she slipped away, to a little girl certain if she just believed hard enough and shut her eyes as she clutched the dying woman's hand, she would be able to follow her to this place called death, to disappear along with her mother. She had been devastated to remain. She was always such a good girl, but she had fought the men like a cat when they came to take her mother's body away.

Amanda had asked Edward to translate the phrase for her into Spanish.

'te amaré por siempre '.

Aside from the very basics of the days of the week and pleasantries, that was about all the French she could remember and all the Spanish she presently knew.

Any time she had attempted over the years to seek out a tutor to help her relearn her French she'd ended the lesson on the first day, paying and thanking the tutor enormously for their time, but feigning a sudden headache. The memories were too strong. They would close around her throat, acting as a vice, and she could never form the words without nearly bursting into tears. Her dead mother was in every syllable of the language. Her baby sister was found there too.

Memories of lullabies sung by her mother to a dying little girl were too much for Amanda. One morning after another abandoned lesson, certain she would embarrass herself if she kept trying to reach into the past for something that was simply already lost, she had made the decision to let her French go in an attempt to let go of their ghosts. She did not speak French. She'd not wanted to utter another word of it or even hear it once her mother was gone. Who would she even speak it to in their big, empty home? Her Irish father, who never had a knack for it and who the sound of French tore his heart out? Trying to speak it again felt like trying to resurrect her mother's corpse and even seemed oddly disrespectful. That was nonsense, she told herself - her mother had lamented her not being fluent by the time she was seven. But by then, mother had fallen ill, so what did it even matter anymore? It happened so fast, all one right after the other. The baby dying. Mourning shrouded the house in a never-ending fog of devastation, and then.... the doctor having a serious talk with daddy about mother. Their beautiful life had been upended as swiftly as one of those magicians who tore the tablecloth off the dining table while trying to leave the settings intact.

Nothing was left intact.

No, she did not speak French, and she had no need to.

"French is lovely", she assured Mrs. Heatherington with a smile,

"But aside from pleasantries, I won't have use for it. I will; however, I am confident I have no problem learning Spanish", she said with a tight smile and a warning in her eyes.

She knew she would be fine even if this ridiculous old woman couldn't fathom it. She was going to live a beautiful new life in the City of Palaces, Mexico City. Now, she told herself, she would learn Spanish instead. A new language for this new adventure and her new, growing family.

Chapter 3

At the very same moment, moonlight fell upon the Tappan's penthouse party in Manhattan, a soft rain misting the streets; down in Mexico City, it was a crystalline night. No rain, yet that same moonlight, through parted curtains, fell upon the name 'Doctor Eduardo Tappan'.

Written elegantly on cheap parchment, rough quality paper in the equally rough hands of a soldier of fortune named Emil Homdahl. The Swede sat at his desk, using the moonlight to read, the rest of the room dark save for the dying embers in the fireplace. He was getting tired, but this was the last bit of reading he had to do before heading off in the morning for a long journey to meet with Pancho.

He was increasingly getting his hands dirty. He loved getting his hands dirty. There were many things Emil Homdahl excelled at, many things in his life; his favourite among them- war. A bit of bloodshed, the occasional thrashing around of other men, he felt was good for the soul of a man.

War and money, he was skilled at falling into both.

Tappan's name was one of several high-profile targets. No, he thought, target was not the right word. Contacts, yes, that was better. Sommerfeld had been very intentional when explaining this part of the plan to his comrade Emil. Emil, the Swede, Sommerfeld, the German Jew. Tappan, the American – and Mexican- doctor, of all things. Yes, this was turning into a strange stew, this recipe of men from all over the world getting involved in the crumbling – and rebuilding- of Mexico.

Emil did not fancy himself an opportunist but a businessman.

Tappan was cooperative and eager; word on the street went and would be arriving in Mexico with the first small shipment. Emil had initially had misgivings about involving someone so academic. After all, "cientifico" had become a slur in modern day Mexico. Tied to that old fart of a dictator Diaz, the scientists of Mexico had shown themselves to be untrustworthy – upper class, ultra-wealthy and very much the white man. They – the upper crust, the socialites, backed the Diaz dictatorship because it kept the poor Indian down, scavenging to get by. Now, to be a cientifico was a bad thing. Scientists were snobs. They were very often mad men, impulsive with dangerous ideas and even greater levels of arrogance. They involved themselves in politics and in the unrest that led to the start of the Revolution. Emil had doubts involving even a trained surgeon. The man had no military experience or background. What good could he be, other than sewing up the occasional wound or digging out the bullets that had to be dug out? Emil had done that himself plenty of times. Bringing some Harvard Blue Blood into anything that Sommerfeld was planning could be catastrophic if the doctor turned out to be soft or big-mouthed like so many Americans were. Emil had never heard of him; no one he spoke to knew who this mysterious Gringo doctor was. Sommerfeld seemed intent on bringing him in.

"No- it needs to be Tappan. Just trust me."

He had reassured Emil over dinner earlier in the evening when they viewed the list together.

Emil had known him a long time and did trust him but wanted more information on the stranger.

He knew better than to press the matter with Sommerfeld, however. He was quiet when he wanted to be and elaborated when he felt you needed the information. Those were the unspoken rules of Sommerfeld. No man ever broke those rules. The ones that had always ended up very regretful or very dead.

Emil took the last swig of his scotch and stopped at the last name, just under Tappan's, one he had missed before. How had he missed this one? The food had been put in front of him; that was how.

This contact was already in country. This name stood out on the list. This one had not been expected.

This one belonged to a woman.

Emil's heart began to pound in his throat and a strong yearning in his body began to grow at the recognition of her name. He knew this woman. He had heard many things about her and been unnervingly distracted the one and only time that he saw her in person, leaving the Cathedral in Mexico City.

He had seen her from a distance, both too far to call out hello without appearing odd and too near to miss the delicate features of her soft and lovely face. She had eyes that drove him to distraction. He asked his companions if they knew her.

"Ah.... yes, the widow." Said with a soft chuckle,

"Stay away from that one, my Swedish amigo", had come the warning blown in his face like so much cigar smoke.

Emil wanted many things in his life. He wanted his side to prevail in this uprising. He wanted to further his career, his reputation, and fill his coffers. He wanted the occasional bit of blood, for sport, for the thrill.

Adding to the list of growing desires, now that he saw her name on that yellow and rough, cheap piece of paper, now that he knew of her willing involvement- he wanted this woman now more than ever. The black ink of the swirling letters of her name were as intoxicating to him as the way her shapely form had moved not twenty paces away from him that morning at the Cathedral.

Emil fell into his bed, still with the paper in his hand, looking up and out at the moonlight that fell upon Manhattan and Mexico and somewhere in the same city as him- it fell over her sleeping form. He needed to sleep but was afraid he would not be able to, now knowing he would get to see her, to speak to her, in a matter of days. Not only would he be meeting this woman, but he would also be giving her orders and working with her. He decided at that moment that he would have some men follow her and watch her house. A large smile spread across his face like the tide washing ashore. This revolution was indeed getting stranger by the day.

Chapter 4

Amanda had enjoyed city living when she was a young newlywed, but after the children were born, she found she often longed for her grand old house in Philadelphia. She dreamed at times of her childhood home. A grand red brick Colonial with its sprawling garden and the peace of anonymity.

Why on earth had she sold it? She would ask herself this question from time to time, in surprise and then quiet realization. Edward had insisted, never admitting to her that they needed the money to help fund their lavish lives in Manhattan. A physician of his stature certainly made enough money to rear a proper family, but he was always striving for more money and more clout. Edward steered their ship without much thought as to what course his wife would like to take. Amanda felt she should have begged him to find work in Philadelphia. She should have never left that house.

She consoled herself that as the constants of life often change without warning, they would have ended up leaving it eventually with this move to Mexico. Yes, she told herself that in times of regret and it did offer a modicum of comfort. Perhaps she was having an easier time leaving New York precisely because she didn't feel as attached to it as she had been to her old family home in Pennsylvania. Silver linings and explanations came in handy, especially when married to Edward.

Her house in Philly had been the perfect backdrop for a loving family home. A plush bed of green velvet, the lawns and gardens had been kept impeccable. The roses her mother had planted overwhelmed the grounds with a fragrance that Amanda imagined Heaven must smell like if it existed at all.

New York City, in contrast, never smelled of anything rose-like and certainly could not be described as heavenly. No, the city was more urine and coal, tobacco, horses, and illness…no plush greenery to stroll about outside of the respite of Central Park, no rose bushes to admire in front of the houses. Instead, it was a cacophony of carriages, people yelling, machinery and the wails of children. It was construction, travel, hurry, rush, go! It was dirt and grime personified.

Her home was as far away from the grunge of the city as could be. In its halls, the outside world ceased to exist and for a while at least, there was no pain.

When the sound of the piano did not fill the rooms, wonderful music wafted through the home on the fancy new machine her father was fascinated with, the gramophone. Their house always smelled of baking bread, and the lavender and oatmeal soap her mother had brought in from the countryside of France. The kitchen had been warm and large, an orangish hue filtering in through stained glass windows above the door. The dining table was always set for five places, even if there were only the four. In no time at all, those numbers dwindled even more.

Her bedroom had been a perfectly white and pristine hide away, soft bleached linens and lace curtains, large pillows with plush, stuffed bunnies and dolls of every description from velvet to wood to porcelain. She dreamed of her bedroom, but most often, when Amanda would roam the halls of her memory during the night, she always ended her little journey in the same room, the library. It was her favourite spot in the house, the fire right in the middle of the room, the unexplained scent of sandalwood always hanging in the air. She always thought of it with fondness, even if it accompanied the bittersweet. The picture emblazoned in her mind of her as a child sitting unladylike across a chair, face buried in a book, always produced a quick smile to flash across her face. She was forever finding sweets left out for her on her father's desk, and her mother liked to press flower petals into the pages of Amanda's favourite books. The petals were gentle reminders of her mother's affection.

Amanda had read everything she could get her hands on from the time she could read. She had been left an enormous and full library in her big, empty house after the last of the family was gone.

She credited her father for showing her the magic that awaited in the books on the shelves.

Paddy, the pauper from Galway, made his way as a fifteen-year-old kid fresh off the boat to apprentice to a shoe merchant in Boston. He read everything he came across, whether he could understand it or not. His literacy had been poor at first, that of an educated eight-year-old, and he struggled for years to read, learn, and read some more. He used this drive of his to build a thriving business he was proud of.

Reading, he had told Amanda repeatedly, was the thing, the habit, that set people apart- not money, not social standing- knowledge and the sincere pursuit of acquiring more. He had delighted her with tales of his travels. He had met many wealthy men who were total fools, with not an objective, original or rational thought rattling around in their noggin. The more money they had, he had told his young daughter, the sillier they tended to be. The ones who were well-read, however, usually turned out to be sound. He had over the many years struggling to become a gentleman, acquired a vast vocabulary, a love of the greats of history, and had refined his speech to that of a noble man, with a watered-down accent that took on notes of American.

He once told his daughter that, "Because I immigrated as a teen, I was able to lose a lot of my Irish accent and, at times, blend in flawlessly. Having a more American-sounding accent has helped me greatly in business. Often people mistake me for English and well-sadly, that can help too."

His bibliophile tendencies meant he introduced her to Homer's The Odyssey, the Iliad, Dante's Divine Comedy, and Inferno.

He had insisted she read all the women authors of the 1800's, from Mary Shelley to the Bronte sisters, Austen and Alcott. It was safe to say her father had instilled in her a love of all the arts, but most especially for the written word.

Her mother Josephine, from Bordeaux, was an accomplished pianist and was the daughter of French poets and lecturers, academics. How an Irish farm boy turned salesman ever swindled a classy French girl into marrying him struck everyone as oddly unexplainable, even if he had been able to present himself well. The two of them would laugh over the years that it was beyond both of their understandings and that he had even won over her parents, making him a miracle worker. The two of them looked at each other with a certain affection that silently said they would have found each other, circumstances be damned. They were comfortably in love – every mundane day had a sweetness to it. The touch of a hand in the evening, a glance at dinner, as if years had not passed since they were nervous innocents first undressing to touch each other on their wedding night. They put the other at ease and simply were happy together. They had a passion that bordered on worship and a solid friendship. Their happiness grew more so after Amanda arrived, all red hair and cheeks. Agatha, Aggie, with more red hair and cheeks, arrived two years after Amanda and died three summers later, following a long illness Amanda could never remember the name of.

She was gone as swiftly as she came, like a little ginger bird in winter, alighting on a barren branch and then changing its mind and swiftly flying away.

Josephine's black hair had streaked with white after they buried the baby, as if some painter of ruined lives decided that she should wear her grief as a portrait for all to see. Amanda's parents always tried to put on a brave face and speak about the loss of the younger girl with honesty and a certain sort of acceptance, but as the years went by, they spoke her name less and less so that Amanda grew to fear mentioning her. Her portrait sat atop the fireplace mantel in the parlour. When the fire was lit, the flames illuminating the toddler's face made her hair seem part of the blaze made her eyes come alive. There were days in the early moments after her death when the only comfort any of them could touch was from sitting and staring at Agatha's angelic face. It became an altar, a shrine to the little girl who vanished. Although she missed her sister so badly at times it would wake her from nightmares, tears soaking her nightgown collar, she was too little herself to understand where Aggie was now that she was gone. Yet she had an understanding at such a young age that her parent's loss must have been unbearable. She tried desperately to always be especially nice, considerate, and well-behaved for her mother and father so that at least they could have a good life with the daughter they had left. Yes, Amanda was a good girl, always and prided herself on that one quality. Her parents had lost so much already that she wanted to give them something intangible - all the peace that she could.

Despite the differences in their backgrounds, Amanda's parents were both avid learners who valued their minds above every dollar they amassed. They instilled that ethic in Amanda, and she was grateful for it. She knew it was one thing that had caught Edward's attention. Her now auburn hair, thick and heavy like velvet curtains, was perhaps the other.

Amanda often found she got lost in her own thoughts, and when reminiscing as she tended to do, she wondered if her parents would have liked Edward Tappan for their daughter's husband. In the beginning, as she was being courted and then first married, she was certain both her mother and father would have approved. As the years began accumulating and she matured as a woman, wife, and mother, she would feel the inescapable pang of uncertainty enter her body. She often felt a pull, as though someone was touching her, a hand on the shoulder, a voice that whispered to her that her mother would not have adored the good doctor. She would not have fallen for his graces and charms; she would have instead warned her daughter. Amanda felt that instinctively, her mother would have picked up that Edward was brash and would have said so. That she wanted someone slightly gentler. For Amanda needed perhaps a touch more softness, a quality that this cardiac surgeon did not possess, no matter how talented or wealthy he knew himself to be. Often, Amanda wondered if what she felt was regret but had no love to compare it to other than that of her parents.

As they packed up the household and said their societal goodbyes, as they prepared to leave all that Amanda had known behind, these thoughts arrived to her now daily, as letters sent anonymously, arriving at her door. Amanda would do her best to ignore them.

Chapter 5

Some New York affairs were always certain to make the papers, and anything to do with Edward or his famous father certainly did. The Farewell to the Tappan Family would surely run on one of the first pages of tomorrow's paper. Anyone who was anyone important in New York had been there to see the popular young doctor and his family off. The newspaper men, the real estate fellas, the heads of companies. Lawyers, doctors, judges, bankers, the stock exchange folks, and all their glamorous wives had been cavorting through the night. The staff would be cleaning the household well into the morning and the mahogany grandfather clock was chiming three times as the tired couple made their way into their bedroom. Amanda's eyes burned from all the smoke, and her feet were aching, but she was delighted she only got sick one time, and nobody was the wiser. Edward had a good bit of champagne, whiskey, and brandy to drink but was now approaching sobriety through sheer exhaustion.

"Well, I'd say tonight was a success, and we know who our friends are, Señor Tappan.",

Amanda smiled at her husband before she disappeared behind the partition to undress.

"Everyone is your friend when you're leaving", quipped Ed as he began to untie his tie and work on his cuff links. He was in a very good mood.

"And it's Señor Tappan Santiago, as I will soon be called down in the old country- Doctor Tappan Santiago."

"Yes, of course, doctor, apologies, I nearly forgot the two

surnames. What will I be again? Tappan, then my maiden name? I get confused."

"Well, with Spanish and Mexican naming traditions, if you'd been born in Mexico, you would be introduced to me as Señorita Byrne Du Clois. After marriage, you drop your maternal surname, keep the paternal and add the husband. You will be, La Señora Byrne de Tappan. There's wiggle room, you know. I'm sure I will just be Dr. Tappan for the most part unless it's something formal.

"All that seems rather a mouthful after just having been Mrs. Tappan for the last seven years. Can I just be Mrs. - Señora Tappan- down there too?"

Edward laughed as he prepared for bed.

"You are married to the most in-demand surgeon in all of Mexico, and you will be one of the wealthiest women that country has seen since the Conquistadors – you can be called whatever you like."

He declared with a cheeky smile and the raising of his eyebrows.

"Edward, don't be smug. You make it sound like we are royalty." Amanda shook her head in disapproval.

She began to arrange the pillows to her liking, not wanting to look at him when he went on an arrogant tear.

"We very nearly are."

Amanda shot him a look, hoping the conversation would end, but she knew better.

"What you don't understand, what you can't understand until you are in Mexico, is that while we are wealthy enough in New York, connected, and known… In Mexico City, we will be kings. We will be Gods."

"Don't be blasphemous Ed, it's not nice."

"Amanda- your life is going to change radically, and the money and status that you've enjoyed thus far are nothing compared to what we are heading into. Prepare yourself to be revered as royalty- there is no escaping it. Not down there. You will be fawned over simply by virtue of your race.

Then there is a pretty face, your hair colour is not very common in any country, and lastly, you're married to the son of the doctor who reinvented surgery in Mexico and saved thousands of Mexican babies in the process. You need to accept that your quiet little life and social events on your schedule might be upended a bit."

"That is not what I want to hear, Ed. And I know well what you and your father have accomplished." She huffed.

Instead of getting angry with her as expected, he was toying with her now, a flirtatious smile starting.

"Well, that's the way things are, and we are only going to climb further through the ranks of Mexican society with every success I have. I'm grateful for the legacy my father left behind, although I have some big shoes to fill, as the saying goes. Do you not realise, my father's success has opened every door in Mexico for this family? Our children could do anything they desire, and they would be not only welcome but pursued– medicine, law, - and government. Between what we already have and what we stand to gain, plus the living standards down there, our fortunes will be vastly inflated, if not our egos as well."

He grinned very pleased with himself, like a man about to get everything he ever wanted.

"Well, you can be glad I'm a modest person by nature, Edward. I don't like the boasting that seems to be all the rage now in modern times, at least among some circles. Have you noticed it has gotten worse?"

Ed gave a small shrug, "Boasting is nothing new, especially among the rich and pompous."

"People used to think before they spoke. My parents taught me to hold my tongue instead of saying something uncouth or stupid. I find it in poor taste the amount of people who – even when they have gobs of money themselves, make assumptions, try to imply, or allude to our standing, all to obtain information so they can sit there smiling to you one minute, then talking behind your back the next."

She sat at her dressing table, brushing her long hair, a look of disgust on her face.

"Why don't they just come out and ask, how much do you have? Or worse yet they will talk specifics about their own circumstances, in front of everyone. My parents would be absolutely mortified. It is gauche, downright vulgar to talk about money in this manner. Tell me the elite of Mexico City aren't like the New York crowd."

"They're not- they're much worse." He said with a wink.

"Surely you're joking.", she groaned.

"I expected the wealthy there to behave with a touch more discretion or class."

Ed shrugged his shoulders again, relaxed and amused, "Why?"

Amanda paused for a moment, unsure. Ed always made Mexico

City sound so cosmopolitan; she just assumed foreigners would have more refinement than most of scummy New York.

"Perhaps it's the Catholicism everywhere in Mexico that makes me expect better manners? Or the European influence? "

She applied her cold cream to her face, always shocked by the cold feel of it, despite the warning in the name.

"Everyone in New York is turning into a heathen. Suddenly, everyone is a Methodist. Or a Jew. Mrs. Mason isn't making her son attend church anymore and lets her daughters out with young men without chaperones. One girl she let go to some new ice cream parlour, along with some fella from Chicago, clear across town. People are vulgar and impertinent. I just don't believe the nice families in Mexico City are carrying on anything like New Yorkers-"

"Are we *gossiping,* Señora Tappan?", he grinned.

This was not gossip, she told herself. This was the decline of morality. The decline of society.

"Don't be cute Ed. People are outrageous, and you know it. Women behaving like men…they're all cutting their hair; the hemlines are moving up and up. That Dorothy, what's her name, Cooper or Parker or she's a writer or something, was saying tonight that if women don't get the right to vote within the year, there will be picketing in the streets and possible riots."

"I don't know her."

"She's friends with Eleanor - but riots, really, can you imagine anything being so important that women would act like- like thugs and lawless mobsters? Eleanor just thinks this Dorothy is brilliant. "

"Tad jealous, are we?'

"Ed, stop it. Of course not, she can keep Eleanor."

Amanda finally took her place beside her husband in the marital bed. Even after all those years, it never felt totally comfortable for her.

She continued talking to keep him from getting any amorous ideas, "Then her mother, the Heatherington woman, started up tonight about money and what they have put into that stock exchange. She nearly flat out asked what sort of money you would be making in your new position in the hospital down there. Everyone is so rude and pushy and inappropriate. Tell me the Mexico City crowd isn't like THAT. Tell me they have some restraint."

Edward smiled at his wife, shaking his head. At times- most of the time- he found her strange. She was far too young to be so old, far too light-hearted to be so serious, and she was infuriatingly level-headed, beyond most men he knew, when she wasn't having one of the episodes.

"You're something else."

"What does that mean Ed?"

She crawled further into the bed beside him. It was arctic, and she needed the warmth.

"You're level-headed, and it still takes me by surprise. I mean to consider for a moment what you were able to do after losing your parents."

"I didn't do much of anything Ed, other than meet and marry you.

"No- you were solid. You being orphaned, it was a feat truly unprecedented- to have lost your mother at nine years of age and then your father at fifteen. The fact that you were alone for four years before we met – "

" I was hardly alone; I had Julia. "

"Ah yes, the housekeeper- but not withstanding your Julia, you were left alone with a fortune as a young girl. You could have easily squandered it away. Instead, you were a proper adult- attended school, read, and played the piano."

"Poorly. I played the piano poorly."

"And you were so utterly mature by the time I found you-….it really is remarkable. I can only credit your parents, that they did such a fine job of instilling in you the virtues…."

He seemed to reach out into the air for the very words,

"…the virtues needed to enjoy an extraordinary life. I'm not sure I would have paid very much attention to you otherwise."

"I beg your pardon, sir?"

"I mean, you are a darling a girl, a real looker but- it was your fortune- no apologies,"

he laughed at his slip,

"It was your forthright attitude and mature nature that caught me off guard. So many of your peers are stupid little girls. That head- that pretty head on your shoulders is not often seen in nineteen-year-olds. You are not vapid; you're not a gossip- well, not much of one."

Amanda gave him a pinch for that.

He continued,

"Everyone likes you. And surely being raised by the maid is not exactly a proper way to finish off your adolescent years. Yet it did you no harm, instead you thrived. You could have fallen into a state of melancholy after losing your folks that left you insufferable- instead, you were a delight when I met you- a happy little thing. Think for a moment if you had, as a young woman alone in the world, fallen in with the wrong crowd. Things could have gone very badly for you. Taken by charlatans, romanced by fellas with bad intentions, abandoned by scoundrels without a penny left to your name- most certainly left with a babe, or several, in arms. Things could have gone very badly indeed."

He took her face in both hands and kissed her forehead,

"I'm ever grateful that they didn't and that you happened to end up being fortunate enough to meet me."

It was unlike Edward to give her such credit. She knew it was the alcohol talking and the high of his wonderful bash that had him praising her. Still, she thought to absorb it while it poured down.

"Well, I really had no choice, Ed when you think about it. It was grow up or ship me off to either France or Ireland. I would not have fit in on some farm with more money than my father's eight brothers and sisters combined, and the people there, although blood are strangers to me. My father always said it was a poverty-stricken country, which is why everyone is leaving it for the US or Australia. What would I do there? What sort of future could I have? I know nothing of farming. I'd have been as useless as a hen that didn't lay eggs. I know books. I know the United States… I don't speak Irish,"

"They speak English now, don't they?"

"Well, apparently, out in the west, they don't. And my father's family, almost all of them only speak Irish; my father and his siblings were the only ones with English.... I could well have been walking into a disaster going to family in Ireland."

She pondered the possibilities for the first time in years as he moved closer to her, his eyes heavy but still wanting.

"Nor would I have been able to settle in France, as there was almost no one left of my mother's family, save one great aunt around two hundred years of age and apparently mad as a march hare."

Ed chuckled, "So it made sense, I suppose, that you stayed put."

"Well yes, I think so. I mean, at that age, some girls are getting married. My father and I spoke about this as his illness was progressing. He said we had to plan for the inevitable and he knew, ultimately, I wanted to remain in Philly, in our home and with Julia by my side. He was concerned that I would feel alone, but that wasn't the case."

At least not all the time, she thought to herself.

"I had my school friends."

She was trying to convince herself now. She brushed away the fact that Edward had run nearly all her friends off from his young bride as not being of good enough social standing.

"I had our lovely neighbours Mr. & Mrs. Shoemaker...we always had a good laugh about that, that my father became a clothing merchant and shoemaker, and we lived next door to the Shoemakers. And the Shoemakers instead were builders. They had no children, so they were staples in our house, always over for dinner and holidays and after my parents died, they were all but put in charge of me. I had Julia and my darling cat, Edgar Allen Poe."

"Yes, wife, I know all this.", he yawned.

Ed hated cats. Ed hated anything that took Amanda's attention off him or their children. Ed never wanted anything competing for her attention. Where his wife was concerned, he wanted her day to begin and end with thoughts of him.

"She was my nanny from the time I was born. My parents adored her, and she was there to console me when I lost them. I don't know what sort of trouble you expected me to find tucked away on a sleepy estate in Northern Philadelphia Ed, but it wasn't as if sharks were circling. I was fine- and happy- with Julia. "

She paused in her thoughts, frowning,

"You know, come to think of it, I have not received any post from her in the longest time. It's been well over a year. I don't even know if she received my Christmas card. I should really call down to Philadelphia and visit her. Do you think we cou-"

"Come now, don't even ask Señora. We won't have time before our departure to Mexico, for a holiday to see a housekeeper. That should have been carried out weeks ago, I'm afraid."

"But Edward, I hardly have had a minute- "

"I understand", he said, raising that same hand he always began to hoist as though he were giving his medical students a lecture,

"That she was much more to you than just a nanny, a confidant, a guardian after your parents were gone, but at the end of it all, she is now nothing more than an old housekeeper on a very good retirement thanks to you and probably doesn't think of you much after all this time. "

He avoided looking directly at the hurt that caused to flash across Amanda's face.

"She has her own family, as do you. You must learn to let go of some things, my wife. You must learn that the past is gone and the details of it belong there, not encroaching on your new life. You are under no obligation to say goodbye to someone from your former life that you have already said goodbye to. It is time to be fully devoted to your present and your – our future."

Amanda sat in stony silence, contemplating if it was worth arguing with someone who never let anyone else win.

Julia was more than Amanda's past. She was the marrow in her bones, as integral to her childhood as her own parents. It was Julia who held her trembling little frame when her mother passed and then again when she lost her father. It was Julia who answered Amanda's whispered questions about her dead baby sister when her parents could not speak her name. It was Julia who put aside her own grief at the losses of her beloved employers to stand as firm as the oak in the front garden for the girl left behind, the girl who had no one, the girl who needed her. Amanda's face flushed red with shame at the realization that she had not kept in touch with her darling Julia for such a long time. She simply had become the sort of busy and occupied that always seemed to find young mothers. Life had gotten away from her, she told herself. And now she was leaving the country without saying goodbye. Her eyes were starting to betray her, rimming with water that she could not let him see lest his jovial mood turn sour.

"Ed, it's just she's old and she was very good to me. My parents revered her as family, not just some servant, you know. Who knows when we will be back this way."

"You tend to live in the past. It is time to move forward. To a new country and a new life! Our little ones demand it and – "he smiled while holding her soft abdomen, "this little one, the first in our family to be born there after my mother, this little Mexican Prince or Princess, will most certainly demand it."

He was pontificating now, mostly for his own ears and it was far too late and she too tired, so she abandoned her idea to see Julia one last time as swiftly as it had popped in her head. She knew he would never allow her even to make a quick trip on the train now, so she gave in, as always, swallowing her disappointment.

"Will I like Mexico, do you think?" she asked as she arranged the blankets, changing the subject, trying not to cry.

"I'm sure you will find it many things - charming and astoundingly beautiful, quaint in the countryside. At times, you may find it frustratingly bizarre and, awful and confusing. The place is absolutely mad- wonderfully hypnotic and mad. Mexico City is more like Paris than New York, but the three cities are very alike. If I can get you out to the countryside or to the coasts, you may decide never to return. As a boy I used to imagine even the soil was magical. The air on the sierras is clean, and the people are warm. The beaches are paradise. I feel sorry for the Gringos who never make it down, as I know what they're missing. I feel as if, at times, Mexico belongs only to me. Yes, you will like it very much. You have an inquisitive mind, and the history and art alone will keep you busy. You can explore."

"I don't think I will be doing much exploring as a mother of three, will I?" she mused.

"We will explore the secrets of Mexico together, all of us."

"When you're not working, that is."

"Well yes of course. Even doctors get to take a day off you know."

"Well, as soon as I see one do that, I will write it down in my diary to mark the occasion."

"Oh, my dear", Edward groaned as he turned onto his side, and any fleeting thoughts of romance dissipated. Was it pregnancy that made women behave like wet blankets, or was it just his wife?

"What is wrong?"

"You women love to complain. My mother did it to my father, always begrudging that he was working, earning hordes of money to keep her. While he was bringing forth new babies and facilitating life.... she was always moaning about his absence. And if he had not been so successful, I am certain she would have found that displeasing as well. She wanted him to accompany her to dinners and social gatherings. She wanted him home with us children more. She wanted him at our dinner table and never ceased to let us all know all the time. It grew bloody tiresome."

He eyed her sternly enough to make her hold her breath in anticipation of what he would say next. Would it be simply an admonishment, or would he bark at her like an ill-tempered dog?

"I hope you won't become one of those women, those types. I mean, you must understand," he continued more gently than she expected,

"I will be inundated with work, lectures, and research. More than anything, we have seen in New York. The ratio of cardiac specialists is astounding. Say we have twenty-five heart specialists in New York State, in Mexico, the entire country, they have six. I will be lucky, number seven."

He had been doing amazing work with his colleagues. The heart was their sole focus. These doctors had spent the previous decade researching and proposing new surgeries and treatments and learning more about this organ than man had ever gleaned. This meant carrying these new procedures out, often, unsuccessfully. It was revolutionary medicine for the United States, and it was time to take it abroad so that others could benefit. He had a mission. Amanda knew this. Ed always said to insure you are the best, you must be the first. Edward came first in everything, and medicine would be no different.

"No, I do understand Ed; I was just pointing out that perhaps our days of adventure and exploring a new country together leisurely are behind us…"

She trailed off at the realization that they'd never even began.

At the beginning of their courtship, he had suggested travel before starting a family, but it all happened so fast. Once Edward had decided they were going to be married, it had never occurred to Amanda to say no. To turn him down was out of the question- or so she was told by all her friends. For all his charisma and good looks, those large brown curls, the startling blue eyes, for all his wealth and fame, it had never really been a question that he asked Amanda, *if* she would be his wife. It was, true to form, more of an order. She mused from time to time it was as if she had practically no say in the matter. She often marvelled at how she had gone from one part of her life to the other, almost unaware.

They married right before Amanda's twentieth birthday, four months after meeting. A whirlwind courtship. He always promised travel and adventure, but he was already a doctor, and they settled into married life immediately. Plans to see the Grand Canyon or to holiday in Europe continued to be put by the wayside. He was far too busy. Although they did spend their honeymoon week in

Niagara Falls, there had been little of the travel plans they'd made coming to fruition.

Amanda had been quite taken with Edward in the beginning. He left her with no choice, and he pursued her relentlessly. Everyone told her this was a match made in Heaven. The ladies in the church assured her God himself had sent this most wonderful suitor to romance her and so Amanda had been swept away in that regard. After God had called her family home so early and left her all alone, she agreed, this persistent man giving all his attention to her, well, he must have been a gift. Amanda chose to see it that way.

The only person who had ever really been hesitant in the pairing was, in fact, Julia Newsome, the long-time housekeeper and nanny. Julia found something unsettling and downright unlikeable about this arrogant young doctor, although she never dared voice her concern. She would have rather Amanda marry someone not quite right for her than to see the poor child alone. She was so alone. It pained her to see Amanda with no family, no warm embrace to wrap herself in at night. Julia wanted more for the girl she viewed as a daughter than an empty mansion and an ageing black cat with their ageing old nanny. She kept her mouth shut and smiled and was as relieved as she was trepidatious when Amanda revealed their engagement. It didn't take long for Ed to let Julia know she would need to retire. Her services as a housekeeper and as the keeper of Amanda were no longer needed.

Ed made it clear from the start that he did not want a long engagement, and being eleven years her senior, he was adamant about marriage and a family right away. Amanda desperately wanted a family again. She felt that she could trust Ed, even if there were times she wasn't sure she always liked him. She felt attraction and excitement when he was around and felt that perhaps the rapid beating of her heart must certainly mean love. For all his positives and his dashing good looks and beautiful speaking voice, he could be, at times, just too much for her and most people. He could be so overbearing, but he meant well, Amanda always told herself. She was so young, and she had never had a serious suitor before. Her beauty got her attention; her sad story pushed many away. There had been a few schoolboys who were mad about her, but the timing was always wrong, as poor Amanda Byrne was forever burying someone. The young gentleman from the all-boys preparatory understood that her years becoming a woman were mired in grief, so there was never a right time to ask her to dance. Then, Ed came along and right away was very serious about her and making her his wife. That confidence he displayed had to it, Amanda felt, an authenticity. He had waited this long to settle down and find that suitable wife and mother to his future children so he must have been a respectable young man looking for someone very special. Whatever his glaring faults, she told herself he must be made up of many more charms, even though she couldn't always name them. From a highly respected family, he could still be a little bit rough around the edges. Certainly, his know-it-all demeanour was hard for him to overcome when, a brilliant surgeon, he seemingly did know it all. Amanda made as many excuses for him as there were days in the year.

They married at the Sacred Covenant Catholic Church in Southern Philadelphia, the bride carrying big, fat white roses, each bud the size of a pastry. Julia and some girlfriends, as well as Amanda's closest neighbours, attended for her, and Ed's side was equally meagre. It rained and thundered, and everyone joked it was a good omen or a bad one, depending on which sort of luck you believed in more.

At twenty-one, she was expecting Arthur. There had been no time for adventure, only the setting up of the household while Ed worked at the hospital. She felt as though she merely turned around and she was expecting again, this time, Amelia.

Now, a new country, language, and life beckoned, and at only twenty-seven years of age, Amanda felt exceedingly tired and old, and yet, as if she had not really lived. She had gone from child to orphan to wife in the blink of an eye. Then mother, now times three. She was unsure if it was this third life that grew within her, depleting resources, taking from her, that made her feel so exponentially drained. Or perhaps this was just life catching up to her, that had her weary and she was mistaken to expect anything else. This was reality, not some Jane Austen novel. This was how it was supposed to be for everyone. Work, children, responsibilities, not adventure, as if she fancied herself the heroine in an epic tale.

Her work was the proper rearing of her children.

It struck her for the first time that she was a tad apprehensive, not about moving to the wilds of Mexico as silly Eleanor had proclaimed, but that a move such as this would take from her all that she already knew. She was as good as blind going into this new world. All her usual New York haunts and habits would be gone forever. She strolls to the markets to get her favourite Brannigan's tea and her favourite honey from upstate in the Adirondacks. Her usual corner of Central Park where she would stroll with her little tots and feed pigeons. The usual characters she came across every day from every walk of life, her routine would be forever altered. She had been so focused on fleeing the parts of this life she disliked she forgot for a moment that she was letting go of everything she knew.

What if she didn't like the new life? What if…she hated to even think it, but the thought crept in anyway, and it sat down on the end of the bed. What if she got sick again? Ed's patience had been tried. The whole episode had been so unexpected, as Amanda had always been so happy, not one for histrionics or nonsense. After this baby, what if she didn't feel good again, like the first time? She wanted to say it to him, wanted to speak the words, but it had been so bad, so much he didn't see or know about that time, and so much that he had been witness to, that she couldn't say it. Everything had been fine after Amelia; it hadn't happened. Remembering it made her face flush red and warm with mortification. She felt like dirt, even remembering her previous stupidity, and lucky her doctor husband did not put her in a sanitorium.

She didn't need to dig up the bones of that upset, long-buried now.

"What if- well, what if we don't get on well in Mexico City or one day we want to return to the US?", she asked after a few moments of silence.

"Ed?"

His answer came in the steady exhalation of breath, a small soft snore of a man falling rapidly into a deep slumber, into a place where questions need not be answered, not even in dreams.

Chapter 6

Four days after the party to end all parties, as tongues were wagging all over Manhattan, the upheaval of an international move had gripped the household proper.

Couriers came all day long, men with packages and gifts from friends, letters to be signed for, and telegrams to be delivered. Servants were diligently packing away the Tappan belongings amid Amanda's instructions. The belongings they were shipping would need to be at the harbour the day before they sailed. There were dockets to be signed and receipts to be kept up with, and while Amanda had an organized system, she had never done this before.

Orla, their long-time nanny, a timidly sweet girl from Roscommon, chased after the rambunctious toddlers, who were wound up from the excitement. It was very dignified bedlam, like a bomb had gone off in the middle of the apartment. Paper and packages strewn about, luggage in every corner with the household staff helping Amanda to launder, press and pack up an entire marriage and the lives of four people.

Amanda was adept at delegating and running a large home, but there was so much to do, decisions to be made, and time was slipping away from her. So much so that she felt harried and stressed and oddly short-tempered; this newest pregnancy felt different as well. She couldn't explain it to herself or anyone else, could not pinpoint what felt off, but she felt strange, and she knew it was the new passenger causing it.

"Shame I can't go with you all",

Orla said to Amanda as she sat braiding Amelia's hair on that bright, sunshine-filled morning, the dust dancing on the sunbeams.

"I might like to see Mexico. I can't imagine how different it must be to New York- how different it must be to Ireland. You must be very excited Mrs. Tappan". She smiled at her employer, who she was going to miss greatly.

In the years she'd been their nanny Orla saw her treatment had been exceptional. Talking with other nannies solidified that opinion and Orla was not looking forward to her new post that was to begin the next week. Mrs. Tappan had kindly arranged for her to come in as a second nanny for the Morgan's, a wealthy banking family who had a large brood of children. Mrs. Tappan had taken her the day before to meet the prospective new employers, and Orla found the whole ordeal overwhelming. The first nanny, the ancient and cement-faced Mrs. Detweiler, whom Orla would report directly to, had been with the family a long time and was regarded as an old battle axe. Orla was frightened of her looming size and presence, her beady grey eyes and of the cold, unwelcoming feel of that house, that was more mausoleum than family home.

The Tappan's had not only been fair employers, but Mrs. Tappan was friendly, chatty, and kind. She did not strike Orla as one bit shy but wonderfully confident. She was always ready to talk to the young nanny, to regale her with stories she had read or been told by her parents. Mrs. Tappan was never one to gossip, she never was cutting or said nasty things to her young nanny- about others or to the girl herself. She was never mean or in foul humour. She always had something interesting to discuss. The nicest part was she spoke to the girl as a friend with a kind tone and even a kinder face. Orla was for the first time in her life, treated with genuine kindness. She was always greeted with a smile from Amanda Tappan. She would ask the girl all sorts of questions about herself and about Ireland. Considering Mrs. Tappan's father was from there, and she had never been, Orla sensed any information she could give her was appreciated, perhaps even treasured. This made Orla feel something she had never felt before- important. No one usually cared what she had to say. Orla even took a secret, silly pride in that Mrs. Tappan's father had been from Ireland. There was an Irish fella that had made something of himself, and wasn't his daughter so lovely?

Orla had never known her own mother, as she had died in childbirth. She had heard Mrs. Tappan speak candidly of losing her mother at the tender age of nine and often wondered on sleepless nights which was the worse fate. To know that your own mother didn't even get the chance to hold you in her arms before she was taken from you and to miss someone you never knew, or to have known the love of your mother and have her stolen out from under you? To have known her smile, her smell, her voice, but only for a brief moment? Did your arms ache from the want of holding her? Could Mrs. Tappan still feel her mother's form against her when she closed her eyes? Or was she like Orla, a blank sheet of paper? No memories to cling to, no lasting anything. Orla had no sense of who her mother had been. No one in the little Irish village ever so much as whispered her name, and Orla's father had been a mean drunk. She had lived a cold and miserable life so that stealing away on a ship to America was her only option, as she was utterly alone. No family, no friends, but with a deep affection for Mrs. Tappan. She mourned her mother too. They could not have been from more different backgrounds, but they had a similar experience, and Orla knew instinctively that was a tie that binds.

Orla had learned a great deal about life and even academic topics from her employer. Orla had never thought of herself as smart, had never had the chance to attend school after the age of twelve and yet her employer of all people, made her feel valued and had shown her that she could in fact, retain large masses of knowledge. Orla had been absolutely stunned- and excited – when, in her first week there,

Mrs. Tappan had loaned her copy of Wuthering Heights to the girl for her day off, insisting she enjoyed it. Amanda Tappan never spoke down to any of her household staff, like so many of her station who treated workers as if they were stupid and beneath them. She treated her nanny as an equal and encouraged Orla to read and, discuss and think and to never be afraid to ask her anything.

"Really analyse the things that confuse you- the more something has you stumped, the better. Figure it out, examine it piece by piece, like a puzzle- life is a big puzzle; it can be frustrating but also highly entertaining." She had told her once.

Although the lady of the house was only five years older than Orla, she seemed so adult to the young girl, and she couldn't help but idolize her. Being in Mrs. Tappan's presence made Orla feel smart, confident, and happy. Her work with the family became her whole life.

"I am extremely excited Orla- I will most certainly miss your company, my dear, but you are going to be so well looked after with that Morgan character. With so many in Mexico crying out for work I have to find comfort in that I will be employing a girl like yourself in need of a wage."

Orla admired her so. She knew that not only was she right, but she was fair. Still, it stung the family would not ask her to go with them.

The children were as lovely as their mother, not terribly demanding or difficult to care for but it was the lady of the house who Orla adored. She rarely saw Dr. Tappan, and that was just fine with her, as he made her supremely uneasy at times.

She didn't care for the way most men looked at her, and every once in a while, she saw the same old shadows on Dr. Tappan's face, but only when his wife wasn't around.

Orla was a well-developed girl with a very mature frame on her by the time she was fifteen. Coming from a lesser station in life, she knew men would always want one thing from her, and other women would assume she was trouble simply because of the way she was put together. She had a heart shaped face that was instantly endearing, a mouth like a cut strawberry half, long pale-yellow silken hair, eyes the colour of green sea glass. She had a sleepy look to her eyes and a delicate neck and this picture was only from the shoulders up. Her form was another tableau altogether, hard to hide its shapely curves under skirts and bustles and pinafores. She was young, pretty, poor, very physically desirable, and worse than anything else- she was Irish. She could not really think of too many others as disliked as her kind, except, of course, for the poor Negroes. New York was not the friendliest of places to either person, but at least she had honest work where she was not mistreated. Most residential staff were not so lucky, no matter their race or creed. Orla knew of one Negro girl working with a very respected family who endured terrible indignities once the front door to the home was shut.

The man of the house had even tried on more than one occasion to force himself on her until she fled in the middle of the night. The lady of the house had known and looked the other way, refusing to acknowledge anything of the sort. Orla never heard what happened to the girl after she fled that house. Word on the street was she fled out west. They had become friendly, and Orla was shocked to learn she had just disappeared. Orla knew, of course, that the Americans treated some differently because of the colour of their skin, and although she was a foreigner, a dirty Irish girl, she knew she was lucky in a way. Her skin was her disguise; she could at least take comfort in that. If she didn't open her mouth, nobody had a problem with her.

The real miracle of her life had been her luck in finding Mrs. Tappan and having such employment. She had her place with a wonderful family. She even had a bit of integrity, a word learned from Mrs. Tappan. She had told the girl to carry herself with it as if it were a shield. No one could take it from her and this integrity, this sort of moral armour, would keep her out of harm's way, so long as she herself safeguarded it. Orla found the way men looked at her implied they did not see her integrity. She wanted the world to know she was a respectable young lady, so she would stand a little taller, eyes forward and pretended integrity was a person walking beside her. As if Mrs Tappan were walking beside her. She would never waver and ignored the crude whispers and cat calls of the society that surrounded her.

It was only in these last weeks that she realised they were really leaving, and she was off to a new post. She feared she would cry when the family left, and she would feel small and stupid for loving her mistress as family. She was, after all, only a nanny; they would have many down in Mexico. She would be forgotten in a month or so by the children.

Arthur was four and a half and was a proper little gentleman. His mousy brown head of silk was always combed, and he often reminded Orla that he needed help to wash his hands. He always carried a handkerchief and was gentle and soft like his mother, although he was tall for his age with a booming, almost manly laugh. Little Amelia, just two was funny and coquettish and always playing, very seldom speaking. She was covered in a delicious layer of baby fat, and had a big round head with pale yellow curls arranged sort of haphazardly, as if the hair on her head was an afterthought, sewn on in a rush by a forgetful dollmaker. Her face was like a cherub, her eyes a startling blue, like those stones the Indians wore.

"Turquoise", Mrs. Tappan had informed Orla one day, "Her eyes are a very light turquoise".

"That is a word I wouldn't want to have to spell Mrs.",

She had made her employer laugh with that.

It was yet another fascinating bite of knowledge the woman knew. Orla thought she must know everything; you'd nearly have to, being married to a doctor. Aside from simply keeping up in a conversation with her brilliant husband, Mrs. Tappan was able to keep him on his toes, evoke laughter and spark heated debates. Orla tried not to listen to the couple's conversations, not wanting to eaves drop, but where Mrs. Tappan was softer and quieter, Mr. Tappan made up for it with his boisterous nature and loud voice, so many times there was no avoiding hearing every word. He was not a large man, but his slight build was more than made up for by bravado and the way he carried himself. His wife often referred to him as the Bull, as he had a habit of gruffly and quickly moving things and people that were in his way. His personality and ego often entered the room before he did, and he was never one to shy away from instilling just enough fear into most people when he had to or to get what he wanted.

Some days, his wife feared he wanted the world, for his passions were all-consuming, his demands often exhausting. She did not fear him as such, but she had good instincts, so she knew when to back off or flat out avoid him. She respected and admired her husband greatly, so she did what she could to not fan the flames of his temper, lest he take everyone with him upon igniting.

Orla sometimes thought she secretly despised the man. He didn't ever seem appreciative or truly happy when he looked at his wife and children. He did have a soft spot for the tots, always preening and going on about his children as if he had produced them all on his own, without the hard work of the fine lady beside him. He annoyed Orla; with his constant mumbled critiques to his wife about this or that and his surly demeanour with everyone. He had a habit of one minute being nice and charming and the next striking out like a viper with a nasty look or hurtful comment as if he enjoyed being vile for the sake of it.

Orla surely thought an intelligent woman such as Mrs. Tappan would pick up on his occasional snide remarks and ill tempers, but she seemed to either not notice them, or they simply did not get under her skin. Orla admired her so- always able to put her family first, whereas Orla was convinced she would throw some heavy object at his head with great force if she were stuck with the likes of him – wealthy or not. Orla thought to be married to such arrogance would require the soul of a nun.

Luckily, the children were fine little people, nothing like their father. Orla had a sense about people, and she could tell – the babes were every bit their mother. She only hoped Doctor Tappan for a father would not ruin them, especially the boy.

Yes, Orla was going to miss the family greatly, but not Dr. Tappan. She could not wait for him and his smug, sneering face, his prying eyes, to be but a distant memory, even as it came at the loss of her beloved Mrs. Tappan.

Chapter 7

The housekeeper appeared at the door just as Amanda sat down to go over the train and boat schedules. They would depart from New York harbour on a nine-day journey by boat down to Veracruz where they would then take the train to Mexico City. They left in three days. She felt ill-prepared and as if she were forgetting a million details. The minutia of this sort of move was overwhelming.

"Excuse me Mrs. Tappan, you have a guest calling to the door. A Mr. Diaz Carrera?"

"Oh, my heavens!" she gasped in genuine surprise.

"Please see him straight away," she clapped her hands in delight.

Although she felt unprepared for a visitor, it was Diego, and he was a welcome distraction.

Amanda, delighted, furtively stacked papers out of the way and cleared a chair at her desk.

"Orla, looking at the time, perhaps the children can go out to the garden, please, for a little walk before dinner."

"Of course, Mrs. Tappan."

Orla ushered the two little rabbits out of the room, but not before Diego Diaz Carrera swooped into the room, beaming at Orla and bending down to touch the children's little faces, exclaiming how big they had grown.

A truly welcome sight, Diego was one of those beautiful people who had no idea how beautiful they were. All women adored him, and oddly, all the fellas did too. He put everyone at ease immediately. He was so charming and good-natured. A gentleman, while still a man's man with no pretence and always up for a laugh. He was handsome and humble, a rare enough combination. He always carried with him and always doled out compliments for the ladies and sweets for the kids.

Tailors loved him too, for he was a finely dressed man who spent a good bit of his time and money in their shops. He was a walking advertisement for them, an impeccably dressed statue of David. He stood 6'1", a slim build, always with a slim cigarette to match that build or a cigar to match his mood, which was always playful. His eyes were green and riveting, hair black as ink, his jawline square, and his skin appeared to be made of porcelain, the colour of snow, just enough of a rosy glow of youth in his masculine face to catch the eye. He looked years younger than his age and had a boyish, impish quality that kept him eternally youthful. Amanda had never seen him sour or disagreeable. His moustache was always neat and as tailored as his clothing. He was what Amanda's mother would have called "a pretty boy", but not in a derogatory manner, but simply because he was such a feast for the eyes. Orla couldn't help but turn her neck again to steal another long glance at him on her way out the door, which he caught and rewarded with an almost imperceptible wink, sending a blush of embarrassed attraction to her cheeks.

He was nothing short of perfect in every way, and yet it was impossible for anyone to begrudge him for it. An old Harvard buddy of Edward's and extraordinary doctor, Amanda had always been very fond of this man, who could charm anyone. Everybody's friend, the wild and darling Diego, was not just the life of every party but could transform a boring Tuesday house packing into an event. He was funny to the point of ridiculous at times and had a manner that had children rapt with attention. Over the years he would even prance out the latest magic trick he had picked up at the World's Fair- executed terribly, but no one cared. Everyone always clapped and laughed for Diego, even when he got it wrong. He came off as a playboy but had a shrewd mind and could get information out of someone without them never being the wiser.

"Ah la princesa!" he exclaimed as if he were a circus host introducing the next act, stretching out his long arms towards Amanda.

"The Irish and French Princess of the United States is now ours- Mexico will be so delighted to have you, preciosa! Mexico can hardly wait for the arrival of the Tappans. And just in time for our new President, Madero! Tell me, have you seen the papers? Very exciting times, my dear. We have finally ousted Diaz! You will be experiencing a whole new Mexico."

His accent was thick as honey, and with his voice booming and his arms outstretched, he positively took over the room with his presence.

"Why Diego, what on earth are you doing here? Does Edward know? You, why you haven't even stepped foot in New York since after I had Amelia- it has been far too long. No, I haven't seen a paper in weeks, Ed has kept me so busy with organizing everything. He did mention awhile back some new President in Mexico, but who can keep up? It is so good to see you; you're looking well; please sit down, sit down; what have you been getting up to?"

A giant, warm embrace and cheek kisses and the general sit down, make yourself at home ensued for a good minute as the housekeeper brought in a tray and set to pouring coffee.

"My work, my work, as any man will tell you, the work keeps us very busy, and yes, Eduardo knows I'm in town; I just left his office.

He knew I was coming into New York- Did he not tell you? Oh, of course, wait a moment," he said, feigning confusion and then snapping his fingers,

"I told him not to tell you- I love a surprise. The look on your face, like you've seen a ghost. Cómo estás preciosa?",

He grinned at her like a cat with a bowl of cream, even raising his eyebrows in a manner most would have suggested was far too flirtatious for a meeting without her husband present, but Amanda had known Diego for almost a decade and knew he was the perfect gentleman. He was simply very enthusiastic in everything he said and did, even when just smiling at a friend. It was as if Diego just loved being alive, and life loved him right back.

Amanda chattered away on the recurring topics of the big move down to Mexico City, the daily life of a mother and wife, and, of course, all things New York. They gossiped as if in a sewing circle as if no time had passed since they last sat exchanging news, and the laughter rolled continuously on like thunder. Amanda did not have any male friends who treated her as a confidant the way Diego did, not even her husband. They discussed the children and their excitement at what they understood about the big move. They traded stories about mutual friends over their coffees and Amanda was so glad of a break from the doldrums of preparing to move, she didn't notice the afternoon slipping by. She could talk to Diego forever about anything, and she was relishing this time with her old friend. Diego elicited from her smiles so large she felt the muscles of her cheeks – the zygomatics – Ed had told her- grow tired and almost hurt. Diego got her up to speed on the newly elected President of Mexico and, heeding Edward's advice earlier, not to mention the word Revolution to his wife, Diego danced around the topic. As far as he was concerned everything in Mexico was going his way. His candidate had won, and now his oldest friend and his family were going to be up the road from him, so he was on cloud nine.

"You certainly did not come all this way for nothing, Diego."

"I told you; old Eddie wanted me to come to check you were packing the china correctly."

They both chuckled, and Amanda shook her head,

"What are you up to?"

Diego drank his coffee black and lit his fat Cuban cigar.

"I am in New York for a lecture with a certain Professor, a Dr. Freud from Vienna. He is in New York for a couple of weeks, giving talks about his work in psychoanalysis. I see I am boring you, my dear." He chuckled.

"Not at all, it's a new field, isn't it? I wouldn't know anything about it, but I'm sure you will tell me…" she gave him a shy smile.

In a moment where the two of them were no longer talking over each other, and the ticking of the clock and the noise of the city were their only background score, she balled up her courage and decided to ask about something that had waltzed through her mind for months.

"I don't mean to change the subject but, Edward told me a little secret….you nearly married? A German girl?"

"Ay yes, Graciela…a lovely girl- born in Tabasco, of German immigrants. Her parents and grandparents from the Dusseldorf. Yes, I did ask her to marry me but- unfortunately, before I could even invite you to my wedding, I discovered she was not, how do you say…" he trailed off, looking for a moment either pained or embarrassed, possibly both.

"Let's say it just didn't work out, and I had to break off the engagement."

"Oh no- my word, what was wrong- I mean, I don't mean to pry, I'm sorry to hear –",

suddenly her cheeks fell, the smile gone, zygomatics at rest.

"Not at all Señora; I will tell you all the story. I met her through a friend of my sister's, briefly at a dinner and then saw her again at my sister Elena's wedding. We wrote to each other and then after she moved to Mexico City permanently to pursue her studies in languages, I began to court her. Gracie is a very smart young woman; she spoke Spanish, German and English fluently from the time she was a child, as well as some native language from the area she grew up in. She wanted very much to learn French and perhaps work in languages. She was one of these modern young women interested in a career before marriage. I thought I'd let her have her fun before sweeping her away to Casa Diaz to be my wife", he explained.

"It turns out that her father, the German, had come to make his fortune in textiles in Mexico and while he brought his German wife with him thirty years ago…….after they had been here, doing very well for about a decade…..he impregnated the maid."

Amanda froze, her eyes as round as the saucer in her lap.

"Come again?"

"Graciela's mother – her real mother- was una de las clases bajas….the maid of all people. Graciela had not known this herself until recently and I can see why she would not have told me. I discovered that her mother's ancestors came from the tribes of people who still sleep in the dirt and walk about barefoot. I couldn't believe it, but when I confronted her with my suspicions, some of the things I had heard, she told me the truth, to her credit. I think most women in her position would have continued to lie or try to. Very embarrassing situation for her; it really is heartbreaking. Her mother was half Indian, half Spaniard, the poor forgotten bastard of some rich European from a little hole in the ground outside of Puebla. So, Graciela was- of the wrong societal position, and I could not go ahead."

"He..impregnated, her father had a- a liaison- with one of the servants, and Graciela was the result? That's actually flabbergasting that sort of behaviour. I'm dreadfully sorry Diego, I really am."

"It could have been a real scandal if I had married her without finding the truth".

"How did you find out? Did you suspect? Was she of a dark complexion or didn't look like the rest of the German family?"

"No, not at all, no more than many people in Mexico. Her eyes were a light green/blue, her hair reddish auburn, not unlike yourself. In fact, her hair is very like yours now that I think about it. She looked totally European, not Indian at all. She is only a quarter native, but the problem was really not even her caste but that her mother was a household servant. We don't intermarry with these people."

Amanda was silent for a moment, the wind somewhat taken from her sails. Diego was such a fine person, she felt he should have someone to share his life with. At almost thirty-seven, it would have been the perfect time for him to marry and start a family of his own, or rather, she feared that time was nearly past. There had been much speculation among their mutual friends over the years as to why Diego seemed unable to find a young woman to settle down with. Some insisted he was much too much of a playboy and simply not ready to commit himself to a life of matrimony, while others, Edward included, had inferred maybe women were not actually to Diego's tastes….a ridiculous supposition Amanda had refuted vehemently.

"Diego-, I'm going to ask something perfectly ignorant, so forgive me, but also, from a place of sympathy, so I hope you will excuse me but…Does ….does it matter anymore? Haven't things changed? I mean, I understand economic and social trappings, but isn't half of Mexico from the mixing of European bloodlines with the natives?

"Perhaps, yes, a good bit of Mexico is an intermixture of race, but many of us are not, and I am not, so I could not. I am Spanish, Swiss and Prussian, un blanco. I could never marry anyone of the natives. It is not done, not in my family. You see, the problem isn't really the girl or the quarter native blood she possesses, which could be overlooked. She is from one of the finest families in Mexico, well on the German father's side, but I could not keep this secret. Then what, bring this *criada* into my life as a mother-in-law? I could not even fathom it. Fine society does not have maids for mothers-in-law. "

"Well, but does this Graciela even have anything to do with her-does she even know her real mother, the maid?"

"Why would I knowingly invite problems into my life? Graciela is a beautiful young lady who was raised as one of the legitimate children of the household, but she was not. She grew up believing this German woman who resents her was her very unloving and cold mother; now, of course, we all know why the mother was the way she was. I'm sorry, but I did not want to have skeletons in my closet. I did not want to have those people, those awful Germans, as my in-laws and then perhaps one day my wife would feel sorry for her real mother and invite this maid into our lives, into our home with our children, no, no, perdona me pero no.

I did not approve- my own father never carried on with the damn maid, for God's sake. I couldn't even look at this foolish man anymore. I lost all respect for Graciela's father. I could no longer meet his eyes. Pardon my language, but to fornicate with a dirt-poor servant is awful enough, but he broke the sacred vows he made to his wife. Now, often, many Mexican women will look the other way to a mistress, but my parents did not believe in the destruction of their promise to God. We were very strict in my household. My father did not approve of the taking of concubines, and I also do not agree with it. It is categorically wrong. Then you consider that he lied to his own child for the whole of her life, and he made the wife go along with it, keeping the baby while sending the servant girl away, who apparently was only fourteen years of age when he took advantage of her. It is sordid in every possible way, Amanda. Also, I did not approve of Graciela lying to me. She should have told me the moment she found out."

Amanda paused, wanting to choose her next words carefully. She could read the disappointment in her friend's eyes. She did not want to cause him any additional pain.

"Was she not lying for a noble cause, Diego? Think of her embarrassment. If she fell in love with you, this revelation about her origins must have been devastating. To keep it secret, to keep her love or even in order to improve her social standing, to save face with you, I mean.... Especially if she had only found out herself, it wasn't as though she tried to deceive you. Why my friend, you could hardly blame her. She must have been in a sort of shock, and then to have to find the courage to speak the very words- I would not have known how to broach such a subject, much less to divulge that to the man I wanted to marry.

Diego, everyone just adores you. She was taken with you, I

imagine, and then this awful news she thought would ruin things between you and now it has. I feel terrible pity for her."

"Yes, I do understand all that Amandita. It does not change the reality of the situation that we found ourselves in."

"Let me ask you, did you love this girl? This Graciela, I mean marriage material and all that, but - did you truly love her?"

After a terribly long moment of silence that left Amanda fearful she had angered her old friend and that he was not going to answer her, he let out a long breath tinged with a sort of sadness.

"My dear- we can teach ourselves to love people".

"Can we?"

"And we can teach ourselves not to love people- those that we know we should not or that we cannot. Sometimes, it simply isn't allowed for various reasons. "

"Señor Diaz- are you saying that we have total control of our affections in this life- that we determine who we fall absolutely, madly in love with? And then we can simply talk ourselves out of it?"

Diego then looked at her in that moment in a way she had never seen a man look at her, it was wistful and longing and almost angry. His eyes flickered over each of her features briefly, as if he was trying to steal pieces of his friend's wife and put them in his coat pocket.

"I think" he began slowly, "that there is much of the bonds humans create that we do not understand. Ultimately yes, we can control most of them by using logic for dictating to our emotions that they must behave in a certain way in response to certain stimuli.

If you are able to will yourself to walk across the street without thinking about it, to propel yourself forward in life, then you can will yourself to love someone or not to love them. We can train-truly master – both the conscious and the subconscious. It takes practice and commitment, but it can be done. Love is a choice. Then, you control the situation. It can't become destructive because its power is contained. It is when you cannot control those awful human emotions that your life can be ruined, many wasted years pining after the wrong woman- or the right woman…if only under different circumstances. This upset with Graciela, who I was incredibly fond of could have been a tragedy if I had allowed myself to become silly over the girl. It would have kept me up at nights, distracted me from my work or even made me throw caution to the wind and marry her out of a sort of psychosis. Much of my work has gone to not only the study of the brain but the study of the mind, the psychology."

He paused to puff on his cigar as if buying time to clarify or justify what he was trying to say.

"No, no, falling in love is an idea, nothing more. Like the architectural drawings for a building, it is a plan. Wonderful if it works, but if there are flaws in the design, it is really very impractical at best and ruinous, devastating at worst….when it doesn't work out. Or, in my case, when you see from the beginning that it will not. Simply wanting something to work is not enough. It is as silly as wishing upon a star for something."

"Diego, now you are starting to sound far too American. You've been spending too much time around these cold New Yorkers. I thought Mexican men were supposed to be romantic! "

"Romance is a notion for children, Amanda. It doesn't exist. There is only friendship, lust, and yes love, this thing that we call love, that yet no one can really define. It is not scientific, and I at my core, am a scientist. Love cannot be measured. Love needs to be made specific and defined because it is so open to interpretation- no two loves are the same; thus, it must be defined with specific terms and rules. It is abstract and romance even more so; whereas you can naturally define friendship, such as ours, there are rules and parameters. You can even clearly define lust and passion, two things that do not require or imply anything other than pure sexuality."

Amanda blushed ever so slightly.

"Perhaps we can even define obsession. But like obsession, romance is not love. And if you romanticise notions of love, of what needs to be real and practical, you will destroy love eventually. Romantic love places upon its victims expectations no mortal can live up to. You have people expecting the poetry, the sonnets of Shakespeare, with no foundation underneath. Romance is a lovely notion you read in a book- nothing more than a fairy tale by Hans Christian Anderson, something from the Brothers Grimm. I'm afraid there is no Fairy Tale of Mexico City, not even for me."

"Well, Diego, you dash my hopes. I was expecting to waltz down to Mexico and wake up Cinderella." She attempted a joke, and even as it left her mouth, she heard it falling flat.

"I suppose Mexico City is just as disappointing as New York in some ways, then?"

"Not disappointing, no Mexico City is never disappointing, as you soon will see my dear, but it is subject to the realities of this life. The reality being we don't always get what we want no matter how much we crave it."

The pair had a forced laugh and drank their coffees in silence until she couldn't let it lie.

"As a physician, you are familiar with Darwin's theory of

evolution. What of his writings on the survival of the fittest? Are we not perhaps strengthening our bloodlines when we add in the occasional half or quarter Indian? Something to do with the diseases found in inbreeding and that cross-breeding is actually good –"

Diego howled with laughter.

"My darling mujer, what have you been reading now? That specific theory of Darwin's that you are now quoting was about plants!"

Amanda paused, her mouth slightly open, the confusion growing over her lovely face.

Diego found Amanda was always so sharp and witty and yet with some very strange ideas. Her brilliant realisations were part of what made people so taken with her. Her suggestion that mixing bloodlines had benefits over racial purity had Diego guffawing, and he was reminded she was no physician, as clever as she was.

"Now Señora, that sounds very American of you. How is it viewed with your natives? Hmm? Did your father want you off with a Mohican? Happy to see you in a tepee?"

Amanda tried to stifle her laughter, her face red with embarrassment and the thought of her marrying some man in a headdress.

"Well, we hardly have any more natives of any kind- they were decimated! Diego, those poor people- the only ones that are left are the remnants of amazing tribes of the native people from all over the United States, and they're just- gone. The government has allocated the few left behind these barren fields – these reservations – I don't even care for the word."

"The only reservations I want to know about are our dinner

reservations", Diego laughed,

"And the reservations I had about marrying this woman- which turned out to be correct."

He smiled with a wink.

Amanda shook her head; she found his cavalier attitude towards love, towards one of the most beautiful parts of life, really appalling. He made her all in the same moment, furious, embarrassed, and tickled pink. She wondered if he would have said the same about being able just to stop loving someone if he had met her before Ed and they had fallen in love? Her face reddened at the notion.

"It just seems to me, if you don't mind my saying, that you seem only to have a problem with the parents of this young lady, which of course, is a factor totally beyond her control. You mention control in relation to love, and then surely you can see how cruel you are being to this girl, how unfair.

You are punishing someone who you were ready to marry- punishing her for the sins of her father."

Amanda could not understand why this was annoying her so. She was somewhat furious on behalf of this stranger Graciela. Her heart hurt for the girl at the thought of losing Diego over trivialities.

"I'm afraid, my old pal, we will never see eye to eye on this."

Diego sat back in his chair. He was becoming frustrated by Amanda's continued innocence and her insistence to make something so broken, somehow magically work. There were certain things that were just not acceptable in parts of Mexican society. No one had any illusions about the propensity for the taking of mistresses, but certainly not the brown-skinned servant girl who scrubbed the floors.

"Diego, just I simply ask, do yourself a favour- if you can't stop thinking about her- if you can't talk yourself out of feelings for her, the way you say you can, then promise me, one day...

"One day what, Señora Tappan?" he asked doubtfully, suddenly the most thoughtful she had ever seen him.

"One day, if you find you are compelled to seek her out, then you simply must try. This life waits for no one, not even anyone as charming as yourself, so sometimes, perhaps we should throw caution to the wind for happiness-"

She choked on the last word as she saw him smiling at her strangely.

"I will one day remind you of this conversation, my dear.", he said softly, sadly.

"No, never mind. I'm sorry. You know your own mind and what is best for you. I'm carrying on like a silly schoolgirl. Forgive me, Diego. Forget I ever asked about her, please. I've embarrassed myself now; I have overstepped-"

"Nonsense, my dear old friend, you can never overstep with me, Amandita."

"It's just Ed went on and on with how highly you spoke of this young woman in your letters, and we were hopeful…"

she began to stammer, supremely mortified, never having made a fool of herself to such a degree.

"…. and it's dreadfully inappropriate to have been gossiping and making our little plans behind your back for an imaginary wedding, we were simply excited. You spoke with such happiness, and we – I just want to see you happy." she smiled meekly at his beautiful face.

"At this moment, I am",

He said so quietly that she could barely hear him.

There was a strange pocket of air in the room of suddenly, an uncomfortable electricity, an unwanted guest sitting with them.

As they sat across from each other and she swiftly changed the subject back to the excitement of the move, and the logistics of the adventure they were about to embark upon, Diego was only half listening as he gazed upon his old friend. There was an uninvited, quiet ache before him that felt heavy in his chest, as if one of the large trunks in the corner had been placed in his lap, waiting to be unpacked. He suspected it had to do with this highly opinionated woman who drove him mad with feelings that he knew better than ever to study or question because, once examined, he was not so certain he could just reason them away. Diego wasn't afraid of anything except the illogical want of wishing their lives had played out differently, perhaps just like a fairy tale.

Chapter 8

The little village sat on the outskirts of Jalapa, a dusty, yellow, and forgotten landscape. It was more shanty town than a proper village, with lean-tos and shacks with metal corrugated slabs of forgotten scrap for roofs.

The girl was not even twenty yet, but she was the kind of tired the very old knew well. She knew only this life with nothing but work and hunger and little to look forward to.

Tired of the whispers that trouble was coming, she sat down for her one proper meal of the day in the darkened and cool corner of her home. Chicken and nopales. Nopales were abundant, an edible cactus that was as flavourless as it was fibrous. While filling, it never failed to disappoint. There was an ear of corn on the wooden table that was nearing spoiled, so she grabbed that too, hoping that her abuela, the grandmother, would not come looking for it later. Nothing that Amparo did please her grandmother. Where the old woman was concerned, there was offence waiting around every corner, like a wolf waiting to pounce. Amparo found she was very hungry this Thursday afternoon after coming in from the fields. Her day had started with the rising sun, and she knew she had hours more work before she would lay down her body in defeat.

"Amparo", came the call of her friend at the door.

Teresita was small, very small. Not only was she short, but everything about her body seemed minute, doll like. Teresita was her friend from when their memory began and was more of a sister to Amparo than her own sisters.

"Look, I brought tortillas I just made. I have plenty at home."

Amparo was glad of it; she was especially hungry on this day.

"Amparo, I am going into the city soon to see about a job. Would you like to go with me?"

Amparo studied her friend, too tired to register her surprise,

"A job in the city? What city, the capital?"

"Si!! En el distrito federal, Amparo."

Amparo had never been to Mexico City before. The thought intrigued her.

"What sort of job, like in a factory?"

"No- even better- in a family home. As a maid in a nice, big family home of some American doctor!"

Teresita always had such good luck.

"If I can go, I will go. It might be nice to take a trip, to have a day of rest. I would like to see Mexico City."

What Amparo didn't say was that she would love nothing more than to get away from her family, especially her old snake of a grandmother, for even just a Sunday afternoon.

"Andale!" Teresita exclaimed with a laugh,

"So, then, it is settled. You will be my chaperone, amiga."

Amparo ate in silence for a moment.

"Tere- what have you heard of this- coming war- the Revolution- I am hearing all kinds of stories, most seem like nonsense. Bandeleros taking lands off the whites and the rich landowners? I heard an entire family of English – well, they were originally from England, I think – I heard an entire family was murdered last week at their hacienda.

“I heard that too, but Amparo….it does not concern us because we are not white, nor rich landowners.

“But Tere, people were killed! That does not scare you? I heard the children were small, eight and ten.”

“Amparo, I don’t like to think about it too much honestly. Any of it. If there is some sort of war going on, all I know is they won’t hurt my family. Well, I mean, as long as we do as we are told if it came down to that – if these rebel forces took over our village and said you, Teresita, come bathe my horse- well then, I am going to bathe their horse. Problem solved. My family have nothing to lose, nothing of value, and we are not the Europeans who have caused so much trouble in this land for hundreds of years. This is one way in which its better to be native. So, you don’t need to worry Amparo. This is not our war.”

“But if you go to work for some rich American doctor in Mexico City- in his home- what if the war reaches the capital?”

“You worry about silly things Amparo. No war will take over the most powerful city in the world- Mexico City is fine, and we are safe because we are not the people the rebels are looking to punish. We are the ones they are trying to do right by. If anything-,” she lowered her voice to a whisper.

“We should be helping them amiga.”

“To hurt and kill people?”

“Maybe, if that is what it takes. Aren’t you tired, Amparo? Of always having to work so hard? Of being hungry? Why do the whites, the French and the Spanish, the English and the Germans- why do they get to come in and take over our land? You heard what the whites did in the United States, eh? Do you want that to happen here? To let them kill all of us? Or stick us on plots of land we can't leave- in our own country?"

Amparo didn't want anyone to die.

"No, of course not."

Teresita sighed, "This is stupid talk anyway; we are just peasant girls. No one will be looking to us to help them fight a war, and no one will expect us to save them. Come with me to Mexico City. Let's go see about jobs that could get us out of this pueblo where nothing good ever happens."

Amparo did not take much convincing. She wanted to see this Mexico City and leave nothing good behind.

Chapter 9

The journey started bright and early on a warm morning from New York down to Vera Cruz. Over the next week the Tappan family would be in the luxurious first-class cabins of the RMS Adriatic. Less than five years old the ship was humungous, state of the art and shiny as a pearl. It was breathtaking, impossibly large, impossibly white and a pearlescent navy on the bottom half. It was touted to be the fastest passenger ship in the Americas. It was massive in scope, stretching for what seemed to Amanda's eyes to be miles from stem to stern. From Canada down to Chile, there wasn't a more glamorous or faster transoceanic passenger ship to be found.

"The papers are saying this Adriatic doesn't compare to that monstrosity the White Star Line is building in Belfast."

Ed told his wife as they boarded the ship.

"The Titanic, they're calling it because, well, it's supposed to be. The first-class cabins are rumoured to be fit for royalty. Obviously, that means we were meant for it. We will sail on it sometime- a little trip to Europe someday soon."

He winked at Amanda.

"I wouldn't know Ed; I haven't read a paper in weeks- it feels like months, actually. Anything I've read has come from papers that are months old that Orla and I used to wrap my mother's teacups for shipping."

She said with a grin.

"Hmmm, Orla, such a lovely girl. I am sure the family will miss her." Ed mused.

"I've no excuse, really, I could have always sent someone to fetch me the day's paper, but I just have been so busy it usually slips my mind. I mean, who has the time to leisurely read when planning to move a family across the world?"

"Absolutely my dear. You've always had your priorities right Señora Tappan. The paper can wait; we have work to do."

"Perhaps I will have time to read while we travel; I can get caught up on what is going on south of the border. I'd like to be not totally ignorant about my new home."

"Nothing really exciting that the English papers would be covering, but as soon as we get down there, you work on that Spanish of yours, then read all the newspapers you want."

"Oh, but Diego mentioned about the new President-"

"Yes, but that is only interesting to the Mexican populace; you wouldn't understand it. You will get caught up in time; no rush."

Amanda adored travelling by boat and train. She simply loved to travel. Although she had never been travelling for quite so long as this trip and after the second day, she thought the morning sickness combined with the motion sickness would surely kill her. She never knew that one's lack of equilibrium could bring one to pray for their own death. Her usual patience and even temperament were in short supply, so she left the children to the new nanny most of the days, as she felt she could not cope. She had constant waves of putrid gasses just behind her teeth and found the bathtub one place she could sit, fully clothed and get even a modicum of relief. She told herself If she could not get a break from the constant motion, she was sure to lose her sanity. There was no way she could read anything, as she could barely suffer through the day, at times not able to lift her head properly. The first morning on the ship, after she lost her breakfast, she tried to look at a paper and felt waves of nausea that put her in a quagmire of a mood for hours. She could not believe how extraordinarily difficult this voyage was from the moment they pulled out of the dock in New York. This was by far the sickest she had ever been while in the family way. Little Arthur and Amelia were happy enough to be entertained by Marta, the new Mexican nanny making the trip down from the US to Mexico. At the same time, Amanda would keep herself busy getting sick into a paper bag or banishing herself to sit in the cool albeit tiny bathtub. She spent a good amount of the trip lying down, but at night, the malaise would subside, and she would perk up to where she could even have dinner. Dinner seemed to be the only thing she could keep down, and the dark of night seemed to offer her equilibrium relief. As soon as the sun went down, she perked up and despite Amanda being mind falteringly exhausted, she still presented a refined, collected picture of utter grace in front of Edward and the other first-class passengers. Although there were moments she thought she was sure to faint, she luckily never did. It would have been terribly rude.

Throughout his life and travels, any time Edward would travel to Mexico from the US he would go through Galveston. He'd found he enjoyed travelling by train down to Texas and then sailing from Galveston to Mexico. He found it faster, even though he knew it wasn't. Ed liked the ability to depart a train and step onto dry land ever day or so, as opposed to being stuck on a ship for what seemed like months. Yes, if they had not had the children in tow and having to deal with household effects and some bits of furniture, mostly sentimental attachments his wife refused to sell, he would have much preferred going through Galveston, or at the very least New Orleans. Up until the previous decade, sailing out of Galveston had been the preferred option, but that bloody hurricane ruined the place. Galveston was simply "washed off the map," as he put it to his young wife over a late-night brandy in the first-class dining room.

"It was as if God himself grew tired of it and decided to redecorate. Or perhaps they were such sinners that He sent another flood to tidy his creation. It's a shame; I really was quite fond of Galveston. I'd often thought in my youth I might relocate there before that storm. And if not for that, I would have gone and I would have missed out on meeting you, dear wife."

The first decade of the twentieth century found the once large island of Galveston made infinitely smaller and dealing with the fallout of a societal killer. The city was struggling to come back from the devastation of the storm and rebuild, as suddenly, investors and developers were wary of the island. The Golden Era of Galveston did not seem likely to return. It had been a much larger and bustling port than even New York, but like anything else, even the most fabulous cities were not impervious to the temperamental moods of mother nature. It had been a densely populated and quickly expanding monstrosity- one of the richest cities in the United States. In just one day, after the storm, Galveston was gone. Ed often pondered how if Galveston had not been victim to that hurricane if, he would not already be established down there, perhaps running the hospital, had it not been washed away. He supposed it was for the best he had not moved there. Those kinds of storms could pop up at any time with no real warning. Staying in New York had been the smart choice. Then, with the luck of meeting his wife and beginning to court her, it all fell into place. Moving Amanda out of Philadelphia, a city Ed referred to as a dump that thought it was something, had been the right choice. He knew now more than ever that the move to Mexico City was not only the right choice for him but the opportunity of a lifetime. He didn't even bother trying to explain to Amanda the scope, the massiveness of the riches before them. She could not count that high.

"I'd like to one day visit Galveston again and take you there of course. "

Always with his promises of plans and the happy couple seeing the world.

Amanda, too would have preferred travelling the United States by train and then going from either New Orleans or Galveston to Mexico, simply so she could have the opportunity to disembark the train for only an hour or even a few minutes. Sailing on a ship while in the first part of pregnancy was something she would be sure not to recommend to others. The lengthy trip was, at times, agonizing, and she found herself willing the ship to cut through the water faster and faster.

The children were in their cabin suite with the nanny, as Ed accompanied his wife as she insisted on making another lap around the ship after their brandy. As badly as she felt with the movement of the water, she found she could almost mitigate the upset by moving herself, as in constantly walking. The day made her feel so poorly that once the sun went down some nights, she refused to stand still.

The third sunset on the water, not a bit of land to be seen, the couple strolled arm in arm as she breathed in the heavy warmth of the night air. It was just sunset, and most of the passengers seemed to be elsewhere. The horizon looked as if it were giving birth to the sky; there was every shade of brilliant pink and purple, and orange with grey storm clouds in the distance. If Amanda had been a painter, she would have wanted to capture this vista.

“Penny for your thoughts”,

Ed muttered as he lit his pipe.

“Just enjoying this view and wishing I had the talent to replicate it.” Amanda smiled.

“That my wife, is yet another thing you will enjoy down Mexico way- the art is incredible, like nothing you would have seen in New York.”

He delivered this promise as if he himself had painted something. Ed was often quite proud of himself, proud of his accomplishments, even when he was not involved in any way. Ed had a terrible habit of taking credit for most things he found pleasing. If you complimented his whiskey, it was because he had sourced the finest. If you complimented Amanda, it was because he had selected the perfect bride. If Ed could have, he would take credit for the very sunset before them.

“Maybe you can even take up painting once we are settled down. I can get you lessons with a local artist, see what my Amanda can do.”

“That would be lovely, Ed. I’d sure like to try. I mean, why not? We only live once.”

“I think that dame Diego is seeing is a painter.”

“The German girl?” Amanda asked.

“Oh, you haven’t heard? Diego didn’t tell you?”

Amanda quickly recounted the crux of the conversation she had with Diego only the other day.

Ed lit another match against his pipe, annoyed that it had gone out or annoyed with Diego; she could not tell.

“He is being ridiculous”, Ed muttered.

“A man like Diego needs to settle down. He is lucky he doesn’t have any bastard children running around, well, assuming he doesn’t.”

“Oh, Edward, that is not very nice to speak of our friend-”

“He’s an idiot.”

“Ed!” Amanda exclaimed, laughing, but saw that he was getting worked up.

“He should have found a girl around the time you and I met and got married. He drags out his bachelor hood instead and now drops a perfectly good match because of what exactly? This lady is twenty-four, prime age for children and he spoke of her like he was really taken with her. Used to go on to me in letters about her hair, for crying out loud. He was very much the love-struck schoolboy. It is strange how he could have turned so quickly, almost like he was looking for an out.”

Amanda studied Ed, wondering silently why Diego would want an excuse not to marry the girl he was supposed to be in love with.

“I don’t think he- well, I don’t know, Diego seems to think we can control who we fall in love with, mentioned some doctor, started saying that we can control our mind in a way I just didn’t think was possible.”

“Oh, yes, Diego has become a philosopher, don’t you know? Has gone into the field of psychology, this quackery no different than crystal balls and fortune tellers, only in reverse. They don’t tell you the future; they use your past against you. Utter rubbish. The traumas of childhood manifesting in adult life." He said mockingly, with his face exaggerated.

"They are simply looking for any excuse to explain away pure bad behaviour. There are sane people, and there are crazy people. The crazy should be locked away in sanatoriums where they are of no danger to anyone. The sane, well, we shall get on with it. Not go looking for excuses to be splashing around in hysterics."

Amanda sensed him tense and saw his jaw set hard and square. He was getting angry at what exactly she was never sure, but in this instance, it was really bizarre so she thought she would distract him.

"Ed, maybe we can return to the cabin; I need to lie down."

Ed deposited his wife to the door of their large cabin suite, telling the Mexican nanny in Spanish that Amanda was to lie down, from what Amanda picked up.

"You rest- I am going to the bar for a few nightcaps."

He was still moody, as if Diego not marrying this young girl had somehow messed up his own plans or at the very least, ruined his night.

"Well, all right dear, don't get too inebriated and fall off the side of the ship." She teased.

Ed shot her a look that was so cutting and dark that it made her regret her attempt at humour.

"That is not funny."

"I'm sorry Ed, I just want you to be careful, and I wanted to make light of it instead of clucking at you like I'm your mother." she rattled off quickly.

This seemed to appease him, and he relaxed somewhat.

The children were already asleep as he gave them a quick glance.

"All right- to bed with you", he told his wife and abruptly shut the door.

He then headed towards his trusted, and Amanda felt his favourite companion, whiskey. She should have joined him, she thought, frustrated, but her stomach began to gurgle unpleasantly, and she needed her bed. She instinctively knew as well that the sudden turn in Ed would mean he would not have been a pleasant companion that night anyway. She prepared for bed feeling low, crawling under the covers as if she had been chastised or they had quarrelled. It was a sad and lonely feeling she could not shake, even as she gazed upon her children in the dark of the cabin.

Chapter 10

When finally disembarking off the Adriatic onto the shores of Vera Cruz, Mexico, Amanda felt a sensation overtake her quite like the pure relief and joy in the moment after giving birth. The long, arduous task was over for the moment. She was ecstatic to not be swaying and able to put her feet on solid ground. Her mood instantly elevated, her smile returned, and she was never more grateful than in that moment. The Titanic and every other ship would have to wait. She was not interested in sailing again any time soon.

Vera Cruz struck Amanda as a beautiful yet strange place, a city that seemed to have eyes everywhere, heavily lashed, watching the inhabitants from behind foggy corners and Spanish fans. Amanda had never been anywhere so exotic, and after disembarking for only a few minutes, she wanted to spend more time there before they got back on another mode of transport. The city was hauntingly beautiful, like a sleepy Garden of Eden. The pace was languid yet still that of a bustling, busy town. Its buildings were beautifully ornate, and the place looked genuinely like parts of New York, something Amanda was not expecting. Maybe all port towns ended up looking similar, she mused, although she knew that was not it. It was certainly cleaner than New York. The streets were artfully arranged and swept clean. The air had a heavy sort of sea breeze to it- filled with the smells of salt, smoke, and the sea. The people were impeccably dressed. The city was elegant. Construction was ongoing but was less chaotic than what they had left behind in the U.S. She was delighted to see palm trees dotting the city landscape in front of newly built municipal buildings and decorated homes. She was unsure if she was simply dreading another two to three days of travel, even by train or if she was slightly taken with Vera Cruz, but Amanda felt as if she could stay there forever.

"Promise me, Ed, we will come back here someday."

"Oh yes, of course. Too bad I can't show you around; old Vera Cruz is lovely."

Edward's mother had relocated to Vera Cruz not long after his father died. Edward was only at Harvard a couple of years ago when the original Dr. Tappan, the famous Dr. Tappan, finally passed in his seventies, in his sleep. Edward's mother relocated with the last of Ed's siblings to the bustling port town. Vera Cruz put a spell on her, like she does to so many who find themselves possessed by the city and Edward's mother stayed, happily relocated there until her last breath. There were whispers as well that she could not bear to remain in Merida, with memories of her darling husband Arthur Mortimer Tappan everywhere.

Amanda and the children were tired and longing to find a hotel room, but Ed was busy instructing porteros to move their luggage from the docks they had arrived at only an hour ago aboard a train.

"Ed, I thought we were staying the night in Vera Cruz to rest and taking the noon train tomorrow?"

"We were going to, but then our ship arrived thirty minutes early, putting us just in time to catch the last afternoon train to Mexico City! Can you believe it? By thc skin of our teeth, we will have made this train- so I moved our departure up. The train today will get us to our home a good sixteen hours earlier."

"Well, all right, but Ed, I'm exhausted. Look at the children; they can barely stand. We need dinner and sleep."

"Both of which can be got on the train we will be boarding in ten minutes, so quit your complaining."

Marta, the new nanny, watched this exchange through downcast eyes. She could already see the wife was kind and accommodating yet struggling and the husband was difficult to be sure. She had no loyalties here, but she already did not like how he spoke to his wife.

The exhausted family boarded the train, and Ed directed them to again, the finest private car on a very full train.

Amanda felt her old troubles whispering to her. Out of nowhere, here they were, turning up again, uninvited guests to ruin the dinner party. There were too many people about, and she was so tired after being on that ship. She was feeling just so very drained. She felt as if she were one of her mother's beloved china teacups, shattered. Little porcelain rosebuds on the floor that Edward would step on. Her breathing became shallow, and she was feeling lightheaded.

The anxiety began to wash over her face like waves, her eyes ocean glass and distant.

Edward read her face and saw she was in distress. Instead of sympathy for his pregnant wife, this evoked more annoyance, which would soon turn to malice if she did not straighten up.

"They will be bringing dinner round shortly - what is the matter with you?" he huffed.

"Ed, I'm fine," she lied,

"I have just never travelled so far while expecting, and it makes one tired."

She chose her words so carefully so as not to anger him but also to try and calm herself as she felt panic rising within her.

Marta had the same disinterested look on her face she always wore so her employer could not see her contempt for him. He was meaner than most. In the households she had worked in before, the men from all different levels in society usually hid any mistreatment of their wives from the servants. It was an issue of respect- if the husband disrespected the wife in front of the staff, it could embolden them and lead to disobedience. This one, he seemed to make it a point to make a show for her. Marta did not know if he was always like this or if he was acting, putting on a performance for her benefit- to either impress her with his power or to impress upon her that she was next if she stepped out of line. She decided perhaps it was the travel and weariness that had this man frayed like a rope, so she tried to ignore his behaviour. She turned to the wife,

"Señora, you want water. I go get you?"

"Yes, please."

Amanda smiled at the new girl, who had turned out to not only be helpful, but also had sharp instincts, seemingly able to anticipate her new employer's needs.

"Oh 'k",

Marta said with a sigh and headed out of the car to find someone on the train to bring them water. A task she thought the loving husband could have easily offered to do, but she supposed men of his station didn't do such things. As Marta set out on her errand, Amanda sat flanked by the children, who were tired from travel but also able to tap into that infinite well of adrenaline little ones could harness through pure excitement. The train began to pull out of the station, first with a heavy jolt and then a slow roll forward that made

Amanda feel as a baby herself being rocked into much-needed slumber.

Edward was quietly observing his wife, not as his wife but as a specimen, with interest, even if he was mildly annoyed. He made a wager against himself in his head that she would begin to weep within the hour. If so, he would congratulate or console himself with the most expensive brandy on the train.

Within moments, Marta arrived, followed by a portero with a cart on wheels filled with drinks, fruit, and pastries. Edward paid for the children to get that fizzy Coca Cola he found disgusting. Marta set up a decanter of cold water next to the now sleeping Señora Tappan. Marta got herself a glass of water as well without even looking at the doctor, who she was growing convinced by the minute was an absolute jack ass of a man. The wife was now stretched out, pale and ghastly white, a sick colour, Marta thought. The poor thing looked more childlike than the children excitedly pressed up against the train window. Edward viewed his wife's pathetic sleeping form and shook his head.

"Tell me", he addressed the young portero, "what is your finest brandy?"

Chapter 11

The arrival to Mexico was one that Amanda had tried not to build up in her mind, but like a child approaching their birthday, she was just on the cusp of delight. She had read everything she could about the great city, one built on a lake by the Aztecs, conquered by the Spanish in the 1500's, with huge influences from all over the world. If those facts alone were not the beginning of a centuries-old fairy tale then she didn't know what they could be. Perhaps the Aztecs did not have any fairy tales, and those were purely European inventions. She knew all cultures had stories passed down through the generations – fables, allegories, all just another way to instil morals, virtues, and ethics, and she understood that the fairy stories she had read her own children were unlike anything they would encounter in the history of Mexico. Mexico's fairy tales were of a much wilder, feral nature.

She was an expert on the history of the United States and could recite names, dates and facts going back to before the American Revolutionary War. Amanda was a proud American; her young country had accomplished so much. While she felt there was much that it had also gotten wrong, she had to keep her opinions on the treatment of the coloureds, the China men, and the natives to herself. She was considered odd even by her most progressive and modern girlfriends.

They had mocked her in school for stating in class that if all men were created equal, then they should all be treated as equals, and so slavery should have never happened in such a modern and free country. It seemed a remarkably simple concept and foregone conclusion, and yet her classmates had laughed and made mocking faces.

As history was a love of hers, she tore into the history of Mexico with awe, with the few books she had been able to get a hold of. She felt it was her wifely duty to inform herself, as she had not previously known anything about it.

She found Mexico fascinating and its history full of wonder.

Why didn't they have slavery? How did the Conquistadors not decimate the natives and yet still wound up in charge, such a different outcome to the United States? Was Spanish the official language, how many native tongues were there, and how many native tribes? Would she see them in the city or were they sent off to other parts of the country? While she found herself becoming ever more interested in her new country, she also had to balance her wonder with the duties of everyday life. As much as she had wanted to devote time to reading, she found there was never enough time. She asked Ed to tell her great stories of Mexico, but of course he did so only when he was in the mood for it.

She held no fantasy that their lives would suddenly become a non-stop holiday. The work of a man and his wife in rearing a family would always have ups and downs and heartache. She had tasted enough loss in her young life to know that more simply waited around every corner, but she could not help but feel optimistic. She imagined she was an author as they set out to write a new novel or a painter in front of a blank canvas. She was going to be able to create her life in Mexico; Ed had all but promised it. She thought of the glorious sunsets she had seen over the water with longing. Amanda possessed none of those talents, but she liked to imagine that she was building something, with a plan for the outcome and hopeful ideas, all the while working for a dream to come to fruition. She felt she was writing a new story for her little family as if she had bought one of those gorgeous little Gidden typewriters she had seen in the store window in New York the day before they left. It had shiny, black, round buttons- or- they were called keys- keys just like her piano. Perhaps she would even take up writing while down in Mexico. Yes, she thought, she would have Edward buy her one of those typewriters, and she would document their family's adventures. She could use a nom de plume and educate the American masses as to how life really was in the "wilds of Mexico".

The closer they travelled each day to the City of Palaces, the more excited she became. She would take up writing. She would become a painter. She would learn Spanish. Her children would have the best of both worlds. How could she have really been nervous about this move when it sounded every bit like a fairy tale? She would have to mention to Diego just how wrong he was. Romance did exist, perhaps between people and places, if not in human relationships. Her family going to Mexico, was the very definition of romantic, she was convinced.

The train tore through the Mexican countryside, marking a path through expanses of desserts and fields of grassland, past rivers and shanty towns and large, bustling cities, many with exquisite, coloured houses and buildings. There was so much colour against the many backdrops of dry and arid land; each new place seemed an art exhibit to savour from the windows of the train.

She was unsure if she expected to see cactuses all over Mexico City or Parisian influenced palaces. Would there be cactuses growing in front of those palaces? Was that a stupid or juvenile thing to wonder? She had peppered Ed with questions but did not want to seem daft or childlike with her impatience. As she strolled the train that morning with a child in each hand, she could not help but get slightly lost in her daydreams. Anything that helped take her mind off her constant nausea was a welcome distraction. That day, she awoke with the knowledge that we were inching closer. Her heart would beat as if doing a little timid dance.

She dreamed the night on the train that she and Edward stepped off the train from Vera Cruz and were greeted by Flamenco dancers. It was night- and unseasonably cold.

Mariachis were handing them their guitars, insisting that Amanda play while she kept telling them in French that she only knew how to play the piano and not very well. Marigolds were raining down on them and just before being whisked away to their villa in the mountains of Mexico City, Amanda pricked her finger on a large spike off a cactus. There was a great rush of blood, and she suddenly felt very sleepy. Did this make her the Sleeping Beauty? She asked the mariachis in the dream. The Brothers Grimm appeared as two handsome young men and then morphed into old, fat men laughing and chatting to her in German. I don't speak German, she told them. No matter what languages were spoken, nobody was understanding her. Then she was turning into Cinderella, their carriage a giant pumpkin. Mexico City, which she had seen in picture books, was trying to stay on top of the lake, great buildings falling into the water, and people drowning as the Aztecs stood by watching, expressionless. Mexico City melted into New York and then swirled into her childhood home in Philadelphia. The door to her childhood home opened, and Diego stood there, gazing at her but not his usual smiling self. Flashes of paintings of Ireland and France appeared, her parents too, both in the paintings and then beside her in the pumpkin carriage. They smiled without a word. Then a flamenco dancer, in her typical dress, was standing right in front of her face, shouting something at Amanda that she could not hear, and then she took the giant marigolds and began throwing them at Amada's face with aggression. Each one that landed its target sent Amanda's head backwards. She felt she was being pelted with rocks, sharp and pointy, aimed at her face. Every flower she saw became a rock launched at her by a very angry young woman.

Amanda opened her eyes to find that she had started crying in her sleep, the dream disturbed her so. It was not so much a nightmare but left an ugly feeling in her as if something terrible had happened, an ache of melancholy that felt so real and left her confused. She could not make any sense of what that was. She simply was over tired- exhausted, she told herself and should not have been having wine with dinner while pregnant- it seemed to get her drunk faster. She felt terrible, and while she was able to explain to Marta, that she needed her help in dressing the children and taking them to breakfast in the dining car, she could not whisper a complaint to her husband. They were now less than two hours away from their destination, and he was in an exuberant mood she did not want to dampen in any way. She felt as if she had travelled the world in her sleep as the train cut its way through the Mexican countryside. Her dream had become not a nightmare but a tad unsettling. She had hoped to forget it. They were nearing their destination.

The reality was Amanda was asleep yet again when they pulled into the train station in downtown Mexico City at four in the afternoon on a busy and unseasonably warm Monday on the first of April. She was parched and not able to rouse herself fully. The train car was sweltering or maybe it was just her. She felt nearly drunk, and the babies tugging at her, the nanny attending to the children's luggage. At the same time, Edward ordered some porteros to hurry up and get the rest of their belongings, was making for a mix of commotion and frustration on everyone's part. Edward started snapping his finger at the young men, a habit Amanda hated.

What he lacked in patience, she made up for, but sometimes she wished he was just a bit kinder to those he considered to be beneath him. He was not alone in his treatment of the lower classes or out of line with the times, but it always grated on his wife, his annoyance with the very existence of anyone not wealthy. He did not view them as people worthy of sharing his space, so he barely tolerated them. He didn't speak to them; he spat orders.

"Good manners cost nothing", she would remind him.

The platform was full of all kinds of people from all over the world, heading in every direction save for right onto the tracks. With some patience and then some pushing others about by Edward, the Tappan family were finally able to meet their carriage and start the trek off towards their new home. Ed loaded the children into the carriage first, the little tots too spent even to complain anymore and then helped Marta aboard and then finally his wife.

He stopped her, taking her hand for a moment, and looked at her with a softness she rarely saw anymore.

"We are almost there now. We are almost to our new life kid, almost home."

Amanda was eager to be done with travelling and sleep in a bed that wasn't moving. She was eager to arrive home.

Chapter 12

Home.

The word carried such meaning, and it was a heavy, thick word. It evoked so much conflicting emotion in Amanda.

Home was where people were born and died and, in between, slept and made love and passed time watching children grow. Home could be a safe comfort or as bleak and empty as a tomb. Amanda had experienced both. Although this home would be filled with children, she was fearful this new life would be so unlike anything she had ever experienced that she would feel lost and alone, even when surrounded by others. She was scared suddenly, for the first time since she was fifteen and realized both the people who were responsible for her very existence were gone from the world. She had, back then at least, an adult by her side to look after her and this time around, she was the adult in charge of three little lives, as she knew Ed would be forever working. She would have a staff of people for help, and she had a reliable and capable husband. Still, her apprehension grew.

She said a tiny prayer as they made their way at a rather slow pace to la colonia. This was one of the finest neighbourhoods, if not the finest in the whole city, Ed had told her. Away from the masses lived these giant estates, secured fortresses for the few, surrounded by money and sheltered from the reality of the common man, especially the common Mexican.

Armed guards stood at the entrance to every wealthy colonia, a detail Edward had assured her was normal and not to raise any alarm- if anything, she would be far safer than she had ever been anywhere in her life before.

"We will be living with the politicians and the financiers- all the most important people." He had informed her while she remained unimpressed. Back in New York, it had been all the most important people she found to be the most work.

They arrived as the sun was lowering to the first set of gates for the neighbourhood, what looked like a soldier standing guard with a long rifle in his hands. He nodded slightly at the driver and again to Doctor Tappan as if he knew to expect them. They made an immediate right onto a long, cobblestone road and then three left turns down streets lined with fruit trees and elm and pine trees.

"Ed, this is beautiful.

"Just wait", He mused.

They pulled up to a set of gates inlaid within a thick, high, and very long white stucco wall. When Amanda looked at the gate before them, she found the heavy, green iron gates almost melting into a green forest, the likes of which had her nearly convinced they were stepping into an estate in Ireland or Scotland or somewhere overcast, cold, and covered in moss. The grounds were not unlike her old house in Philly in many ways. The gates were opened by two men on the other side, and they began the ascent up the carriageway to the house. Hibiscus, jasmine and plumeria lined the approach to the house, the smell overwhelming.

Then she saw it, La Casa de la Flor de Naranja, the House of the Orange Blossom, so named because it seemed someone had decided to stick a giant orange grove amid a bustling and growing city and an impressive Parisian Chalet had sprung up in the middle of this massive grove.

There were giant trees lining their approach that, by the sheer size of their trunks, Amanda knew they had to be hundreds of years old. There were fruit trees she found unrecognizable; Ed told her those were called mangos. There were rose bushes reminiscent of her mother's. Along with the dappled sunlight of the willows and tall birches overhead, all the different foliage of the massive canopy gave the grounds a sleepy feel. Amanda was taken with its beauty and the serenity behind the walls of the property when they had just passed through a city of commotion and noise that rivalled the pace they had just left behind in New York. It was so quiet and peaceful behind the tall, thick white stone walls. She loved this new home instantly, having not even stepped inside yet, her eyes filling with water. She was always so soft and fragile when expecting.

Ed helped her down, and she simply stood, taking in her new home, nearly forgetting to breathe. It was Goliath in size, and she felt tiny standing in front of it.

The great brown oak doors were thrown open to reveal craftsmanship Amanda could not have expected. The City of Palaces was already living up to its name. The porteros had their luggage heading upstairs before she could straighten the hats on the children's tired little heads. Ed ushered them inside the doors, and Amanda found the front entrance smelled of oranges, and she realized with joy her favourite smell of her childhood home, sandalwood. Had Ed done this, she wondered? There were marble floors of white with veins of grey and gold, and a staircase that became a balcony welcomed them. Oil paintings of Spanish nobility, Emperors of Mexico and what looked like the gentility and aristocracy of England, posed with their hounds, all lined the hallways in both easterly and westerly directions.

"Well, Señora?"

Edward beamed, quite obviously proud of himself as if he had laboured to build the house himself.

"This is not what I was expecting Ed. This is impressive, even for us."

"Welcome home, Señora. Bienvenido a Mexico."

"Did you become the Emperor of Mexico?"

Amanda marvelled, looking down one hallway that seemed to stretch forever.

"Not yet." Ed quipped as he began by taking the family on a tour.

The kitchen was the first stop, where they were met by their housekeeper Guadalupe, who had agua fresca ready for the travel-weary family. Guadalupe was short and soft with warm hands and spoke nearly perfect English.

"My father spent some time in the United States, and he taught me well",

she beamed as Ed made introductions.

"Guadalupe ran our house when I was just a boy, and I had to track her down and steal her away from her former employers."

"I was just a jovensita of eighteen when I began working for your husband, Señora ", she smiled at Amanda.

"He was the most rambunctious six-year-old I had ever seen, but I became so fond of the Tappan family.

What Guadalupe was too kind and intelligent to say was that Eduardo was a monster of a child, but the pay was the highest in the city.

The house was of the most modern standard, built earlier in the decade and updated as late as earlier in the year, with electricals throughout. Fully powered, all indoor plumbing, water closets with giant clawed bathtubs and the most modern toilets. The ceilings seemed to sparkle, but Amanda attributed the effect to the waning daylight. Her bedroom was large yet cosy, and she asked her other half to forgive her as she crawled quite unladylike across their massive new bed and laid across it, sighing with sheer relief and tiredness. The house tour was cut short, as Amanda had "run out of steam", Ed had teased,

"As if you were the locomotive."

"I will have Guadalupe draw you a bath and start a fire."

"A fire? It's so warm."

"Yes darling, we are up in the mountains. As the sun goes down the temperature will drop even in the spring and summer, and we will need the fires to warm up the rooms of the house.

Guadalupe was a pleasant woman in her fifties, from Monterrey. She had worked for Edward's family long before his father passed, and so she had known Old Doctor Tappan very well. She was happy to be back with such a prestigious family. Within moments of formally meeting the new Señora Tappan, Guadalupe was helping her to undress and step carefully into the bath. Amanda's belly was just starting to round into the form of a peach, soft and pink.

A more well-rested woman would have enjoyed her bath in a luxurious ivory tub with soaps made of goat's milk and honey from Michoacan; bubbles on the water frothing and smelling of jasmine, but she soon started to nod off in the water. With Guadalupe's help,

Amanda got out, dried off and slipped into a fresh nightgown. Once she was assured that the children were being fed supper and tucked into their beds by Marta and her husband- who was chasing around the place like an excited boy, she decided everything else be damned; she needed sleep. Whether from relief or exhaustion, she entered under the bed's blankets, heavy as the train that had brought them there, and closed her eyes in her home in Mexico City.

Chapter 13

Marta, the new nanny, was from Puebla just southeast of Mexico City. She had travelled to New York to marry her lover, a Mexican boy with some French on his mother's side. He was talented and spoke fluent English and looked like a white boy. He was going to train horses in the United States while she learned English and gave him babies. She would be a cook outside the home if needed. They had made plans.

Her French boy got sick one day. The doctors didn't know what it was at first or what to do once it was too late. He had been fine on Monday, sick on the Tuesday, and dead on Wednesday. He was only twenty-six when he died. The name of the illness she knew had the word "men" in it. She was only confused by this. Men. Man - that was what her love was. He was a man, the only one she had ever known in an intimate way. There had been many apologies by the doctors in the small hospital as if they had made a mistake. The men had made a mistake, or he had died of men? Her head was cloudy, and her English lacking.

Marta had been at his humble funeral and had seen them lower his pine box into the ground in a part of New York she didn't know the name of, but later was told "Buffalo- like the animal."

She had been in shock, their landlady had said. She had little English, the Polish woman, but she stumbled through her English, and Marta stumbled back, and they got by. They understood each other. Marta understood that this woman felt extremely sorry for her and had let many rent days come and go, but now it was time for Marta to leave. She could barely find any work and decided to take the position of some highbrow family leaving the U.S. to return to Mexico. It had been sheer luck she had heard the Gringo speaking perfect Spanish outside the hospital, and she approached him in a haze of desperation and hunger. Doctor Tappan had looked her up and down and read that abject poverty and wanting to return to Mexico was enough to convince him she was the better option to bring with them. Better this pobre instead of that Orla girl. Marta was the much safer option.

Marta would be happy to return to Mexico too, lest she end up begging in the streets. No Gringo babies for her. No reason to learn any more English, although it had started towards the end of her time in New York, to get better, she thought, even if those doctors spoke too fast for her to understand everything.

Dr. Tappan hadn't cared about her English or her problems or her dead fiancé. They couldn't take the Irish girl with them. She hadn't talked yet, but Ed was sure over time she would, and after all, it had been a misunderstanding on her part; she would surely make a huge ordeal about it one day to his wife, so here was Marta. Marta would suffice.

Marta met Orla briefly on the first day of her new job. She had been given instructions to meet the family down at the docks at 7 am, and she appeared that bright morning with her one little red suitcase. Her love had been dead for exactly two months; her heart turned to brick. Marta had been taken aback to see the old nanny, a fine-looking girl, like one of those portraits on soap boxes that promised to make you forever young and beautiful, hugged and then hugged again the Tappan children, misty-eyed. When the Tappans had moved just a few feet ahead, so as not to be overheard amidst the racket of the ships and the dock, Orla came in close to Marta's ear, grabbing her arm and whispered,

"Watch out for the Dr.", before rushing off without looking back.

Marta had sensed something about Dr. Tappan she didn't like but since her Armando had died, she thought that she just didn't like anybody. He was not particularly friendly, but as employers go, that was to be expected. That was not the issue, but she could not put her finger on anything. She would watch him the entire journey down based on what the pretty blonde girl had said.

The arrival at the house in Mexico City had been uneventful; although Marta knew of the ongoing Revolution, she was not worried about it. There was no one revolting against her kind. She was happy to be home and devastated, in equal measure.

Amparo and Marta shared a large room in the basement, with two tiny bedrooms in the back across from each other. Marta looked at the lazy-eyed idiot with pity. There was a pecking order with the servants in this and in every house. Guadalupe, being the housekeeper, being the oldest, and having the lightest skin out of them, was obviously in charge. Amparo was as brown as the dirt Armando had trained his horses in, as the dirt they had covered him in. Her face was flat and broad with a nose that made her look as if she'd fallen off some Incan pyramid and landed face first. She seemed not to say much- whether she was dumb or just quiet, Marta didn't know or care. Marta wasn't interested in anything that the peon had to say. Marta herself was not much darker than Lupe, with beautiful honey-coloured skin that darkened in the summer sun but lightened every winter to a beautiful pale gold. Marta had flecks of gold in her light brown eyes and refined features. Marta was Morena, but she was not una India ignorante, like that ugly thing in the bedroom across from hers, and that was good enough for her. Why she could nearly pass for one of the family. Marta would have had a beautiful family.

Amparo was strange in every way. Lupe noticed it too. Strange shuffling walk. Strange way she would talk, if she did at all. She would make strange faces when she should show no emotion or annoyance, such as when speaking to her employers. She was odd. Guadalupe was not sure where she came from or how Dr. Tappan had chosen the household staff that he did. Perhaps he had found her in the streets begging and felt sorry for her. She never asked, and Amparo never offered up the information. Save for the fact that Amparo had worked in the sugar cane and corn fields since she was a young child, nobody knew much about her. Neither Marta nor Guadalupe, were even sure the girl had any thoughts in that head of hers. She seemed a blank slate of personality, a barren field with nothing to offer in her soil. Mostly, she just went ignored. The older housekeeper and the young nanny could have great conversations-recipes shared and talk of the Tappan children, jokes shared between amigas. They were cut from the same cloth even if Lupe was the boss with her own big bedroom on the first floor off the kitchen as if she were family.

Amparo did not fit in. She seemed to frighten their American mistress that first night. La Señora Tappan had such a lovely, steady grace yet you could see she was unnerved by the girl, dark as sackcloth, quieter still. Amparo smiled at inappropriate intervals so that one couldn't help but think she was daft.

Amparo went about her merry way, never knowing anyone thought about her at all. She liked this new family and this new job. The lady of the house was very nice, and the children were not annoying like the siblings Amparo had left behind in the shanty town she grew up in.

They fed her very well, and they paid her. She had her own room with a sink basin for washing, a mirror, a closet, and a chair. She even had a uniform to wear, which was a source of pride. Her bed was firm, so it felt nice on her back but still so soft that some mornings she hated to leave it. It was surprisingly nicer than sleeping on a mat on the floor like at home. She was learning more Spanish, something her own grandmother would never have approved of.

The Spanish Imperialists had taken over their lands, according to the older woman. Brought the white man to destroy them. No child of hers would speak that European trash talk, the tongue of the wicked. Spanish, German, English, French, Portuguese, Swedish, Italian, it was all the devil. The white men with their blue eyes and their raping of the land and the native women. To make mixed mestizo babies, to make more enslaved people to look after their blue-eyed Spanish children. No, Amparo's family were never to be a part of that, yet as time passed, things in the country had changed. Spanish was everywhere in the land; it was the official language, and it was becoming all that was spoken, with more European languages coming after it, taking over. English, French, German. Those people were everywhere, like vermin. There had even been an influx of Lebanese into Mexico with their Arabic talk.

Natives were no longer speaking their mother tongues but bowing to these intruders from across the sea. Amparo came from a proud native family of Zapotec Indians, even if her mother had given her a Spanish name, much to the chagrin of her anti-European grandmother.

"These pale-skinned killers with their one God and their Christianity and their Jesus",

she would mutter,

"And what of our Coquihani, the god of light, hmm? Is there even a word for that in their Spanish? And you go and name your daughter as if we are the same as those invaders!"

She would spit the accusation at her daughter, even in front of

Amparo.

Amparo was a good daughter, even if she was slow and at times, lost in her simple thoughts. She meant no harm to anyone and tried to win over her grandmother. The pressure began to ease as Amparo's mother continued to name her subsequent children with Spanish names. Jose, Antonio, Rosalinda. While infuriating the grandmother, it took the heat off Amparo. Her mother would only speak Spanish, further infuriating the grandmother, who inhaled her rage and then threw it back out again in a hurricane of accusations. Amparo always felt it was as if her grandmother enjoyed staying angry, a way of living she could not understand.

Amparo worked long days outside, the sun and mosquitos pouring down on her, oblivious to her toil. She had done this without question for the whole of her life, so she never imagined there was another way. Her kind didn't end up in the homes of the wealthy, tending to their chubby babies. They worked the land; they were the land, and it was a life Amparo was fine with. Happenstance had her accompany her friend to the house of the rich American doctor in the city to see about a job.

"Doctor Tappan and his family have not yet arrived.", said the tall man, Doctor Diaz, who met them at the house.

"They are due next week, and I need to procure a full staff."

He looked at Amparo, asked her some questions and decided they both could come work- Amparo thrice weekly. That schedule changed when her friend Teresita fell and broke her arm, and so then Amparo showed up on the Sunday alone. After a lot of whispering in the corner with displeased faces, Amparo was told by the woman Guadalupe and the doctor Diaz that when she returned from her village on Wednesday, she could stay in the place of the other girl. Amparo packed a small cloth bag with her meagre possessions and said goodbye to her mother. The women- even the scowling old grandmother, agreed this was a wonderful turn of events for Amparo. This could mean lifelong employment in a comfortable home instead of back-breaking work in the fields.

Guadalupe instructed Amparo on her first day that she was to bathe or shower every other day and use her wash basin the other days.

"I will not tolerate smelly villagers in this household."

She informed Amparo that she expected hard work, manners and compliance or she would find herself back in the fields. Amparo seemed to be only half listening but nodding along, a habit that would immediately come to grate on Guadalupe's nerves, causing her to ask the girl and then ask again if she had heard her instructions.

"I will not tolerate impertinence, laziness or vulgarity of any sort. I-"

Guadalupe was going to go over all her formal rules, including that male suitors should never appear at the place of employment, but then she stopped herself, realizing she would not have to worry so much about that with this one.

On Wednesdays, Amparo and Marta did all the floors of the house, sweeping and mopping and dusting rugs, while Lupe minded the children and had something constantly cooking. The other days, Amparo swept and, dusted and polished the house on her own. She made all the beds. Marta tended to the children, from dressing to bathing to entertainment. Lupe cooked nonstop and barked orders at the two girls, the gardener, the carriage men, the workers, and the delivery men.

Amparo was happy with her work and her life, unaware that the other staff barely tolerated her.

Marta barely tolerated anyone. She didn't resent the children; they were lovely in manner and easy to care for. They were past the point of diapers, something she was not looking forward to when the new baby was born. If life had been in any way fair, she would be expecting her own little one by now, and the only soiled diapers she would have to scrub would be those of her own baby. The only foul messes she would be covered in should have been of the children she made with her lover.

People had assured her she was young and pretty and would love again, but Marta did not like many people, so she doubted that immensely.

Guadalupe listened to her tell her story one day in the kitchen as they were making the tortillas.

"And then, after Armando died, I came here."

Marta explained to the older woman without a hint of emotion.

"Pobres", Lupe shook her head.

"Was it meningitis that took him?"

Marta looked up, eyes wide,

"How did you know?"

"You said the doctors said "men", it is the only sickness I know of that sounds with the English word men in it. I could ask Dr. Tappan to be sure, but the symptoms and the sudden sickness make me think….you mentioned his neck. I am certain that is it. A girl from my village when I was younger, she and her sister both had it, years apart. It is terrible; they both died. I'm sorry flaca."

Lupe sometimes called Marta "flaca"- skinny. Marta was not sure if it was a term of endearment or a reminder; she had gone very thin. Lupe had nicknames for everyone in the house. Amparo was "tonta", which meant dumb.

Marta's curiosity considered Lupe's offer to ask the doctor if it had been that – meningitis, but her pride did not want the older woman too much in her business.

"No, I – I will ask Dr. Tappan myself one day."

And she felt a tiny flame of embarrassed rage that she had not thought to ask the doctor herself. Marta used to think she was halfway intelligent, but ever since the experience of losing Armando, she was never again quite in her right-thinking mind, she felt. She was always a little fuzzy, always a little lost, but still able, unlike that baboon Amparo, to do her work to a high standard.

Lupe tried to comfort her.

"One day, you will meet some nice gentleman; you're so young, you will love again and go on to have your family, and at least you had Armando- you were married, you knew love- look at that pobre diabla Amparo, esa tonta- no man will ever love her. At least you had Armando", she said with a shrug as she went about starting the caldo de res.

Marta knew in a way that Lupe was right. But Armando and the United States had been Marta's ticket to freedom from a life of servitude. Here in Mexico, her future daughters would never marry a doctor like the one she worked for; she would never be anything more than a servant. It was hard for her not to feel anger at times at where destiny had led her because Marta knew in her heart that she was so much more than a servant.

Chapter 14

A warm and bright morning, almost a week in their new country, found Amanda sitting at a huge mahogany table in the biggest dining room she had ever seen in her life, staring down at a plate of uncertainty.

"What is this?"

Amanda nodded to the plate full of pink squash.

"Papaya", Amparo smiled.

"You eat- is good for bebe. Es buena para los ojos."

She pointed to her lazy eye.

Amanda had asked Ed many times about what he had called the marvellous cuisine. He loved to brag about the delightful foods on offer in Mexico. His descriptions of cheeses and candies and breads and soups she'd never heard of had her eager with anticipation to try some new and exotic foods. She was convinced that when her sickness finally went, she would be able to really, joyfully eat. There were many dishes she looked forward to, along with a great mixture of things that she did not think sounded appetizing, such as the idea of eating any sort of cactus or cow stomach. Yet there were many dishes that Ed insisted were more delicious than anything she had ever eaten before; the chilles rellenos, sopa de fideo, tinga and mole would end up favourites, he assured her.

On this first morning in her new home that she had been able to make it downstairs for breakfast, she sat unsure. This papaya was a different matter. It was nearly an offence, this pregnant-looking fruit mocking her own condition back at her. It had a feminine shape with a fat belly, and she kept getting whiffs of a strange odour.

"It appears to be full of eggs- if I didn't know any better, I'd say this was caviar".

"Caviar?" Amparo shook her head, confused,

Amanda found it tasted of vomit and smelled of it too. Surely, this fruit had spoiled; it had to be. She spat it out into her napkin, horrified.

How could anyone eat this?

"Can I have instead perhaps some toast please? This is not, no, this is not to my liking."

Before he ran out the door to meetings, Ed assured her if she had not been expecting, she would have been able for it, but Amanda was too sure this fruit would never be anything she wanted on her plate.

"Toast?" Amparo looked at Guadalupe with confusion as she poured the orange juice.

"Pan tostado.",

Guadalupe grumped at the girl,

"Tostado- toast. Son casi igual las palabras. Toast- toast- pan tostado",

she repeated, hoping to drum the words into the girl's head, and then she sent her off scurrying to get the lady of the house something palatable she would recognize from her former life.

Amanda was having a hard time making sense of the girl Amparo, who was small, dark, and very different looking to anyone Amanda had ever seen before. At times Amanda was certain she could see the girl muttering to herself. The girl's eye was distracting at first, but she tried to ignore it. The first night, she was so exhausted from their journey that she had to remind herself not to stare at the poor girl, who they said was only twenty-four but looked as if she was fifty. Ed said she had been working in the fields since she was eight years old, very hard labour and so was delighted to be a servant in a lovely home. Her English consisted of a few words she was being taught very quickly and her Spanish was almost fluent, but she originally spoke some tribal tongue of the mountains. Guadalupe had told Amanda what it was called, but Amanda was certain, as adroit as she was with languages, that she would never be able to pronounce it.

Eleanor shrieking at her drunkenly from the going away bash came back to haunt her. She didn't really think there would be Mexicans who didn't speak Spanish, but seeing as how immigrants were flooding into Ellis Island every day with little to no English, she supposed nothing should surprise her. She had to remind herself that neither Spanish nor English were the mother tongues of any of the Americas. It was a strange and humbling realization.

Amanda was beyond grateful the older housekeeper Guadalupe was fluent in English even if Marta and Amparo were not. She was a warm and friendly woman with a genuine smile, even if her eyes told you she was sceptical and watching. She seemed to have wasted no time and already had things in motion in the house, had everything in order and on schedule. Guadalupe liked smooth sailing; she liked efficiency. The little Indian Amparo was anything but efficient. Guadalupe liked Marta however- felt an affinity straight away. Guadalupe found she looked at her the way one would a daughter. They slid into their quasi-familial roles with the ease of putting on slippers. The staff were settling in, as was the family. One thing everyone agreed on and took delight in were the Tappan children. They were small and darling and not fussy.

The children were having a terrible time adjusting as they were having entirely too much fun staying up all night with the excitement of this new palace to explore. They looked at the house in wonder, convinced it was a castle. Their father also made sure to tell them it was a castle. They played hide and go- seek behind every heavy door, and they slid on their bums on the cold Mexican tiles of the kitchen, brown and smooth. They ogled the copper of the bathrooms, every fixture an ornate Rococo masterpiece, chubby little fingers tracing every line and curve of every fixture and door handle. They pulled the long chains to flush the toilets for fun, for these toilets were far more interesting than the ones left behind in New York, they decided. They wandered the many halls and the six bedrooms, not including the maid's quarters, where they were told firmly, they were not allowed. They spent a lot of time in and out of the little enclosed garden courtyard in the middle of the house.

They told anyone who would listen, very loudly, that they were going out once again to smell all the different sorts of tropical flowers, but really, what the two mites had on their minds was the dipping of little hands in the fountain. It was utterly charming, this large fountain where a stone mermaid sat on a giant conch, a real pearl inside of it. True to form, it was as if the sirena, the mermaid, was calling out, beckoning the children, making it all too tempting for a pair of tots not to play games in that fountain and occasionally splash each other before being found out.

The second day there, Ed had wasted no time in attending El

Palacio de Francia department store and ordering everything they needed, from more bed linens to the silver to what looked like thousands of the most beautiful beeswax candles from Acapulco.

Amanda knew he planned to use the remnants of his inheritance to buy their new home. She had carefully expressed to her husband that it would be best to conserve the leftover money until his work schedule solidified and their coffers, which had been heavily depleted in New York, could fill up again. Amanda was uneasy with the idea of conversion rates and different currencies and couldn't tell you how many pesos went into a dollar or vice versa. She tried not to be concerned as she still had a good bit of her inheritance hidden away at the bank in Philly, to fall back on in case of any upheaval, but she did like keeping a helpful eye on their cheques and balances. Ed however, thought he knew better about finances and never shied from reminding her of that. She, in her placid and agreeable nature, would merely shake her head and smile, as she knew Ed always insisted on the best of everything, and he had in eight years never led her astray financially. They had always had the means for whatever their fancy, so there was no need to worry now. They had been renting their luxurious apartment in New York for the entire time they lived there, and Ed had insisted on not only buying once in Mexico but outfitting the new hogar as if for a king. He had warned her- they had people to impress, a family reputation to uphold. There was something about this opulence, however, that made Amanda's heart race, but she tried to ignore it, as she was always seemingly worried about something.

The first week of adjusting to this new world was supposed to find Amanda resting, but instead, there was only chaos, and she found herself spending too much time on her feet. Even the air was different in Mexico City, and she would find herself catching her breath after a flight of stairs. Ed would remind her the different altitude- much higher than New York- meant the air was thinner. That and her condition found Amanda forced to slow down.

Trying to acclimate herself and the children to the ways things in this new house worked, where things were proved there was a new lesson every day. Getting used to using hot water differently for bathing and having to boil water for drinking- little strange new things she didn't have to think about in New York. Guadalupe had told her about the water the first day they arrived.

"You must never drink or allow the children to drink the water straight from the tap, Señora . You must only take from the pitchers in the kitchen of the water that has been boiled. Not even when in washing your teeth must you drink any of that water. Dysentery."

Lupe then took her to the cold cellar- the large closet off the kitchen that served as a drying room for the fruit and vegetables.

Marta and Amparo oversaw the washing of clothes and linen, the scrubbing of floors and the minding of children while Lupe did the cooking, promising to teach Senora Tappan the best Mexican dishes after she had settled in.

The constant stream of visitors, old family friends of Edward's and dear friends of his parents, even politicians and military men and their wives had Amanda feeling like an old shoe, worn out and flat. She would sleep all day and still be exhausted and then had to put on a fresh face and fresh dress to meet with strangers. Whether for an hour or a minute, she continually found herself on Ed's arm for introductions and trying to play hostess while unsure of the expected customs and nearly falling asleep standing. Ed had promised to get her up to speed on the who, what and where of everything but the pace in the house those first two weeks was like a derailed train, flying off the tracks. She would ask Edward questions that he often thought she should simply know.

She found meeting all these new people, yet not really knowing anyone left her feeling every day as if she had a chore to do but didn't know where to start. Like her hands were empty and she didn't know what to put in them. She felt quite useless other than as an ornament on her husband's arm, some decorative piece to be ogled and then gingerly put down, then ignored. She didn't have terribly demanding obligations, but she felt she could never relax fully. She kept having to force her shoulders down as they kept creeping up to her ears from tension. Ed started to bark at her about her posture, as she was prone to slumping when tired, which he noticed seemed to be all the time now.

"Stop carrying yourself like an old lady",

Ed had snapped at her right before meeting some dignitary who had stopped by unexpectedly and woken her from a much-needed nap.

When not in his office in el centro, Diego was an immediate fixture once they were in the new house. It had been he who had found this spectacular French style chalet for them and arranged the purchase ahead of their arrival. Amanda was happy to have another adult around who Ed would listen to, at least most of the time. She was grateful to Diego for arranging everything and for finding such a house. She found her new home, with its white stucco exterior walls and chocolate roof tiles and shutters, to be breathtaking. She simply had never seen anything like it anywhere in the US. The French doors, the giant windows, with the details and layout of a small palace, it had been everything Ed had promised her, down to the carpets and rugs fit for royalty. At times Amanda pondered if her husband really did believe they were actual royalty. He acted like it a bit too often for her liking. She dismissed her overactive imagination that seemed to insist Ed's ego had tripled since they arrived. No, he was excited, thrilled, she told herself; he would settle down soon once he was acclimated to their new life. No one could possibly be so arrogant.

Edward's upbringing may have had a hand in his superior attitude and lofty expectations. His own father had been not only a revolutionary in the field of medicine but a handsome, wealthy American son of great military men, leading all the way back to a certain General in the American Revolutionary War. The first Doctor Tappan could trace his roots through the Americas back to the pilgrims, all bloodlines leading back to Mother England. After being widowed twice, he decided a change of scenery and an opportunity to provide medical care to those who really needed it would be his newfound life calling after his children from his first marriage had flown the nest. So, as a forty-six-year-old he had ended up in Merida in the Yucatan Peninsula and unexpectedly fell head over heels in love with Mexico.

As luck would have it, he then fell in even deeper love, a near obsession with a twenty-two-year-old Mexican girl named Susana Mercedes Ramirez Santiago. The daughter of a lawyer of Spanish nobility and a Dutch socialite, she could trace her family back two generations in Mexico before her lineage jumped back over the Atlantic. Susana had two much older brothers who had left the household and a little brother who had drowned in Acapulco. Being the only girl in the family, and the only child in the home, she lived a life of luxury few could find in 1800's Mexico.

She was not long in marrying the older American doctor, who the whole town of Merida revered. Doctor Arthur Mortimer Tappan, learning Spanish for his patients, suddenly became almost fluent overnight to win the heart of the young woman. His attempt charmed her, and he married his young bride, thus beginning his second family. Edward came along, and two sisters and then another little boy before Susana seemingly could no longer fall pregnant. The years flew by, and it became an impossibility because she rarely saw her husband. He was so busy with his work she sometimes went days without him next to her in their bed, so too it became rare anything could transpire in that bed. At thirty and with four children the young wife worried her husband no longer found her attractive. The stunning beauty he had discovered less than a decade previously remained, yet she saw the flecks of early grey in her hair. The passing of time in her once perfect skin. And the weight she had put on her once perfect frame annoyed her, her round face and chubby cheeks the bane of her existence. Her breasts and hips, like mountains, she remained every bit as desirable, but he seemed to have cooled in his passion for this young wife. The idea was then born in her mind that perhaps it was she who was somehow past her most fertile time, never once imagining that the problem could be her by then fifty-four-year-old husband and his abilities that had suffered the consequences of time.

Susana, or Ana Mercedes as she was called, raised Edward with the knowledge that he would follow his father into medicine or die trying. There was no failure allowed. After she was widowed, her expectations grew exponentially. Her children would be a legacy, that of the great American physician and the fruit of European nobility. Some said that Edward received a great dollop of arrogance from his mother and her Dutch and Spanish aristocrat ancestors, while others blamed the talent and success of the Good Doctor Tappan for the hubris running through Ed's veins.

However, those who really knew his parents would tell you that while indeed they were certainly impressive individuals, despite both of their accomplishments, they were assertive instead of arrogant and proud without being obnoxious. They both possessed an innate and sincere humility that Ed seemed to be lacking from the day he was born. La Señora of the house never found it enough to sit around on her laurels, basking in her good privilege. She travelled, she studied, and she worked her home and family as they were the most noble vocation. She instilled their deep and abiding love for God. She had studied opera and knew every word of her Bible, all by the time she married the much older American. She raised the children with a firm yet just hand, showing them all that hard work and study, along with religious devotion, were the tithe owed for being born into such great circumstances. Still, she remained humble before God, and it vexed her that Eduardo, her firstborn son, was pompous from the day he could speak.

"Nobility, and our wealth, is no excuse for ignorance or laziness."

She would tell the children as she doled out chores despite their fleet of servants. Edward would groan the loudest when his mother would send him to the stables to help the farm hands brush and bathe the horses and clean their stalls. He felt this sort of menial labour was beneath him, yet his mother knew he needed more of it. He needed to be broken like a horse. She wondered if she did not beat him enough. Was that why he had this streak of…temper, defiance, pig headedness. His little sister Leonor had it too, but not to the same degree.

Ana Mercedes would have taken to Amanda as a daughter-in-law very well, but she passed before they got the chance to meet. She would have respected the younger Señora Tappan's ability to keep her husband in line without him catching on to what was happening. She had always known that Eduardo was her hard-headed troublemaker, often lamenting to Dios,

"Where did we get that one?"

Doctor Tappan had made a name for himself at Harvard and perfected his technique for caesarean section in New York. He was the first doctor to introduce the use of ether in Mexico, for both the dangerous surgery and for run of the mill labours. While he performed thousands of caesareans in the United States and Mexico, he always tried to avoid it unless it was truly the last resort. Still his practice ended up becoming mostly that, and as he was amazingly successful, he found a popularity in Mexico that at times surprised him. The residents of Merida wanted to canonize him and embarrassed him with such proclamations.

"Don't I have to be dead first?"

he would joke in heavily accented Spanish, before swiftly bringing up something else.

Even saving the lives that he did, the Good Doctor Tappan was a humble man, kind to his core. His own father had been a Reverend and so he had been raised to live a humble existence, giving thanks to God for every safe delivery and never wanting to take the credit. He had no interest in being a sinner or a saint, but the saint he was painted as. Those were blessed hands, according to the folks in Merida. He never lost a baby. Some stillborn were unavoidable, and sadly, a few mothers could not be saved, but if the baby was alive at the start of the labour, they were alive when it was over as well. He never lost a baby. Those were blessed hands.

After his death, the town did erect a statue of him in el zocalo, the town square in Merida. Edward claimed to his mother that he was far too busy at Harvard to make the long trip from Boston to Merida to go see a statue and hoped she understood. Rather, Ed was more dismayed at the thought of having to return to his hometown to have to encounter his father's ghost, looming up over him, enshrined in bronze. His father had been nearly perfect in life, and here he was now, forever perfect for all to see and compare his son to. In a drunken temper after the news of his father's passing, he had let it slip to Diego,

"They will one day erect a statue of me by God!"

Diego, equally young and drunk, had placated his grieving pal, with a clap on the back,

"Sure, of course, they will….but it's not a competition."

"Life",

Edward had assured him pouring another brandy,

"Is most certainly a competition, and I intend to win."

"En contra de tu papa…against your own father?" Diego had laughed.

"Against…everyone, amigo, against everyone."

Chapter 15

Amanda found herself spending most days and every morning in the garden. She fell in love with it immediately, her own little refuge. It was exactly what she wanted, but she had never imagined it would be so expansive, so welcoming. It flooded with dazzling sunshine every day, it seemed, and on the odd overcast day, the garden still held a peculiar and magical pull that Amanda could not ignore. After years of city living in New York, she wandered these gardens, marvelling that it was all hers. She asked Edward who was responsible for its splendour – every plant, tree, and flower so painstakingly arranged as if painted.

In every view a tableau she imagined God himself the designer.

Ed had told her he didn't know who the gardener was, nor did he care,

"Someone on my payroll, I'd imagine", he would say dismissively.

He often did not understand what his wife was mumbling about. It was only a garden after all, not one of the Seven Wonders. Amanda could not understand how Edward could be so blasé about the beauty of the natural world. Edward could not understand how simple his wife could be at times.

The mermaid fountain, the gates, the pergolas and benches, and the climbing vines of ivy and roses all seemed to merge into a living tapestry. The cacti, the plumeria, tulips, lilies, the fruit trees, and the front lawn of the house was spectacular, but here, tucked away in the back of the house in her own secret garden, Amanda knew, as tired as she was and as much acclimating as she had to do, this move would work out just fine, so long as she could rest in this spectacular setting. This place had been built just for her. She felt renewed in the garden, happy to sit staring off as the children played at her feet.

One early morning, Amanda sat taking her coffee in the garden when the most vivid and giant butterfly she had ever seen flew slowly down and landed just on the bench next to her left arm. Another two inches, and he would have landed on her shoulder. Amanda was still as could be, unsure if she should even breathe, imitating the mermaid's frozen demeanour right back to her, her eyes never leaving the magnificent orange and black wings that seemed to glisten in the sunlight as if they had been spun from gold. Her winged friend stayed for a few wonderful moments as if he too were evaluating her strange beauty, appreciating her as much as she him, before taking off again and flying off above the lime trees. The wings were nearly the size of her tiny palm. The interaction delighted Amanda. She didn't know the first thing about butterflies, but she knew whatever kind this was it was huge. The king of butterflies, she had never seen anything like it – not in New York, not even in her beautiful garden in Philadelphia.

"Those are the Monarchs",

Guadalupe smiled after he had flown away. She brought la Señora agua de Jamaica and a light lunch for her to enjoy outside and had caught a glimpse of the childlike glee on Amanda's face to have a Monarch so close.

"That one didn't land on you, but if one does, either on your head or hand- they say it is a loved one back from the other side Señora. That our dead fly down to show us they are forever with us through the Monarch."

"They are not the same as the Monarchs we have in the US

surely? That was giant!"

"Yes, Señora, they are the same- they vary in size, of course, and we see a lot of the big ones. They leave the eastern and northern lands to fly down to Mexico every year, right around the time of the Day of the Dead. And they stay with us in large colonies until about the end of March, then the colonies break up, and most of them leave to find the milkweed they need to reproduce. Many generations are born within the year. That was a very big butterfly indeed."

She smiled to herself as if she knew some secret of the Monarchs.

"Just like people- some stay, some go, some travel much further than others. They have their reasons, I suppose like we all do. They reproduce and then they fly off to find… the place."

"The place?", Amanda asked.

Guadalupe was pensive for a moment before she smiled and said,

"The final resting place of a butterfly- when they know that they are dying, the place they choose to stay until they die. Legend says it is where the butterfly is happiest, so it is unique to each individual butterfly- again like us humans. Sometimes, they continue to try to fly until they can no longer - until their wings are spent and torn, and they must rest. I have found them in the masetas- the flower pots out here, in fountains, in the dirt. You will see many Monarch butterflies in Mexico, much more than any other kind, but you will also see hundreds of other kinds. We have the most beautiful butterflies in the whole world Señora, you will see."

"And why is the Monarch supposed to be our deceased loved ones, as opposed to, say a bird?"

"Well, Señora, this was a Mexican tradition long before Mexico as we know it existed. It was the Aztecs who first foretold that the spirits of our departed loved ones returned to us in the form of hummingbirds and butterflies. Then, over the centuries, this belief grew. Every year, right after the Day of the Dead, like clockwork, millions of these orange and black butterflies return to the same places, the same way at the same time, to do the same things. But it is not the same generation of butterflies, but their offspring that somehow know to return. It is so mysterious that these creatures can tell time- down to the day, they know what to do and where to go as if guided by an internal ...cómo se dice....esa cosa...compass or by some inner voice or higher power. They always return to the land of their mothers. And they reproduce many times throughout the year, but it is the very last generation, the ones that migrate back to Mexico in November- the fourth generation, that live the longest. They have more work to do than the previous generations, it seems. Señora, it is something to see – to look up in the sky above the fir trees on the first and second of November and to see clouds of Monarchs. They are mostly found in groves in Michoacan, by the rivers, but we have many that make their way around the city. The butterfly knows what it is doing. At this time of year, we don't see too many of them, so it is especially wonderful that one that size has wandered into this garden. This is one of their birthing seasons, but up in Canada mostly and where you just came from. Maybe this one followed you from Nueva York, si?" Guadalupe said with a grin.

There was no seasonal explanation as to why that Monarch visited the garden, but Guadalupe enjoyed watching the interlude between the young woman and the lost butterfly.

Chapter 16

The first fiesta in their home ushered in a housewarming, the scope of which left Amanda shaking her head in dismay at her husband. She thought the going away party Ed had thrown in New York was over the top, but this night would leave that in the dust. She didn't know how, but he was able to outdo himself yet again with an overwhelming amount of food, people, liquor, music, and decorations. He had even joked - or threatened he would hire alpacas and a donkey for the children to ride but swiftly decided against it, fearing the mess they would make. He couldn't chance to get manure on his new Persian rugs.

Ed had a group of Mariachis wondering the house playing classic Spanish and Mexican songs. "Cielito Lindo" rang out seemingly on the hour. Ed insisted these types of troubadours were a staple at any and all gatherings. Servants Amanda had never seen before the weekend came and went, dressed in typical Mexican dress, all greeting her with,

"Buenas noches, Senora Tappan".

Bright paper streamers and garlands that looked as if they'd been cut from the most delicate lace, in every colour of the rainbow, had been placed tastefully on almost every wall and surface, yet the effect was not over done but instead joyful. Giant Marigolds in new department store vases dotted every room. The staff brought around trays with fruit and cheeses and smoked fish. Plates of sugared candies and fruits frosted in granulated sugar, twinkling like diamonds, dotted every horizontal surface. The tequila flowed like the water cascading over the mermaid fountain in great waves and as if it too, were recirculating.

Amanda had heard of but never been offered tequila in New York, and while she admitted she didn't hate it after trying it, she found it burned like fire in her throat to an unpleasant degree. She enjoyed the warmth in her belly, and her passenger must have as well, for she received a nice kick of thanks - or no thanks as the concoction made its way around her body and that of her little guest. She found the taste quite lovely in fact, especially with fresh lime, as she'd been instructed to take it. She baulked as Diego and Ed laughed as they threatened her with some sort of tequila called Mezcal that, for some reason, no one would explain to her, had an actual worm in the bottle. At first, she thought she had heard them wrong, being constantly overly tired as she was. However, further discussion made her realize they were serious.

"Alrighty boys, that's quite enough of that",

she shook her head as she sat on the sofa in the main sitting room, feeling queasy at the thought of it and secretly wanting her bed. The French and their snails, the Mexicans and their worms. It seemed lately all food was repugnant, but this was a step too far.

"If you try and feed me a worm like some demented bird, it will be funerals for the both of you."

She warned the pair as they guffawed at her reaction, already well on their way to inebriated, several guests enjoying the show. The house was packed full of people, the sound of the place making it almost impossible to hear. The cigar and cigarette smoke danced through the rooms as if it too, were an invited guest. With all the windows open, soft, mild air, smelling faintly of woodsmoke and pine needles, was allowed to drift into the party for an effect that was refreshing yet comforting.

They were, on this night, the toast of Mexico City, it seemed, at least according to her excited husband. Everyone had to say hello, and everyone had to get a moment with Ed. He was dressed in his finest suit, looking spectacularly dapper. Amanda watched Ed flirting with all the women, too used to his antics and too tired to care.

Even as her belly swelled daily and she felt more and more short-tempered and confused, everyone around Amanda was having a grand old time. She wished this fiesta could have waited another week just to let her get settled but no, Ed wasn't having it.

"Time is of the essence", he had told her,

"You must get in good with the upper crust while you still have their attention. Plus, we don't want to seem rude by postponing when so many are anxious to welcome us and give bendiciones."

"Of course, Ed, you're right,"

she had acquiesced days before, only half listening. She had known already she would not change his mind, so why did she waste her now increasingly short breath? She couldn't understand, after all these years with Edward, how there were still times she felt she didn't understand his motivations even though she knew him so well. Why all the posturing and attention given to the upper crust when he had always fancied himself atop those highest tiers of society anyway? Who was he trying to impress when he valued his own opinions over anyone else's? Ed was acting like he had to make someone happy, but it certainly wasn't his wife.

After the children were paraded like ponies about by their father, they kissed their mother goodnight before being taken upstairs by Marta.

At the start of the evening, everyone was happily attending to the expectant lady of the house.

As conversations meandered, however, the more people drank, the less they seemed to pay attention to Amanda at all. Aside from the occasional person stopping by to congratulate her or say hello, she sat largely ignored, staring at her fruit plate. Even Diego was occupied telling bawdy jokes and flirting. Amanda was struggling to keep from dozing. She had, in less than a month, gone from not showing at all to showing a good bit, but she wore a long loose peach sequined shift dress that hid her blossoming tummy, so guests soon forgot her condition, and many guests would chat to her for a bit before being pulled away by Edward's magnetism and nonstop stories. Not her usual chipper or friendly self, all she wanted or could think about was her incessant want for sleep. It was like a nagging thirst, and nothing could take her mind off it. She plopped herself at one end of the luxurious velvet sofa and tried to stifle the occasional yawn.

Her mood changed- the very energy of the party changed when the Russian arrived.

At around nine o'clock Ed disappeared and, a few moments later, escorted a stunning stranger into the dining room, commanding everyone's attention. She was there on his arm, his old childhood pal he had told Amanda about only in passing, once on the train. She was the younger childhood friend of the family. Ed had been born in New York and raised in Merida, with plenty of time spent in the U.S. growing up. Raquel was raised in Merida, and their families had been close, so the story went. It struck Amanda as odd that he had never once mentioned her before. Then she saw her and assumed she knew why.

Promptly discarding Edward after a few hurried hellos, Raquel Vanin Goya sauntered over to be formally introduced to Amanda, but not one to wait on Ed for that introduction, she swooped Amanda up and into her arms and, with an exclamation in Italian of "Ciao

Bella!", and

enveloped her in a perfumed hug. She gave Amanda a tight squeeze of a long-ago friend and two rapid-fire kisses on each cheek.

Raquel took Amanda's face in her hands and gazed dramatically at her,

"My God, Edward never told me how stunning you are.

All I heard from that old bastard was he had married himself an American girl, a Yankee, like his daddy. You are like a cameo my darling. They should put this face on currency; what do you say hmm? On bank notes or at least the coins?"

She beamed at her new amiga, her eyes large and sparkling.

"Que gusto conocerte finalmente- oh, I'm sorry, your Spanish isn't there yet, is it? "

"Señora Tappan may I present to you Señora Goya-"

"Oh, please Eduardo, buzz off! This is who I came to see- call me Raquel, por favour."

Amanda could only stammer out a "hello" as she stood in front of this magnetic woman who dismissed Ed with the wave of her hand like shooing a fly. Ed, foul tempered on his best days, only laughed, charmed.

Amanda found this overwhelmingly delightful and her interaction with Ed made a slow smile grow across her face where moments ago she had been practically scowling. Raquel slithered her arms around her like a cat tail, one arm around Amanda's growing waist, another clasping her arm, leading her away from the men,

"Tell me, how are you finding Mexico- are you ready to return home or to become Mexicana? Have they given you the chocolate? Tell me you have had the chocolate!"

"I'm finding it wonderful, just a touch all-consuming so far, but yes, the chocolate is marvellous…."

"Of course, it is so much to take in, all you have to deal with and carrying a new bambino. I must say Señora Tappan you are very brave. So brave, a young woman to leave all she knows, bringing little ones to a country you have never seen before. Without the language and with all the madness that is going on presently in this country!"

She said it with a half laugh and a genuinely warm smile.

Raquel continued,

"And of course, lest we forget, you must be the very bravest of souls to have agreed to marry Edward."

Amanda couldn't help but laugh quite loudly at the truth of that statement.

Raquel's presence was intoxicating. Her aggressively friendly nature, instead of putting her off, put Amanda at ease instantly, even if her energy was all-encompassing. Raquel treated her instantly as if they were the oldest of friends, but it was not an act. There was an ease to her person- Amanda thought if only everyone was so welcoming, dealing with people would be much easier. Raquel held her tequila in one hand and her cigarillo in the other, her curvy frame doll like, yet she commanded the attention of those around her. She wore large emeralds and diamonds at her throat, little emerald flowers on her ears.

Raquel wore a copper-coloured silk evening gown that was of the latest Parisian fashion. A little fox stole, frozen forever in time, wrapped around her shoulders, its eyes mirroring Amanda's tired and pallid complexion back at her. She realized aside from not feeling her best, she didn't look her best and Amanda suddenly felt as plain as water. Everything about this woman was exuberant. Her voice, her laugh, her booming personality all large, coming out of this minute package. She had eyes a colour Amanda had never seen before, a misty dark grey with bright green pebbledash. Amanda had not done much with her face or hair that evening, a basic chignon, a touch of rouge and felt she must have looked like peeling wallpaper in comparison to Edward's old friend, or perhaps Amanda suspected, old flame. She didn't think any man would not want to be seen on the arm of a woman like Raquel. All the men in attendance seemed to drink her in.

Her face belonged to some forgotten Greek Goddess Amanda had read about as a child curled up in her favourite chair in the library. Raquel seemed to have stepped out of the pages of Homer's Odyssey. She was Helen of Troy, launching ships.

Her mother had been of Spanish nobility, like so many it seemed to Amanda, born in Mexico City, and her father too of some semi royal Russian bloodline from St. Petersburg.

"Although all that royal talk never impressed me",

She whispered low to Amanda as half the party attendees claimed some sort of noble blood.

Raquel had been born in Moscow and raised in Russia until the family moved to Mexico when she was ten and so she admitted giddily that she had the best of both far ends of the world.

Amanda could not help but smile as this woman rattled off her life history.

She spoke several languages, English, Spanish, Italian and Russian, all fluently and could piece meal her way through French and Portuguese. She had, as a young widow, began a fur import business.

As insecure as Amanda felt at this celebration, she also felt something else. The appeal of her new friend was undeniable. She had never met a more confident woman. With all the important people in the house that evening for a massive revelry, Raquel's focus and interest were solidly on Amanda the whole night.

Raquel was an amazing storyteller and left Edward in the dust as far as likeability. Amanda suspected she knew why Ed hadn't ended up with Raquel- this woman was simply too much for him to compete with. Edward bristled at competition, and so he certainly would not have involved himself romantically with someone who could so easily upstage him.

Raquel swept Amanda off her feet onto a settee and had food and drink over to them as if it was her house, giving orders and insisting everyone attend to the mother to be. Raquel began to give Amanda the information on everyone in the room, who was who and their varying degrees of importance, all the while keeping away from a catty sort of gossip that Amanda hated.

"You see the lady in the lavender gown? That is the wife of one of the most important men in Mexican government, at least for the moment. She is a French Jew from Canada. I will have to go over and say hello to her at some point in the evening, but she is as boring as watching paint dry. Really lovely lady despite that, and she does love her fur coats. The gentleman standing next to her is the grandson of the Emperor Maximillian. And if I am correct, that is-"

Raquel cut short, surprised to see, of all people, Emil Homdahl in attendance. In a tuxedo, no less, he was so handsome he was nearly unrecognizable. She found it odd that Ed would have invited him but made no mention of it to the young American. Raquel's heart began to beat faster, and she decided she would ignore him.

"Ed has pulled it off I have to say- I'm impressed. Edward really is in some very important circles. Seems that was all he ever wanted from the time we were kids. Old Eddie and his want of people and their attention. But do you believe, all these important people, you are the most interesting person here Señora Tappan?"

Amanda felt herself blushing,

"I cannot imagine that to be true, but you are very kind."

Amanda did not expect to wind up anything other than feeling miserable during this party. That night, however, Raquel proved not only to be a wonderful distraction from Amanda's exhaustion but also a delightful new friend. She sparkled when she talked and really listened to Amanda instead of pretending to listen.

"I have so many people for you to meet!"

Raquel insisted, wide-eyed, arms outstretched in a typical, dramatically expressive and Latin way.

"Oh, I would love that; I would love to meet …anyone," Amanda admitted.

It struck Amanda that with the exception of this new woman, she had not one real friend in Mexico City yet if you didn't count Diego. She knew it was early days, but she had not given any thought to the fact that for some undetermined amount of time, she would be quite friendless. She often felt friendless in New York, but she knew she did have friends there when she needed them. Her friends may not have been a constant, but she also acknowledged she was a bit of a loner, which had never bothered her before. Of all the things she had considered and worried about in moving, it had never occurred to her that it might not be easy meeting and making friends in a new country as an adult or even as a mother. She hoped Raquel would change all of that for her. It was refreshing to find someone who off the bat, was so candid, genuine and friendly. Amanda knew if she had met Raquel in New York, it would not have been any different, they would have become fast friends. A woman like Raquel would have known how to handle Mrs. Heatherington and all the other insipid fools overtaking Manhattan.

"Tell me, Amanda,"

Raquel lit a cigarette and offered Amanda one. Everything was turning Amanda green, so she declined.

"What did you see yourself doing with your life before you met trouble over there?"

She nodded to Ed, who was at the far end of the room, singing Cielito Lindo with Diego and a group of gentlemen at the very top of their lungs, while Emil stood back from the group, sipping his whiskey and smiling.

"I…." Amanda trailed off as soon as she began. It had been so long since anyone had asked her that question.

"When I was a little girl, I knew that some women were fortunate to have professions outside of their homes. My mother had worked briefly as a governess and French teacher before she married my father. She didn't need to work but said she knew the experience would be good for her. She knew she wanted to travel. She ended up with a family in the South of France, an older American couple and their kids, which is eventually how she ended up in New York, where she later met my father. She said taking that chance, risking something, is what led her to my father and to her family. I always admired my mother's adventurous side. So, I suppose that was one reason I was so happy to come see Mexico."

"I like your spirit!" Raquel said, nodding as if she had come to a decision.

"When I was a little girl, I was fascinated with painting, and music and everything literature. I played the piano growing up, though never as well as my mother. I attempted to paint, and that was a dreadful endeavour. I do not possess within me the ability to paint or draw anything."

"That makes two of us, darling", Raquel agreed with a sly grin.

"I had no illusions about being anything other than a mother, and that is what I always wanted. However, both my parents had led such fascinating lives before they settled down. They had both travelled a good bit throughout Europe and North America. So, I think I always secretly wanted to be a sort of explorer. I loved the books where the women got out and did something and saw the world, you know?"

This was a revelation about herself that she had not known before this moment. No wonder she agreed to Ed's idea about relocating the family as easily and quickly as she had. Not even giving it a moment's thought, she had responded,

"Absolutely, let's go!" to Ed's delight.

She wanted adventure, travel, and some experience that belonged to her. How many of her friends in New York could say they knew Mexico? How many of her future Mexican female cohorts would have spent much time in the U.S.? The trip down on the boat and train alone was more travel and excitement than many married housewives often got the chance to experience in a lifetime.

"So, my dear sweet Eddie found himself an adventurer?"

"Well, there's not much adventure in motherhood, I'm afraid."

"Ah yet, here you are. You are on an adventure, certainly."

Raquel leaned her head back to study this most fascinating creature. Not a wrinkle had yet touched Amanda's face, not a grey hair on her head. Time had not found her, or life had not yet destroyed her. She was practically a child, albeit a beautiful one. Raquel wanted to be annoyed by her natural loveliness but instead had to admit that she was positively angelic, both in face and temperament.

Yes, she liked this Yankee very much. She would be her protector, the tequila whispered in Raquel's ear.

"What about you Raquel, any desires to be a pirate or the like?"

"When I was a girl, I trained to be a ballerina. I was born into a ballet family, and at my lessons from the time I could walk. I danced with some of the most prestigious companies in Russia as a child before we moved here to Mexico.

I was very young, but I kept up my practice here, determined to be the first Russian Mexican ballerina to take the world by storm. I would rule the stages of Mexico City before I took over New York, London, and Paris, before heading back to Mother Russia, a star, a prima ballerina. The Nutcracker had only just been performed in Russia when I was a girl of fourteen or so....my parents were old friends of Tchaikovsky, and I was going to be the first to perform the Nutcracker in Mexico; I just knew it. Instead, before I could return to Russia to learn the role... I fell off a horse in Chihuahua, on holiday with my family. I was seventeen. I broke the left side of my pelvis, and so, that was that. No more dancing. I taught lessons to little girls for a while and to help me recuperate and to keep me from walking with a limp."

Amanda was stunned, "I am so sorry-"

"It's all right," Raquel smiled.

"All the men in the ballet were queer anyway. Although I do walk with a limp when it rains."

She shrugged, "Such is life. At least now I can eat! Oh, perdon, mesero, otra tequilita por favour, andale, gracias" She smiled at the waiter walking by.

Amanda marvelled at her reaction,

"You seem to speak of this as if it was not hugely disappointing; I admire that."

"Well, you know.." Raquel trailed off wistfully.

"It was a very long time ago, and you must understand Amanda, that although I had made these magnificent plans of what sort of life and career I would have on the stage- I was lucky to be alive. After Canela – that's the horse, she was named Cinnamon, Canela. She was the most beautiful golden ginger; I don't know colour- even my English is not good enough to describe her. She changed colours in the different lights, and she appeared to be covered in velvet. I knew the horse; I had ridden her many times before when we would go down to visit our cousins and stay in their hacienda. It was a family horse, placid and loving. She got spooked; something out there frightened her, maybe a….aye cómo se dice en ingles…un alacran….eh, yes a scorpion stung her, who knows? She took off cómo un demonio- like a devil, crazy, and she nearly killed us both. I could not walk for many months, but Canela, she could not walk at all after we fell. She crushed us both, and they had to put her down."

Amanda felt worse by the minute for Raquel. What a horrible thing to have happened to a young girl.

"I lost my sister…when I was very young. When I was five."

Amanda never told people this, and she was startled at the words that fell out of her mouth like a broken string of pearls.

"I'm sorry, you were telling me your story; I shouldn't have interjected."

Raquel smiled sadly, taking her by the hand,

"Of course, you should have. "

The women sat and studied each other, a moment in silence.

Raquel downed the tequila the young waiter brought her, knocking it back as if she were not a lady but still managing to look demure and elegant while doing so.

"We all have our pain from our losses Amanda. We come into this life to meet and make peace with our pain."

"It just seems so random; some people escape unscathed, and others get the lion's share of loss…You think it's unavoidable for everyone – great loss and great pain?" Amanda asked her.

"Oh yes, friend. It is a requirement!" she said, beaming as if this was a wonderful revelation.

"Regardless of any financial circumstances, even regardless of health and family and everything that we take for granted, we come into this world from the unknown and into more of the unknown, and we are given so much just by being here. And then so much is taken from us, in great waves of madness and, all at once, devastation. Then, at other times, in very tiny pieces that we don't always notice at first. We all lose in this life, Amanda. We all lose someone or something that we love in the end. It doesn't have to be a tragedy, losing. We can take it and create art… It is part of this being human. We are given so much and so God asks much of us in return. It's very much a balancing act. As if the creator of this universe….demands equilibrium. I'm sorry about your sister."

"I'm sorry about your accident." Amanda smiled at her.

"Well, you know, if I had not fallen off that horse and gone to the specific hospital that I did, I would never have met my future husband. He was in for a broken foot, also from a horse, and he saw me and started coming in, well hopping into my room to talk to me. At first, I thought, who is this escapee from the sanitorium? Why is he here trying to chat to a girl who is broken in half? But he insisted and never gave up and never missed a day's visit in twenty-seven days. As dreadful as he found me, bruised, broken, in body and spirit, he never treated me like I was broken or destroyed. He never talked down to me or treated me like some fragile, stupid little girl, like so many people had started to after my accident. To reward him for his stubbornness, we married two years later."

Raquel downed another tequila,

"And then He died when I was twenty-eight."

"Oh Raquel",

Amanda was speechless, near tears, but Raquel just gave her another rueful smile.

"I had eleven wonderful years with Andres. We had our son

Jaime. We enjoyed our life."

"How old is your son?"

"He is about to be fifteen. He is the love of my life. If I had to give up the first loves of my life- my life on the stage, Andres, in order to have my sweet, special boy- it was worth it. Every moment of pain and suffering and disappointment was worth it for that boy. I would walk through the fires of hell for that child- I will have him over to meet you. He is back next week from his military school. Home for the summer. He wants to be a commander, and someday, he wants to be President of Mexico. I laugh and beg him to consider anything else, such as the priesthood. He only laughs at me. Then I beg him to be an actor, and he says to me, so wise he says to me, 'Aye Dios, mio mama, why would anyone in their right mind want to be an actor?' I am joking, of course; I do not want him to be an actor. He is a wonderful child."

"He sounds lovely."

"Amanda, I think you and I are going to have some adventures here together. Even as you have the new bambino, we shall make the children Mexican, and you as well."

"My word is that a threat?" Amanda teased.

Raquel winked at her new friend, the Yankee, over another tequila,

"No, my darling….it is a blessing."

Chapter 17

Edward had a large office at the back of the new cardiac wing in the hospital San Angel in the central of Mexico City. He had a team of two doctors and eight nurses under him. He was second in command of the Cardiology Department under Doctor Henrique Soto Hernandez. Edward supposed he would have the ageing doctor's position within five years, maybe sooner if he played his cards right.

On Mondays, he lectured the medical students at the nearby University. His lectures in the small room were always packed, a cadaver on the table most days. His first-morning lecture was his Spanish language lecture, while the following was always in English. There were young men from all over the world and as far away as China who had come to learn from the gifted hands of Doctor Tappan; of this, he was sure.

He knew the hospital and university staff viewed him as not only an amazing doctor but that he could offer lectures in flawless English, only opened their doors to more potential students, meaning vast revenue streams. Edward knew his approach to medicine was perfect, but he needed to impart his wisdom to the men coming after him. He had the gift, the touch, just like his father. Surgery of any kind was a delicate and stressful endeavour, but Edward was full sure that he made it look easy to the young student doctors. On this day, there was no cadaver, but Ed didn't need one for this lecture.

What he needed was to find out was, who in this newest crop of Mexico's physicians was the stupidest and who, if any, were right on his heels. He had to see the competition and decide if they were dangerous.

"Can anyone tell me who Doctor William Harvey was?"

A small doctor in the front row with blonde hair and spectacles raised his hand.

"Mr.......Spencer, is it?"

Edward called on him.

"Yes, sir, Doctor Tappan. William Harvey was an English Physician who in 1628, first described blood circulation."

"Very good Mr. Spencer. I am going to presume your English accent isn't the only reason that you know this English physician and that you are keenly aware of your medical history. That you have done so much studying over the years in preparation to become a doctor that I should be able to ask you anything, and you would know the answer."

Young Mr. Spencer sat silently, quite convinced from what he knew about Doctor Tappan that there was a catch coming or this was a trick question. Doctor Tappan was often so vile to his students that many now tried to remain as quiet in the lectures as they could get away with being.

Edward continued,

"In 1706, Raymond de Vieussens, a French anatomy professor, first describes what?"

"Mr. Spencer?"

"The structure of the heart's chambers and vessels, I believe

Doctor Tappan."

"Excellent,"

Edward moved on to the next victim.

"In 1733 Stephen Hales, an English clergyman and scientist, first measures what…Mr. Ling?",

He asked the young man who had come from China.

Mr. Ling delivered his answer in very good English,

"Blood pressure, Doctor Tappan."

"Yes. Blood pressure is the very telling metric we have as doctors to tell if someone's heart is in trouble, or if it is fit as a fiddle. Without these great men and their work, we would be in the dark still as to the most important organ in the body. Some would argue that the most important organ is the brain, but without the workhorse, the powerhouse of the heart to pump that elixir of life we call blood to the brain…the brain is useless. It all goes back to the beating of the heart, or what I like to call the Organ of God. And when we save human life and fix broken, defective hearts, we are one with God, doing His work. You must never forget that. You cannot be but a simple man when working on the heart; you must be a God in your own right."

What Mr. Spencer could not know at the very moment that he himself found this speech to be utterly distasteful and near blasphemous, was that most of the other sixty young men in the room all thought the same thing, in various languages. These were also the sort of basic questions one would cover in their first year at school, so it seemed Tappan was indeed trying to trick them.

Edward continued,

"In 1816, Rene T. H. Laennec, a French physician, invents the stethoscope. My God, what a miraculous device. Nothing makes me more pleased as I look around at all of you fine gentleman to see you all wearing yours. We would be nearly blind, deaf and dumb if not for trusty stethoscopes allowing for us to hear inside the hearts we are working on. However, what I am about to discuss with you today is the most exciting topic we shall explore outside of surgery. Just a few short years ago, in 1903, Willem Einthoven, a Dutch physiologist, developed what, can anyone tell me? This is a most modern development and, as such, will not be in your medical texts, but I know the genius in this room will know the answer."

The room remained silent with that sort of unease at knowing the answer yet still feeling as if you do not know it. None of these confident and highly intelligent men felt they wanted to take this gamble with this man. And then Mr. Spencer raised his hand again.

"The electrocardiograph machine?"

Doctor Tappan smiled. He had found his protégé - or his future rival.

"Very good, Mr. Spencer. Very good. Now what I want to talk to you all about today is a new phenomenon, first documented only earlier this year of 1912. We are on the brink of the most modern of medicine, gentlemen. Never forget it.

An American physician and former colleague of mine, Dr. James B. Herrick, has been writing papers and giving lectures on the nature of heart disease- stemming from something he has called "the hardening of the arteries.", whereby the arteries themselves seem to stiffen and-"

"Perdona me, Doctor Tappan," Philomena, his secretary, interrupted his lecture abruptly. They both knew he hated interruptions, but she stood in the doorway to the lecture hall with a look on her face that said her news was urgent.

"Revert to your texts; use this time to study while I am away, gentleman."

He followed Philomena out into the hall on the way to his office.

"What is so urgent that I should be called out of my lecture Sen Señorita Garza?"

"It is urgent; the Dean is in your office and wishes to speak to you. Apologies, Doctor; you know I would never want to interrupt you."

Philomena Garza never wanted to be in the same room as her boss, much less do anything to add kindling to his ever-smouldering bad temper. She had already contemplated resigning her position three times that very week.

Edward entered his office to find the Dean of the university waiting for him.

"Señor Hidalgo, what do I owe this pleasure to?"

The Dean, Sergio Hidalgo, was a tall, thin man in his early sixties, bald as an egg with spectacles and always in an immaculate brown suit. He skipped the usual pleasantries and went right for the throat.

"Doctor Tappan, I am leaving town this afternoon, but I needed to speak with you. We at the university feel we may need to review your contract."

"So soon?"

"You will remember, this was a temporary position, subject to evaluation. We are happy with your performance thus far, but I am afraid if you are to continue with this university, we will need more of your time. I understand between your own practice with Dr. Sanchez and Dr. Arroyo, and you also have a position at the teaching hospital that, this may prove to be a burden on your schedule."

Edward picked up on a tone that implied the Dean no longer wanted him there, and he tried his best not to bristle but meet this conversation with a smile.

"Dean Hidalgo, there will be no burden."

"What of your lovely family? Your young wife? How will the homestead take your precious time with them being reduced further? I had a wife once, you know. I remember how they can be.", he said with a chuckle.

Edward wasn't going to let a little thing like that stand in the way of a permanent professorship at the most esteemed university in Mexico. Amanda would understand or learn to accept it. There was no other alternative.

"I assure you, my wife will not utter one word of complaint. There will be no discord in my home over my working longer hours. These women, I find, will accommodate what you instruct them to, especially if you make them wives at a young age."

Dean Hidalgo nodded,

"Yes, well we will see. I will stop by again when I am ready to make your position here official. In the meantime, keep up the good work here. Your dedication shows. And, yes, by all means, do keep the little woman in line. An American woman, isn't she?"

Edward paused at the odd tone again in the Dean's voice.

"Yes, my wife is from Philadelphia."

The Dean cleared his throat and then chuckled again nervously,

"Well- we will try not to hold that against her, eh?" Bueno dias, doctor."

Chapter 18

They sat on a bright Sunday morning in the garden, Amanda and Raquel, one fascinated by stories of the other, over café and bolios.

"The way you ignored Eddie at first, I would have loved to have been there to see it. I am sure that drove him insane." Raquel laughed.

"One thing I remember from when we were children is Eduardo Ricardo Tappan Santiago does not like to be ignored."

"I often think it was my lack of interest at first that made him chase me the way he did. He didn't court me, he hunted me.", Amanda revealed.

The women chuckled, both knowing it was true.

"How did you meet Eddie?"

"The 1904 World's Fair- St. Louis, Missouri. I went with a girl from school and her family…. he came up to the flower stall I had gotten talked into helping with- he bought a dozen red roses off me and then gave them to me."

"Oh, lovely…" Raquel conceded, eyebrows raised.

"We began to chat, and it turned out that I was from Philly and that he had been working in a hospital there. He begged for my address so he could write to me, and a few days later, when I arrived home, I had a stack of letters from him already. Most of them were postmarked from St. Louis- he wrote me three letters before he even left the World's Fair. It all happened so fast. I liked his penmanship, and I liked what he was saying, and I liked how relentlessly he pursued me. That probably all sounds very daft, I know."

"No, not at all kiddo. Sounds like Eddie knew exactly what he was doing and going after what he wanted."

Old Eddie blindsided this girl and swept her off her young feet, Raquel thought to herself, with a sense of unease. She quickly decided to change the subject.

Raquel insisted that she come with her to the Ladies Social Club of Mexico City, an exclusive chapter on the Calle Reforma, in a great modern building.

"It is time we get you out!"

"I wouldn't be able to say a word, Raquel."

"Don't worry about that; many of the ladies in these circles of society speak at least a bit of English if they are not fluent. And this is a good way for you to practice bit by bit your Spanish while meeting new people and making new friends. Don't be shy; it doesn't suit you."

Amanda opened her mouth to protest but found Raquel was right.

"I will call the house to collect you on Tuesday at one o'clock. We will arrive at the club for a late lunch, drinks, and introductions. Wear something stunning."

Tuesday found Amanda's hair and nerves a mess.

"Señora," Marta appeared in her bedroom,

"La Señora Vanin Goya is downstairs."

"Thank you, Marta".

Amanda sighed heavily as Guadalupe buttoned up the back of her gown.

"I'm nervous", she told the woman.

"Señora, we Mexicans, we don't bite- the ladies at the Social Club are going to love you. You are so charming.

"My Spanish is dreadful, Lupe. I'm embarrassed; my mother spoke both English and French fluently- flawlessly- these women will think I'm some red necked yokel from the States."

"Well...your Spanish is not the best, perhaps, but how good is their English? Until they can say the Lord's Prayer in perfect English, like I can, I would not let them intimidate you, jefa," she gave her a wink.

Amanda smiled. Lupe had taken to sometimes calling her "jefa," which meant "boss," and for some reason, she could not understand this tickled Amanda. She was feeling an affection for Guadalupe and her warmth that felt familial.

"There she is!" Raquel beamed as Amanda made her way gingerly down the stairs.

"Do I look very pregnant?" she asked her new friend.

"I'm worried these ladies will just think I have gotten fat."

"You look wonderful and very obviously as though you are carrying. My God, half of the women there will be expecting themselves, I'm sure. Stop fussing!"

The motor car pulled up to a beautiful red brick building flanked by palm trees with two doormen who looked as if they served a royal family, in tops and tails of red and navy. The inside of the social club was art deco and the most modern gold and green and black colour schemes. The glamourous feel of the building, for a moment, sent a wave through Amanda as if she was not dressed appropriately.

"Do I look all right?" Amanda whispered again to Raquel, who assured her the chiffon and silk, gold and beige gown was perfect, as were her matching gloves, bag, and hat.

"You will be fine",

she reassured her as they were led to their table in the large open dining room.

The room was all glass with an impossibly high ceiling and plants everywhere. It was as if they were in a giant terrarium, the people giant spiders. The shiny brass fixtures dotted throughout, the plants, and the mosaic-tiled floor was too beautiful for Amanda to properly take in as she was ushered to a table almost in the centre of the room. It was set for two.

"We won't be having anyone you know joining us?" she asked surprised.

Raquel smiled,

"I always sit at this table for two, but you will see after we eat, we will move to one of those larger tables, with fifteen or more women, for drinks and apéritifs and dessert, but first there is a little dance we all do. We all can't wait to greet each other but we also must pretend like we are not in any rush to greet each other."

"Oh," Amanda said disappointedly,

"This sounds even more complicated than the social etiquette in New York."

Raquel picked up her menu and smiled at the American,

"Oh, it is- much more complicated than New York, London, St. Petersburg. New York is small time here. The machinations of Mexico City are legendary…New York is for girls, sweetheart. Mexico City, el Distrito Federal, is for women!"

The waiter appeared swiftly; Amanda had not even glanced at her menu as she was still trying to take in her surroundings without also looking like a slack-jawed little girl.

"Welcome, Señora Vanin Goya, always lovely to see you", the waiter purred, in perfect English, much to Amanda' surprise.

"Hello, Adolpho, how lovely to see you. I will take a Manhattan, please; I am parched."

She gave a dizzying smile that seemed to influence the waiter as he smiled back at Raquel in a way that said he was taken with her.

Amanda felt overwhelmed by the menu, all of it in Spanish and asked Raquel to order everything for her, down to the drink.

"A mimosa for the lady- you will love it- orange juice and champagne, really delightful. Not too heavy. I think we will start each of us with the foie gras and the aspic and watercress tarts, please, Adolpho."

And as he returned with their drinks, the first two ladies made their approach. Amidst cheek kisses and exclamations of how long it had been since last seeing each other, Amanda was introduced to great fanfare.

"Mucho gusto Señora Tappan."

"Hola mucho gusto; I am afraid that is the extent of my Spanish."

A big-eyed blonde switched seamlessly to English.

"Not to worry, my pleasure."

Raquel introduced sisters Beatriz and Helena.

"This is *the* Señora Tappan? What a beautiful wife the good doctor has landed himself.", the second, shorter blonde said with a smile and heavily accented but still perfect English.

The pair fussed at the women and chatted amiably but bid their goodbyes as they were just leaving and had to hurry to another engagement.

Their lunch arrived and Raquel got Amanda caught up on the who is who.

"These women will end up in your social circles, so let me advise you on who to avoid and who to cosy up to.", Raquel said earnestly.

"Those two sisters are the daughters of a judge, Ernesto Garcia Williams from Chihuahua. His mother was an American from

California, whose family made a mint in that California Gold Rush and his father from Tabasco, well he- the judge, marries himself a Finnish woman, who after she had the two girls here in Mexico, ran off with a police officer almost 20 years ago. They say she went crazy drinking absinthe one night and tried to murder Ernesto, but when she failed, she simply packed a bag and fled.

"How did she try to kill him?" Amanda asked aghast,

"With a rifle! But she couldn't get it to fire, so the story goes, so old Ernie is still around, sour as bad grapes, not a nice man- I mean, who would be in that situation? But his daughters are lovely, even if they were raised by the maids and his mother."

As they enjoyed their appetizers and then sopa de fideos and another round of drinks, they were approached by a tall woman with jet-black hair and eyes the shape of almonds. She was older, but her hair did not betray her with even a strand of white.

"Ah, Henriquetta, amor", Raquel stood to greet the President of the ladies club, and Amanda attempted to stand, but Henriquetta insisted she remain seated.

"Please don't get up. My oldest daughter is expecting as well; we just found out."

Raquel registered shock,

"You- an abuela? Already, my dear, if you have a child ready to have children, oh my goodness, I am not far behind. "

"Oh, isn't it something? Just dreadful, the way the years go flying- but I must say her father and I could not be happier- also because there is talk they may be moving to Washington, DC, and to be honest, perhaps that is a good move. Things here are so concerning. But enough of that- please, won't you join us for coffee at my table?"

"Of course, Henriquetta, we will join you in a few moments.

"Lovely; I look forward to making more introductions."

Henriquetta glided back to her table elegantly when a gentleman approached Raquel, who had already stood and turned towards him.

"Wait here Amandita, just one moment", she threw over her shoulder while removing a large brown packet from her bag and suddenly walking swiftly to the bar, where she handed it to the gentleman, who simply nodded and bowed slightly to Raquel. He turned on his heel with the package and walked quickly away.

What a bizarre encounter, thought Amelia.

The pair did not exchange a word but simple, silent glances.

Raquel caught the look on her friend's face as she sat back down.

"That was – oh, It doesn't matter. Business, it is so boring! Let's go mingle with the ladies, shall we?" she asked in a light and breezy manner that implied a change of subject.

Coffee was served to the table of a dozen women, all in beautiful dresses and hats, all done up as if they were attending the opera. Raquel was quick to make introductions as she knew everyone at the table, and Amanda was welcomed amid a sea of hellos and holas. Everyone was warm and smiling, genuinely pleased to make her acquaintance.

As the afternoon wore on, Amanda felt her confidence growing. The women who spoke English were genuine and friendly. The ones who only spoke Spanish, still treated the new girl with warmth. A kindness in the eyes, eagerness in the smiles, told Amanda, that even though she did not yet speak the language, she would, in time, find her footing.

"I really cannot thank you enough for this, for pushing me to come today.", she told Raquel later.

"Of course, kid- I told you, you were the one I wanted to be friends with. Just a shame I have to put up with Edward to get to you."

Chapter 19

Arthur and Amelia sat attentively with their mother on their favourite bench in the garden. The one closest to the mermaid fountain, it had the best view of the crocus beds, brilliant white and in full bloom.

It was a blindingly bright summer afternoon, delicious sunshine bathing their faces and bare arms, warm without being too close to hot or uncomfortable. The air smelled of sticky sweetness, and the hum in the distance told Amanda they had a beehive in some distant corner of the garden. It was a perfect day to nap in the hammock, or wander the garden, not to sit inside at a table learning lessons.

"But why must we earn Spanish?" Arthur asked, "I believe I already know how to speak it mother."

"LEARN Spanish. And it is because your father has taught you very well, but you don't speak it- not yet and neither do I. Your father can't teach us alone; he is very busy with his obligations at the hospital, and we need help. I do not speak or even understand enough Spanish quite yet and so I want us all to be able to communicate and chat with anyone and everyone here in our new home. I don't want us to keep having to ask if they speak English. A few lessons with this nice lady who is coming today shall make it easier for us to speak to Guadalupe and Marta and Amparo every day. Plus, I would like very much to surprise your father one day soon by all of us just jumping into a conversation together. Wouldn't that be nice?"

"I speak Span", Amelia grinned, her thumb finding its way back in to massage her tender back teeth.

"Take your finger out of your mouth, please, Amelia", Amanda corrected.

The Spanish tutor was lead out to the garden by Amparo, who forgot to introduce her but simply said, "Señora Tappan, ju have guest.", before scurrying off to go prepare a tray of cold drinks.

She tried her best, but Amparo often forgot large parts of her job, like making basic introductions. Amanda found this trait oddly amusing.

"You're early; how lovely." she beamed at the young lady dressed in all powder blue, standing and offering her hand.

"Hello, I'm Mrs. Edward Tappan, and you are?"

"Señorita Mayer, nice to meet you Mrs. Tappan", the young girl replied in perfect English with no trace of a Mexican accent. She sounded as if she had just stepped out of a doorway in New York.

"You came very highly recommended by Señora Vanin Goya. I've been looking forward to this, but I'm afraid the children are quite reluctant to sit down for lessons, and I've been trying to persuade them."

Señorita Mayer flashed a large and beautiful smile of perfect teeth behind a perfect mouth.

"Well, that is perfectly understandable on a day like today. One would expect the children to prefer a day at the seaside than being stuck inside repeating words."

She smiled her large smile at the little ones, already winning them over.

"I find that sometimes the best way to break the ice with children and to get them interested in their lessons is to engage in movement instead of simply sitting at the dining room table. This garden is lovely, there's no reason why we couldn't start our lessons out here, walking around among the flowers. I then simply speak to the children in both languages while pointing out flowers, for example, or that lovely fountain with the mermaid. Then, I will tell the children that the fountain- esa fuente - has a sirena- mermaid in Spanish. Then, I have them repeat it. I start with basic words and phrases before advancing to full sentences by the end of the session."

"That all sounds wonderful."

The tutor then turned to the tots standing at their mother's side,

"Buenos dias estudiantes. Yo soy la Señorita Mayer. Y tu, cómo te llamas?" she asked Arthur.

"Yo me llamo Arturo", the boy replied slowly, with a grin that said he was impressed with himself and his proficiency in languages.

Amelia just giggled and hid behind her mother's skirts.

After a tray with limonada was brought out to the small metal table, Señorita Mayer began by taking the two little ones by the hand to explore el jardin; she informed them it was how to say the garden.

Amanda was right behind them when Guadalupe came out to the garden to fetch la senora.

“Perdón- Señora Tappan – ju are needed in the house. Señor Diaz is here to see Señor Tappan, but there is some confusion.

Amanda looked at Guadalupe puzzled,

“Edward left for the hospital hours ago. Did he return home?”

She addressed the tutor,

“I’m sorry, forgive me, but I’m being called away. Please continue with the lesson without me. I will return as soon as I can. Is that all right, children?”

The tots nodded in unison, and Ms. Mayer reassured Amanda that she could handle them.

“Please take your time”, she told Amanda.

Amanda followed Guadalupe in through the open French doors, through the dark and cool sitting room and dining room, to find Diego wandering about, pacing in the kitchen.

“Well, hello, Diego, what seems to be going on?”

“Buenos Dias .....I don’t know what is going on. Eddie said for me to meet him here at mid-day before we were to set off to the new hospital in Chapultepec together. He had some people he wanted me to meet in the administrations. But I called to his office this morning to see if we could just go from there instead, and his secretary said she had not seen him at all. So, I come here expecting he has taken the morning off, very unlike him, but perhaps he is under the weather, and I see he is not in his office here…the maids telling me he set off from this house before eight in the morning. Do you know where he could be?"

Amanda found this odd but tried not to let anything show on her face in front of her staff.

"No Diego, he was gone by the time I woke. I haven't seen him since late last night. I was asleep before he even came to bed. I left him working in his office….again."

Amparo appeared at the kitchen door at the same time wails started in the distance,

"Señora, the little one, she fell in el jardin".

"My goodness, I will be right there, Amparo, thank you. Come with me Diego, for a moment, will you?"

She threw the question over her shoulder as she was already racing back out to the garden to the increased cries, hoping not to find Amelia very hurt.

"Well, my little clumsy one, have we hurt ourselves again, darling?"

Amanda found the tot standing next to the tutor who was talking soothingly to her, Amelia with a bloody knee and soaked face.

"She seemed to trip Señora Tappan-"

Señorita Mayer said and then looked up and saw Diego in the doorway and fell silent instantly.

Amanda, already crouched down and taking the child in her arms, missed the moment between the Spanish tutor and her dear friend, totally oblivious to the heavy silence that entered the garden even as small screams escaped the child.

Guadalupe appeared with iodine and a clean cloth, and the women tended to the injured knee. A few moments passed; Amanda focused on the tiny leg before her. The tot became quiet and settled once her injury had been given attention when Amanda stood to turn her attention back to Diego.

“Oh, Diego this is la Señorita-

“Graciela”, Diego interrupted,

“Graciela Mayer, we are acquainted.” Diego said matter of fact, his voice thick.

“Yes, we are, hello Diego”,

Graciela said staring up at him, her cheeks flooding scarlet, a shade to rival anything in the garden.

Amanda stood confused for a split second, just on the precipice of saying something stupid, of asking how they knew each other, when the answer slapped her in the face. This was the Graciela, the German. The illegitimate child, the woman Diego had loved but abandoned.

Time stood perfectly still for a moment, the trio taking in the uncomfortable pause, when Diego snapped too.

“Right, well if you will excuse me ladies, I must get back to…work. Always lovely to see you both.”

He muttered with a quick half bow and spun on his heel.

Amanda followed him to the front door,

"I will see you out".

"No need, please. If you find your husband, perhaps you could have him telephone me at the hospital. I will see you, Amanda."

He said almost coldly as if he was annoyed with her.

The front door shutting left his lovely cologne in the air in his absence. Amanda breathed it in, confused and longing, afraid he was upset with her. She didn't know and could not have had any idea of who the tutor she hired was.

She did not understand why her own heart pounded, feeling as if it was going to jump out of her mouth. She felt for the both of them- supreme embarrassment, but also something else for Diego. Instead of being preoccupied with where her husband could be, she was more concerned about when Diego would return.

She returned to the garden to find Graciela busying herself with repeating the name of a certain flower to the children in Spanish, her face, slack and ashen, pointing towards the dirt. She did not lift her eyes as Amanda joined them for the remainder of the lesson. Her collar betrayed her, wet with drops that could only be tears.

Chapter 20

The long summer days of her first Mexican summer Amanda found were stretching into nights of solitude that, instead of bringing her peace, put her on edge. She had made it through long days back in New York, filled with bouts of loneliness when Edward was busy with work, and it had not affected her the way the expanses of time now did. She was used to being alone, in one way or another, so she grew accustomed to ignoring it and busying herself with a million little tasks. She always managed to fill her time with pursuits that made her happy. This became much easier after the children were born. She was indeed busy, and her life was filled with purpose. When not tending to the children or household to some degree, she often wandered the markets of New York, looking for the best quality fruit and vegetables, the finest wines, and coffees to keep stocked at home. There was a certain cheese Edward liked, and her favourite flower stall was right beside the shop that sold it. She always tried to sneak into Central Park and take a few moments to herself to enjoy the views, pretending she was able to paint them or even half convincing herself maybe one day she would try. She admired paintings in galleries, attended museums, perused the library, or went looking for a new dress or hat. She filled her days with her children, visiting the occasional friend, dealing with those in her circle she had to endure and her happiest pursuit of reading. She found she filled those days of her marriage so easily. There was always something to do; even though she had the help of household staff, there was always something that needed attending to. Then Ed would arrive home to dinner with the family. Some days, he arrived home much, much later. In both scenarios, he always arrived home ready to spend time with his wife and children. She found, looking back, that she rarely missed his presence. Now, in the new house in Mexico, Amanda felt she missed him a great deal, even when he was in the house.

Mexico was proving to be so different in so many ways. It was an upheaval that, to some extent, Amanda had prepared herself for, but some things she had not expected, so there was no way to prepare. There was a strange coldness to Edward now, as if he was always in a bad mood. Amanda felt there had been a shift from the second or third day after they had arrived. She told herself he had not settled yet into the new routine, odd as he at least knew and loved Mexico. She would then offer up his new and hectic position at the hospital as an explanation. Lecturer, one of the head cardiac surgeons, performing the most modern of medicine all in a country where even he had admitted the hospitals were not fit for purpose, would be enough stress for any one man. The best hospitals in Mexico were on par with the worst in the United States, and while Ed felt he would change all that, for the moment, he had to endure the state of things. Of course, she told herself, he would often be out of sorts.

Aside from tending to her children, Amanda found she really had nothing to do most days in her new home. At first, this freedom was a welcome turn of events in comparison to what she had just left behind in New York.

She was happy in those first weeks to give her body and the body of her unborn baby the sleep they demanded. She was happy arranging furniture and knickknacks and unpacking and making their beautiful Orange Blossom House her home. She was happy to sit exhausted yet content in the garden and hope for an interlude with a Monarch butterfly. The days seemed longer here somehow, with more unfilled hours and boredom creeping in. And she had noticed in her boredom that flashes of *before* crept into her mind. She was not sure if it was the old feelings returning, the problem coming back or if it was only the strong memories of that time haunting her.

Perhaps the long, lazy days of summer were to blame, as well as Amanda's constant state of sickness during this pregnancy. It was uncanny how her first pregnancies had left her feeling fantastic, and this time, she was often nearly bedridden. It had started in New York- the unpleasant retching. She had a bit of that with her first two children, but it had subsided usually by the third month. This time, she was just getting going in the third month. The boat trip from the United States and the train they had taken through Mexico had both been wonderful experiences for her yet also largely abysmal, due solely to her illness. The exhaustion a woman endures while pregnant had not shown any signs of abatement, and the feeling sick, followed too often by the act of getting sick, seemed to drag on through her days. As the first fortnight of excitement and meeting new people died down, Amanda found herself now longing for a bit of the hubbub she had been decrying only moments ago. However, most days, she was simply far too ill to go downstairs or even get out of her bed. Edward assured her this amount of sickness in pregnancy, though rare, can happen. He called it by some Latin name while waving his hand dismissively. Amanda refused to tell him she was starting to have the upsetting thoughts again. They had first appeared in the days after having Arthur. Strange moments of feeling upside down, she had found herself standing in their New York kitchen for half an hour, staring at the spoons, at the knives. Edward never really knew the extent of the malaise.

She found Ed's absences profound and her illness infuriating, even as she felt a bit selfish for wanting. How could she get to know her new city if she never went out into it? On the days she felt well enough to step outside, she never had any real company to take her anywhere. The staff were busy with the children and household.

She understood he would, of course, be busy with a new hospital and a new schedule, but she found herself resentful. She did not think he would immediately drop her and the children like heavy packages just inside the door. He had promised her that he would spend time with them in the beginning, the very first few days and weeks. It had turned out his idea of spending time with the family was the first three days after their arrival, occupied and distracted, before he dashed off to his work. Amanda did not want to be the jealous and needy sort of wife that she knew Edward found loathsome, but he was more a ghost than flesh and blood presence. He was an entity spoken of but rarely seen. She felt her resentment growing alongside her belly.

She knew how important his career in medicine was to him and to the family. It was more than their bread and butter; but it was his passion, his obsession, perhaps his truest love. His work, however; would always be there; his family would not. He would always have new patients that needed him and yet his children would grow and one day leave the house empty. His work would remain as his family aged and changed. These were moments Amanda knew all too well would never return. Not usually one for outbursts, she wanted to grab him by the lapels of his coat and yell at him to notice his own children, to hold them, to listen to them, to see them. He was very good at showing them off as if they were some expensive pieces of art he had purchased, but he never spent time with them at all anymore. Amelia barely recognized him at times. With a new baby coming, she felt they were growing apart. She felt resentful at being left to wonder whether he would be present for the birth.

Amanda began to have moments where she thought she might set upon him in a rage if he was ever there. Many of their conversations happened after he'd arrive home hungry, exhausted with just enough time for a bath and a couple of brandies before collapsing in bed beside her for three, maybe four hours. So many conversations in the middle of the night, in fact, to such an extent that Amanda was beginning to question if he was there, waking her, chatting about some new exciting development in his work at five a.m. or if she was simply dreaming and talking in her sleep to the coat rack in the corner of the room. If she had been her usual self, she would have put a stop to it, but her sleep dictated everything now, and she simply was too tired to deal with her husband.

Raquel and Diego made themselves staples in the household; at least, at first, they certainly tried. They seemed aware of the need to watch Amanda, to check on her wellbeing, even if Ed had left her to the maids. They both came by at least twice a week, but even so, they had their own obligations. Their visits naturally became shorter and more impromptu; their presence felt less and less. Raquel couldn't make every week to the ladies' social club, and Amanda would not go on her own, nor was anyone expecting her to. Amanda understood the newness of having the Tappans in Mexico would have also worn off a bit for even dear friends. Life went on. Days were filled with busy schedules. People take each other for granted at the best of times.

The quiet of the house was imposing, and it struck Amanda as unsettling. Every day, she, the two children, Guadalupe, Amparo and Marta, were there and yet it was so strangely quiet. Save for the soft humming of Lupe as she stirred her sopa, made the tortillas, her occasional vocalization of some old forgotten Mexican love song, the halls and rooms remained like that of a monastery. The silence felt so large that, at times, Amanda found herself whispering as if the silence was an entity to be respected.

The children were entertained by their sweet, jilted, tutor a couple of days a week. There was always someone in the household to mind them, so while Amanda was relieved not to be on duty all the time, affording her the rest she needed, she even found her little ones pulling away a bit. They were still babies, and yet when they had each other, they were occupied and content. Soon after their arrival in Mexico, they rarely came looking for her. She knew that was her fault, being as ill and useless as she was. They would join her in her bed, a comforting snuggle with mother, but soon would grow restless to stretch their little legs and play about the house.

Amanda told herself as soon as she gave birth, everything would right itself; everything would feel normal again. That thought always begged the question, had things in their home, New York or this new one, ever been normal? Being in a new environment seemed to show cracks in Amanda's marriage that she had not wanted to find and that she did not know how to repair.

Chapter 21

Raquel was a widowed and captivating socialite; her dance card was always full. The men of Mexico City were taken with her and those without wives all thought themselves suitors, while even those with wives thought they would eventually be lovers. With her young son attending military school on the far side of Mexico City, her days were devoted to the trials and tribulations of being a business owner. There were no women in the fur industry, not outside of Russia or Paris, who were running a company on their own. Most men in Mexico could scarcely believe Raquel had set up her company *after* the death of her husband.

Most assumed it had been a joint venture or that she had been forced to take the helm after his passing. Instead, it was an idea born amidst grief and fear. With her connections and family in Russia, in just a few short years, Raquel had Vanin Furs, the number one importer of furs into Mexico and held her own with importers in the United States. She had spent the last year breaking into the New York market. She had even sold two of her fur coats to the writer Edith Wharton after the publication of her novel, "The House of Mirth". Raquel's signed copy sat on the bookcase directly to her left in her office. The American journalist Nellie Bly was a dear friend; her scathing articles on the corruption of the Mexican government led to her being not so politely asked to leave Mexico- she and Raquel corresponded regularly. Raquel was friends with artists, intellectuals, suffragettes, and hell raisers.

Everyone thought Raquel to be quite tenacious and not to be crossed when she was much softer than she let on. She did what she had to do in a world where she was alone with her son and her business. She was much more like her new American friend Mrs. Tappan. She had begun to think of her a good deal. Something was troubling Raquel about Edward's young, doe eyed wife, and she felt something was troubling Amanda as well. She had decided upon meeting that she would keep a watchful eye on the American. Edward being Edward, Raquel knew the young woman would need her.

Raquel's next goal was to venture into South America's markets, eyeing Buenos Aires and deciding to go after the elite of Argentina, Venezuela, Brazil and Chile. If all went well, she would then set in motion Colombia and Peru. The winters of South America varied from some parts experiencing biting cold to others with much milder temperatures near the equator, but so much was woven through mountains that fur was not a silly venture like some men had tried to imply. The demand was not quite that of Russia, or other extreme northern territories around the globe, but Raquel was cornering the market hold on Latin America. Sometimes, she would laugh to herself over a glass of wine before bed to think she had wanted to be a ballerina. Still, she was alone and enjoyed it. While she missed the company of a man, there was not a man who could compete with her dead husband for her attention. Most bored her within minutes.

Raquel took great joy in visiting the Tappan household. She would greet her new amiga and after some prodding and nagging, get her to agree to try and get out of the house.

"Venture into the city with me, leave the children behind with Guadalupe. I will take you to see the Cathedral, and upon seeing it, you will want to talk to God."

Everyone had informed Amanda that now was not the time for her to venture anywhere solo, as in her delicate condition and with her lack of fluency and not knowing her surroundings, it was far too dangerous.

"Out of the question", Ed had assured her.

If Raquel or Diego were not with her, she didn't leave the house. Amanda had not been totally prepared for this and felt unable to question Edward on it. She could not verbalize why this detail, although for her safety, felt like a betrayal of a promise.

One Saturday morning in August, Raquel appeared at the house at eight in the morning, ordering coffee up to Amanda's room and cajoling her now large belly out of bed.

"I am taking you on an adventure, my Yankee, my Gringo! Get up! Out of bed with you."

And she took to tearing open curtains and rummaging through Amanda's closet for proper and comfortable walking shoes.

As the women left the house being driven by the chauffer in the automobile, they did not see, once they left the heavily armed front gates of the colonia, that another automobile took off slowly behind them as they made their way to the Cathedral.

The following rainy Tuesday Senora Tappan went to the vegetable market with Lupe. She was so pleased to be out from behind the high walls of her Orange Blossom fortress; she simply wanted to take in everything she could get her eyes on. She was walking too slowly for her housekeeper's liking, although Lupe was too kind and subservient ever to hurry her mistress. Amanda was distracted by the colourful array of some rather odd vegetables she had never seen before.

"What's this?", Amanda would whisper to Lupe in English.

Lupe would answer in Spanish,

"Eso es nopal- cactus, Señora."

"And this one?" Amanda held up a small, purple, bumpy thing.

"Pitaya, Señora".

Amanda had Lupe purchase one of just about everything.

"That was wonderful Lupe. To think that was only the vegetable and fruit market. I could have stayed there all day if I wasn't so tired all the time."

Lupe had only been half listening to her jefa, unable to shake the feeling that they had been followed through the market. A ridiculous thought she tried to dismiss, even though she found herself stopping from time to time, her head swivelling.

Lupe had her own opinions on Edward. He was rarely home to take his wife or the children anywhere. In fact, he had not stepped outside their front door with his wife and children by his side since the day of their arrival. Lupe felt an exhalation of relief upon returning Amanda home after the market.

As the weeks went by, Amanda grew to feel she was a prisoner. She would have moments of increasing nerves at the thought that she would be utterly defenceless and lost if suddenly outside the grounds of her Orange Blossom House. She knew to expect her life would be different to what it had been in New York. She knew to expect it would take some time to settle in and become accustomed to everything being new. She never imagined that she would feel so trapped. As her belly grew larger, she grew more lethargic and more restless. She tried to distract herself with how much she loved her new home- she could see herself growing old in that garden, her grandchildren visiting that same mermaid fountain. The first few weeks felt so odd, but she was happy to see the children went on about their business as if they had always lived in the Orange Blossom House. She took great comfort from them and imagined that if they had adapted, she would too, one day soon. The visit to the beautiful Cathedral and then the market a few days later had lifted her spirits, but she looked at Raquel and her exciting life with a hint of envy she could not admit to her new friend.

Chapter 22

Raquel was standing over Edward's desk, rifling through his papers calmly and deliberately, when he entered the study. She wanted him to see that she was coming behind him, checking up on just how he was handling their affairs.

"What do I owe this intrusive pleasure to, querida, at this time of night?"

Raquel did not smile as she looked up from his desk.

"Eduardo- I just had to put your exhausted wife into her bed. This pregnancy and this move have taken too much out of her."

"You're basing this summation on your long friendship, I suppose?"

"Por favour Eddie- don't bullshit me.

"You know vulgarity doesn't suit you, Raquel."

"Eduardo, I am a woman, a mother, and I know things. I know you.

Tell me this – how much does she know?"

"About what specifically, my dear?"

Raquel was getting annoyed at his playing coy.

"About everything – this house, how it was paid for, Mexico, about the Revolucion? About the two of us and our invo- ?"

"She knows what she needs to know, which is not that much. It's fine for her, to be a mother and a wife to be a tad kept in the dark for now. She doesn't need the added worry currently. Plus, she would not have the head for this."

"Her not knowing is adding stress and worry- she is not a stupid young lady. She senses something is amiss. Now, I can lead her in the opposite direction but for how long, hmm? Do you think that she won't eventually figure it all out? She gave up a great deal to come down here with you so that you could pursue your dreams and other….so that we could …" she trailed off, huffing. She crossed her arms defiantly.

"If I had known that she was pregnant again, I would have never let you bring her to Mexico."

"Let me bring her? My own wife? You would have stopped me how?"

"It was one thing with children, but a brand-new baby in this country at such a confusing time for her, for everyone in Mexico. You bring her here, this young American mother, in a vulnerable position. Maybe, if she had stayed in New York just long enough to have the baby, surrounded by her family and friends and her home and life-"

"My wife doesn't have any family; save the man you're looking at and our children. She had no family whatsoever left in New York or Philly, or anywhere else. They're all dead. And her friends were but a few. How long would she have needed to stay in New York before moving down here with MY children? It would have been delaying the inevitable, and for what? I needed to be here. You know that, and you know why. I wanted my family here with me, where they belong."

"Eduardo, if it were not for me and possibly Diego, she would not have a person in this world to talk to other than your little tots and the maids who don't understand her. You are her main confidant, and you have kept so much from her. I can tell by the way she talks, the things we have discussed, that she hasn't any idea of what you are really-"

"I have only done what any respectable and responsible husband would do. I'm protecting my wife and children. Plus, the baby- we cannot control the timing of such events. This latest pregnancy was a bit of a surprise but surely is just another blessing in a sea of good fortune."

"The tides of this sea are tumultuous Ed. We must be very careful how we navigate the waters. We worry not just for ourselves, but we have our passengers to think of. Anything that you and I get wrong in this situation affects my son, my boy, too, not just your family, who I have become extremely fond of in a short time. There is a lot of talk out there on the streets of this city. I worry about some of the things I hear. Nobody seems to know who the victors in this whole mess of a war will be. Nobody can even try to predict the outcome, and we have involved ourselves for what, more money? I fear we have put ourselves under scrutiny. I am almost certain we were followed when I took her to the Cathedral."

"Nonsense", Ed huffed.

Raquel continued in a torrent, "I'm becoming concerned about my business, my investments, our investments. I am concerned that when Jaime leaves school, will this trouble devour him? He wants into the military so bad he can almost taste it, and there have been days lately when I want to abandon ship and take my boy away from here. My God, Ed, I even went to see a bruja; I lowered myself to go and get my fortune read. And when I asked her about the future of Mexico, she said she saw nothing but blood."

Ed shook his head, disappointed.

“That is not like you Raquel…superstition, el mal ojo…come on, a crystal ball with some gypsy? You are too intelligent for such charades.”

“Perhaps- but the truly intelligent Ed, examine a situation from all the possible angles, even the ones that seem ridiculous. I don’t necessarily believe in prognosticators or soothe sayers, but I have seen some very interesting things in the presence of a Mexican bruja, so I am inclined to believe some of these natives…know things.”

She tried to shake off the chill of the memory.

“Let me just remind you- that your lovely wife es una innocente” she moved towards him and dropped her voice down to a whisper as she put her arms around his waist,

“…and especially if she were to find out what you and I have been up to…she might not like it very much. She is like a little Russian nesting doll, giving you smaller versions of herself, one after the other. She should be treasured, Eddie. Women can be fragile when they are bringing new life into the world. You need to keep an eye on her, protect her, and if you don’t, I will.”

With that, she gave him a kiss on his ear, leaving a red stain,

“You remember my words, corazon.”

Chapter 23

The cold November morning greeted the household with fog surrounding the Orange Blossom House, filling the grounds and the garden with gauze-like whiteness that was nearly blinding.

Amanda had woken again in the middle of the night, unable to sleep from the discomfort of her now behemoth stomach. Along with the pain jolting through her body and the constant heartburn, Ed's comings and goings disturbed her already wretched sleep.

The dawn found her downstairs, where Lupe was already diligently at work, cooking, brewing coffee and giving orders to Marta, Amparo, and the grounds staff.

"Buenos dias Señora Tappan! Can't sleep again?", Lupe called out the kitchen door to her mistress, slowly swaying about like a ship in high winds.

"Si…….buenos dias Lupe", she called out.

"I will waddle back to bed soon."

"You want my hot chocolate? Maybe help you?"

"No, Lupe, later. I just need to pace."

Walking slowly though the house often helped Amanda to later crawl back into her bed and sleep comfortably. Whether it was the stretching of her puffy legs and feet that helped her feel better, or the movement simply got her circulation going, she was not sure, but she knew it made a difference. Just walking even seemed, at times, to help soothe her heartburn. Amanda came to quietly stand in the dark sitting room and peer out into the garden as the day broke, but the light was slow to appear. Through the straining of her eyesight and through the wisps of thick fog hanging about clinging to the plants, she saw them.

She tried to count them at first, one by one, and when she got to eighteen, she opened the door to the garden and stepped out into the still air. There were eighteen, then twenty, then twenty-seven butterflies, she counted. Twenty-seven monarch butterflies had flown into her garden and had taken over the bench and the mermaid fountain. Amanda caught herself holding her breath as she ventured out among them. Afraid to scare them off, she inched towards them for a closer look. It was a bizarre phenomenon to witness these creatures amidst a dense fog. They did not seem to belong here in such strange weather conditions. Could the butterflies see through the fog to fly, she wondered? How could they?

"They have stopped here for a rest on their way back home.", Lupe whispered from behind her jefa.

Amanda turned towards her; unaware the woman had come out to check on her.

"These are definitely headed back to Michoacan?", she asked quietly.

"Oh yes, Señora. Today is the Day of the Dead. These are the very ones that are headed back to the Oyamel Fir trees. What a sight to behold. I have never seen so many at once in a private garden like this."

Amanda cautiously moved forward and sat down quickly on the bench.

She wanted a front-row seat to the performance of these minute dancers.

Within moments, a monarch flew over and landed on the very top of the mountain of belly that housed the newest Tappan. Amanda smiled gloriously, remembering the story that Lupe had told her in the summer. She imagined it was her mother Josephine come to say hello, and for the first time in a long while, she felt great joy and peace. Suddenly, two more monarchs lifted from the fountain as if they had quite enough to drink and looking for a better spot to rest, joined their companion atop the round belly. Amanda stared and suddenly felt not joy but grief. There were three. A bittersweet and lovely helping of the grief she held for the three of them, for her family, swelled within her. It felt like pride and longing and pulled on her as if she was being dragged down.

Amanda's eyes met Lupe's who was caught making the sign of the cross, a small smile at her lips. Amanda thought she might like to cry with the happy memories and the devastating reality that they were all gone. For a magical moment that felt as if it could pause time, she sat in the white fog of her beloved garden with her butterflies on her pregnant stomach, all of them together. The butterflies seemed to still themselves as if they were waiting for something. A tear rolled down her face, yet defiantly, she would not wipe it away. There was no one present to make her feel bad for it. Edward was never around her anymore, so she felt she could just be in the garden, in the presence of Lupe and the butterflies. A soft breeze entered the garden and as if a messenger meant to move the monarchs along, they all started to lift into the air high above her head and began to circle frantically before all starting to disperse. All but one left her belly, and Amanda counted them as they all left over the top of the garden wall. All had flown within seconds, yet one remained. And then the last of the monarchs flew slowly up and over her head, lazy in its movements, as if reluctant to leave her. It finally flew up over the wall, to catch up to its compañeros. As swiftly as they had appeared, they were gone, like the lives of the very humans they visited. Amanda would never utter a word of this to anyone, but she felt them, each of them, with her. Lupe could see the tears on the face of, not her mistress but a young girl, for in that moment she was small and fragile.

"Come Señora," Lupe said finally, affectionately.

"Let me make you something warm to drink and return you to your bed so that you have sweet dreams.

Amanda got up slowly and followed her into the house,

" Yes, I think I would like that very much, Lupe; thank you."

Lupe stopped to look at Amanda in the dark of the sitting room and took Amanda's tiny hand in hers, an unexpected warmth.

"Rejoice Señora. Do not be sad. They were here!" she whispered excitedly.

Chapter 24

The night before the baby would start to make her appearance, another baby appeared in the hall outside Amanda's bedroom door. There she was, pale, achingly beautiful with her red hair, wearing one of Amelia's nightgowns. Amanda gazed upon the intruder with wide eyes. The intruder stood gazing at Amanda, small but very real. With a surprised look on her face, the intruder said,

"Oh, you're awake!"

Amanda rubbed her eyes. She was hallucinating. Had she been drinking again?

"I have missed you, sister."

She said to Amanda in the voice of a child of seven or eight, an age she never got to.

"Who are you?" Amanda choked.

She had awoken from her slumber to strange noises in the house, noises like flames that could be heard even over the sound of rain and distant thunder. She had thrown on a robe, looked at a sleeping Edward and ran to the hall to go check on the children and to find the source of the noise. As she closed her bedroom door and looked up, she met eyes like her own- eyes like their father's.

"When Irish eyes are smiling…" the little one began to sing.

"Who are –"

"You know well who I am, Amanda. You had to watch me die."

Amanda fell back against the wall. It couldn't be. She was

hallucinating; she must be. She looked down to her pregnant stomach to find a flat belly, no baby to be found.

Amanda began to hyperventilate.

“My love”, the vision said.

“Do not be frightened. Mother says it will be all right, but you must come with me right now. I must show it to you.”

Amanda didn’t remember following her dead little sister down the hall to the top of the stairs.

“Be careful- these stairs are dangerous”,

she said with a sweet smile that sent terror through Amanda’s body.

Suddenly, they were at the front door, which stood open wide, even in the middle of the night.

Flames engulfed the entirety of the front garden. The lime trees, the wisteria, their carriage, the motor car, everything burned. Amanda could hear the flames, could smell the fire, could feel the heat. The gate in the distance, men running away from it, all on fire. The men were ablaze, screaming.

“Is that the sound I heard?”

Amanda asked her beloved apparition as thunder grew louder overhead and flames grew taller in front of her eyes. The heat could be felt on her face. Surely, the house would ignite at any moment.

“Amanda?”

Her sister called.

Amanda looked at her so close she could almost touch her……she lifted her hand, tears streaming down her face. The monarch butterflies started to land on her little sister, started to land in her hair, the orange of their wings melting into the red of her hair, flames dancing.

"Are you real….?" She sobbed.

"HE IS LYING TO YOU!" her sister's ghost suddenly shouted angrily.

Then calmly,

"He is lying. Mother says it is going to be all right. "

"Do you know how much I loved you?" Amanda whispered through tears.

"Why did you leave us? Why did you have to go? You killed us all the day you died."

"Amanda, it is going to be all right; I am going to sing our song, shall I? When Irish eyes are smiling…or maybe one for our new home…Cielito lindo…canta y no llores..do not cry.."

The blaze grew, and it started to move towards the house. The butterflies were igniting, some flying straight into the flames. Amanda felt the heat, felt her skin start to burn.

The heavy oak front door of the orange blossom house slammed shut and Amanda shot up in bed so fast she hurt her back.

Awake, she heaved a huge gulp of air into her lungs and looked for Edward, who was once again not in their bed. She was alone, with no dead little sister, no flames, the room cold. Her belly remained huge with its passenger stretching and giving a few swift kicks against being awakened so rudely.

Amanda felt a strong compulsion to check the hallway and be certain it was simply a bad dream and not her losing her sanity, but before she could begin to swing her legs out of the bed, her body froze.

Her face contorted into a grimace, a wave of pain lighting up her back and abdomen like a night sky torn by lightning. She grunted through that first warning of what was to come. She waited for the next one, and when fifteen minutes had passed with nothing more, she knew while she would be in labour soon enough, she wasn't quite yet, and she wearily laid her head down in preparation, hoping to get more sleep before the moment that she dreaded began again. She didn't have the strength to even wonder where that nightmare came from but could hear the echoes of "he is lying to you" reverberating through the room and through her body. She knew that was true as she lay in the dark, waiting for the fear to come.

Chapter 25

Birthing children had largely remained unchanged over the years and across the globe. It was always the same in the end. It was always a dangerous endeavour yet as compulsory to nature as breathing. Amanda's first two children had been surprisingly easy deliveries in the penthouse in Manhattan.

The new century was seeing more and more of a push towards women being taken into hospital for parturition. Ed thought it was the American Medical Association's wanting to take over obstetrics in totality from the midwives. He was glad his father wasn't alive to see it.

"I would definitely prefer to have the baby at home, "

Amanda had agreed with Edward's suggestion early on.

"I find hospitals to be…I don't know, where sick people go? No disrespect to you, dear, as you spend all day in one, but this new era of women having to go into the hospital to do the most natural thing in the world? It just seems a bit over the top."

Ed would not have let her give birth in a hospital if she had begged him. He knew too much about them, too much about infection, and distrusted the mortality rates.

"Absolutely right, my dear. These people trying to assert their status and wealth by having hospital births attended by physicians. It won't last. My father never birthed one baby in a hospital, not one. Babies should be brought into the world in the comfort and safety of their own home, not a hospital where I was just cutting on someone's artery in the next room. Distasteful, really, when you think about it."

Her first two times had been attended to by a midwife and a nurse Ed had worked with before. Margaret, Mags the nurse, curly red hair and a smile as big as her bottom; her background was obstetrics and midwifery, and nothing much worried her. The midwife Nancy had delivered three hundred babies by the time she was twenty-five, and she was much older than that by the time the Tappan children came along. Ed claimed they were the most competent pair in all of New York. With his own father having also been a prominent obstetrician (THE most prominent obstetrician in Edward's mind), he had always felt confident that the ordeal would turn out all right in the end. He always had a peer at the ready in case they needed a physician to intervene, just in case of a caesarean or other complications. Ed trusted his own medical prowess above that of anyone else's, but he knew too well the folly, the danger, in involving oneself as both doctor and husband, never mind father to the person being born.

He had no interest, should things have gone awry, in having to position himself in a compromised situation of a doctor amid panic because the patient was his own wife. He avoided any medical involvement that would end with her blood bathing them both. Accordingly, he also had no intention of seeing his wife spread out in agony and gore; her own body he derived so much pleasure from turned inside out. No, he had pondered obstetrics for a while; following in his father's footsteps was a nice notion, but he had been honest with himself and others- he simply did not want to have to see women that way. He did not pale or pause at the sight of blood or human muck, but he did not have the stomach to see the fairer sex ripped in half like so much wet paper. He found the whole birthing process to be distasteful. He had decided to study the heart instead, for he found it the most fascinating of all the organs. The very vessel responsible for pumping our life within us, never stopping, never resting, the most valiant of soldiers. Nothing could compare to it. More than anything, he wanted to restart the ones that paused and heal the ones that made people sick. It was even more God like than bringing a baby into the world.

Amanda had been given laudanum, a lighter, more polite version of opium and had, with her midwife and nurse, conquered her labours, both in under eight hours. She appeared to her husband to be a perfect machine for bringing forth new human life into the world in an effective manner. He supposed, as young as she was and as healthy, that she could repeat this performance five, six, seven times, maybe more without fail. He looked forward to keeping her with a child as often as nature allowed.

Each child was born strapping and pink, with all the necessary parts, hungry, with full heads of blonde hair. They put on weight and were robust, of fine stock. Ed always knew he had chosen correctly when he first laid eyes on nineteen-year-old Amanda. He knew he had to move swiftly, for a prize such as she would not be without a string of suitors for long.

The mother herself would not ever divulge to her husband how her skin had torn in a most uncomfortable way and, how the midwife had her sitting in poultices of bread and milk those first few days after each delivery, how they had stitched her up with what felt like ship rope. She could share so much with her lover, but so much had to remain hidden away. Only Edward and the midwives would truly know just how lucky they'd been that Amanda never had any complications, extraordinary bleeding or infection set in. Neither half of the couple had any reason to believe that Amanda's third birth would be much different in Mexico City to the others in New York.

Had they been in some forgotten pueblito, somewhere with more donkeys and mosquitos than people, perhaps then Edward would be worried, but in Mexico City he knew they had available to them the finest and most modern of medicos found anywhere in the world.

"After all," he would say smugly to his wife and her ever-growing form, whiskey sloshing around his glass while in one of his moods.

"We are white and wealthy, so we will never be without in Mexico- your wellbeing always comes before that of some.... indigenous maid birthing in a closet like a stray cat. None of this everyman being equal nonsense like they're trying to push in the United States."

Amanda would chastise Ed, who usually only said such vile things when drunk.

It was no secret to anyone in the household that la Señora Tappan had struggled in her first few months in Mexico. Everyone agreed she was so strong to have the fortitude to deal with moving to a new world with young children and another one still yet to make his or her appearance. It was a running commentary among the household staff and friends of the family agreed - she must be something else to handle Edward, who most agreed was difficult on a good day.

Certain whispers floated around the house in the air like so much dust in sunlight. Whispers in Spanish, whispers in English, some whispers full out loud conversations, pondering why anyone, wealthy American or not, would dare to, or even want to, emigrate to a country in the upset belly of revolution. Why come to be an ethnic minority, part of the loathsome ruling class? It was those very Europeans who were being murdered, even after centuries in Mexico, their family lands stolen and taken back to give to the poor, the indigenous, and the rightful owners of Mexico. Why come to a place where you could end up with a target on your back? Whispers began that he must have tricked her or that she was "un poco tocada", a little touched in the head.

Mexicans all over the country who wished for peace were starting to eye their prospects in the U.S. and still others were considering refuge in South America. Those lucky enough who could stay with family in Spain, France, and other parts of Europe were debating staying put in their beloved Mexico and riding out the storm or hiding out in Europe, as it was, for the moment, a stable and peaceful continent. Amanda had heard several of the women at the Social Club discussing this. How many of those Mexican women would have stayed put to give birth in the same circumstances? The ones not so concerned with peace, those heavily embroiled in the war, wanted violence, wanted to stay, rebel fighting against rebel fighting against the elite ruling class. Many of the elite felt they had as much right to Mexico and refused to flee. During this upheaval boiling into war, life went on, and babies were being born all over Mexico. It was odd, however, to everyone who knew them and anyone who met Amanda that they would have moved to Mexico City at this time, and her being pregnant.

Circumstances in the City of Palaces were deteriorating quickly. As Amanda's pregnancy carried on, her little stowaway unaware of any upset in the world outside, the Revolution dug its claws deeper into the country.

They had arrived in a calm and welcoming spring early in her pregnancy, but the time had evaporated.

The end of November found that time upon them. This day would bring forth Amanda's first Mexican-born child, but she knew by now this was the birth of her family into turmoil. Her mind had been wandering for weeks as her suspicions grew. She was unusually cold as she bid Edward to send for the nurse and informed him she was in labour. He gave her a kiss on the cheek she did not respond to, but Ed just assumed she was in the throes of contractions. She allowed him to help her up the stairs and into their bed, but it did not go unnoticed when she snatched her arm away from him in a temper.

"I will leave you to it.", He said not unkindly.

Within a minute of his departure, she was up and out of bed, the contractions coming faster than she expected, and lying down was far worse- she needed to be upright; she needed to move around. They were coming faster and closer and stronger- one nearly brought her to her knees, and she held onto the bed post, the force of the contraction rattling her teeth.

"I can't do this again", she whimpered to Amparo.

"Si Señora", Amparo nodded reassuringly, feeling sorry for her.

Amanda decided she needed to pace. She roamed the halls of her Orange Blossom House, which she had grown to love so much, roamed them because walking helped soothe the intensity of the contractions. She wandered like a lost banshee, moaning softly, caressing the walls with pain, resting for moments, all with Guadalupe and Amparo shadowing her. Guadalupe had her rosary beads in hand, whispering very softly the Lord's prayer among others to beg God to safeguard the baby and mother through this birth.

Amanda's moans would stifle in her throat as if she did not want to give some unseen force the satisfaction of hearing her suffer. She would press her face and breasts and belly into the cold walls and feel relief. She would turn and press her back and hips into the corners of halls and doorways in a strange dance. It made total sense to her body pulsating through the enormity of the pain but surely was an odd sight.

It struck Amparo as different for sure; her employer was usually so dignified, and here she was flailing about. She understood it had to be a horrible experience, perhaps one she might not want to ever go through herself.

It struck Marta as beautiful. She had never had more respect for la Señora, then in those moments, watching her go through what Marta knew had been stolen from her own future by cruel fate.

It struck Guadalupe as bittersweet, remembering her own births. How could they have been so long ago when she could still remember the feeling of the rolling pull of her little ones inside her and how they had crashed into the world like waves in a storm?

Finally, after hours of pacing through moans and tears, Amanda returned to her bedroom and undressed down to her nightshirt, her half-naked and swollen figure illuminated by the orange glow of the fire. The end was close; she needed to let go and let Mother Nature have her way. This child was big and late and felt so different to her experiences back home. She felt as if this was her first time enduring this; she felt uneasy, and that made the pain magnified through tension. Every part of her body throbbed and ached and seemed to hover just a breath away from terror. Guadalupe brought her a whiskey and the nurse who brought with her a black medical bag and the chloroform.

"What did – what is this, chloroform? Why not laudanum, as I've always had? Did you inform Edward- he will want the final say in this? I can't take chloroform; I will be knocked out totally."

Her voice was rising in her panic.

The nurse spoke English,

“Señora, desculpe, we have not been able to acquire many medicines as of late. The war has made it to where-

“The War?”

The room fell silent, all the women looking from one to the other.

“So, it is a war then; it is a war that I have brought my children to?”

Amanda asked though heavy breaths and clenched teeth, trying to keep from full-blown hysteria.

Finally, she had confirmation from someone outside this house of what she had suspected for months. Amanda felt so stupid at that moment, embarrassed.

“Señora”, Guadalupe held the glass to her lips, nodded fiercely and made her take a swig of the whiskey.

“Don’t talk of such things; you need to remain calm. We will only give you just enough of the chloro-

“Or you can do this without it”, the nurse shrugged abruptly, in nearly perfect English.

“It’s not as if women haven’t been doing this since time immemorial without any help from pain medication. The pain is God’s way anyhow.”

This Mexican nurse, childless herself and quite merciless, did not like this American woman who was so soft and weak she could not handle what God had given her. She did not think this arrogant and rich gringo deserved this blessing. She knew she could have handled the pain if only she had been given that chance, but no, it was not to be for some. The irony of a barren midwife was not lost on her, never on her.

"I am no martyr", Amanda gruffly replied, "just I can't handle this amount of pain. This is by far the worst I've ever known. I will take whatever we have."

Agatha was born some twelve exhausting hours later, after whiffs of chloroform that left her mother spinning, after Amanda pulled against ropes tied to the four posters of her great bed, after shrieks of agony rang out of her like church bells and blood washed over her feet.

Amanda had considered Agnes, but in the end, she decided to name this little one after her lost sister, Agatha. Agatha Flora came at five in the morning after a tremendously difficult birth, just in time to greet the dawn. She was the largest of the children, weighing in at just under ten pounds, which Ed would later boast was down to the rich Mexican cuisine and the tequila, even though his wife had barely been able to get sustenance into her this pregnancy and had lost so much weight her clothing swam on her. The baby was as bald as porcelain, with startling emerald green eyes and except for a strawberry birthmark the size of a kiss behind one ear, she was perfect in every way. The newborn seemed very sleepy and hazy due to the chloroform, which the grumpy nurse had assured Guadalupe would wear off by the next day.

"She did good."

she begrudgingly admitted to Lupe, whose face gave the woman nothing in return.

"Yes, my jefa, she did wonderful as I knew she would.",

Lupe said through smugness.

This one was so different. This time instead of feeling elated, Amanda felt vacant, her heart comatose, her face catatonic. She was glad it was over and relieved the child was alive and seemingly healthy, but she felt as if some part of her was dead, and she felt a shame and guilt press down upon her that loomed as large as the Orange Blossom House. She felt as if she had been buried under the house, the tonnes of mortar and cement pressing her into a soft grave. She wondered, quite calmly, if perhaps she was dying and if they would bury her under the lime trees.

The medicine, she thought, surely it was the effect of this poison she'd been fed. The guilt she birthed alongside her new daughter seemed to steal her voice, and she could not form a sound at the babe or at anyone else in the room. With her first two births, she had been elated even in her exhaustion, cooing and talking softly to her new little family members, smiling, singing, and whispering promises as she kissed their little heads, smelling them.

This time had been different.

She prayed throughout the ordeal that God would shut down her womb and extinguish it like one of the candles or oil lamps she watched around the room in the moments of pushing, straining, and expelling this newest child into existence. She dared never utter such a thing out loud, the desire to be done having children. What would people think? Not even thirty yet with only three children, surely people would find her disgusting and lazy. It was her very purpose in life, and yet she had known for months that she could never do this again, and the birth solidified this notion in her mind. She was categorically finished. If people knew these hidden desires in her heart, the shame would be too much. She had always wanted a family, a large family. She had always imagined having at least five or six children, but instead, that picture she carried in her mind was now replaced with a large allotment of resentment. What would Edward think of her? Would he be disgusted or, more likely, enraged? Surely the important and brilliant Dr. Tappan would want another three at the very least.

They had spoken on it many times over the years both agreeing to a large family, as many children as God blessed them with. Now, she wanted to renege. She was certain she could never go through this again; she would die, she knew it. As she stared at the infant, she marvelled at the thought of women who bore children dozens during a lifetime. She remembered her mother speaking of the mothers who came before, Amanda's own mother had been one of eight children, her grandmother one of ten. The woman before her, Amanda's great-grandmother, had birthed thirteen. The one before that, some great, great, unknown Frenchwoman without a name, had made it to twenty live births before her own demise at thirty-eight. Surely, that would have killed any woman.

That ancestor had spent more than half of her life heavy with a child, birthing a child, bringing a child to the breast, burying the children that didn't make it. Her whole existence had been to multiply, even as she herself was infinitely divided until nothing remained.

Amanda did not want any more children. She thought it a cruel and clever blessing that the horrors of labour were so quickly forgotten. No, not forgotten, but dimmed, turned down, like the oil lamps she kept focusing on. The memories were never fully extinguished but dimmed down to a hazy level where one was quite certain it was never as awful as they had imagined it. Then, once again in the throes of labour, presented with no way out, the full reality of the excruciating chore would flood back. Suddenly, all too familiar, those whispered negotiations with God, pleas for a good and safe outcome for both mother and baby, would begin again.

"I'm more tired and sore than I ever have been",

Amanda murmured to Guadalupe as the nurse cleaned and dressed the baby, Amparo tending to the fire. The sound of her own voice startled her, as if someone else had said it to her while she was being held under water. Her breath was off kilter, very shallow, then suddenly a great crashing wave of inhalation that would open her shoulders up and back. Not exactly a sigh, bigger than a sigh.

The entirety of her sex organs pulsated and throbbed so intensely she was nearly numb. As if she'd been sat in flames, the embers remained, still glowing. This was not anything like her previous times. No, she would never do this again.

"Pour me more whiskey, will you?"

Guadalupe poured three fingers into the glass and helped her mistress to get comfortable in the bed, arranging pillows to support her jefa. With the doctor's wife most intimate parts cleaned and bandaged, and, with her now dressed, she took the baby and placed her in her mother's arms.

"I shall go to Dr. Tappan; let him know you've finished."

She looked at the wreck of a woman before her, pale, covered in sweat, baby in one arm, whiskey in the opposite hand. Although La Senora Tappan had powered through like a war horse, it had been one of the most traumatic births Guadalupe had ever witnessed for sure.

Guadalupe, unlike the sour old bat of a nurse, quite liked the strange American. She had never felt so sorry for anyone than she did for her mistress in that moment.

"Or would you like a few more minutes to yourself, Señora?"

Amanda gave a small laugh, her voice full of water like she was on the edge of sobbing,

"Sure- go get him. Let him see his baby of the Revolution, his Mexican Princessa."

Guadalupe eyed her in the firelight. It was becoming more and more obvious that the Dr. had brought this woman here under false pretences and with no knowledge of the situation in Mexico.

In one flash of a moment, as fast as the smell of sulphur hitting the air off a match, Guadalupe understood. She understood now why the Dr. always insisted she bring the newspaper straight to him. She understood why he always told his wife he couldn't find the days periodical and would get her tomorrow's paper, this time in English, for sure. She understood why he burned his telegrams soon after reading instead of throwing them into the wastepaper basket for Amparo to empty. Why he appeared to be keeping secrets from the entire household. Guadalupe felt a distaste for the doctor, like dirt in her mouth.

Le estaba engañiando. He was going out of his way to fool his wife.

Now more than ever, it became as clear as the crystal she polished why all the military men came traipsing through this house and at increasingly odd hours. The furtive glances, the conversations immediately cut off, sometimes mid-sentence, whenever she entered the room to bring them their coffees and liquor. Guadalupe had sensed the man of the house was involving himself in the troubles, and now she knew. The fooling the wife was only part of it. Dr. Tappan spending less time seeing patients, less time at the hospital, suddenly appearing home at odd hours and agitated. His presence at home was ever increasing, yet he continued ignoring his wife, who was becoming a whisper of herself.

Guadalupe had always thought that she herself had been so unlucky in life – a good for nothing husband, being born into a life of servitude, never much money. Her list of complaints was many, and they vexed her- her cantankerous daughter, her son who had almost died from the polio- but she did not stand to lose anything should trouble appear at the front door of this particular house. If war came calling, she knew that with her low station in life and her lovely native skin, she would most likely be fine. Surely the rebels had no reason to harm the housekeeper, one of them, she mused.

La Señora, on the other hand, a doctor's wife with a big house, big blue eyes, a big bank account and an even bigger reputation, had much to lose. The treasures la Señora Tappan had to lose were sleeping down the hall, little fair heads innocently dreaming away on large and warm pillows, totally unaware that there were powerful and angry men fighting over their very future. Guadalupe felt fear for this family, a premonition that formed a pit in her stomach and made her bladder weak. She shook her head,

"You should have stayed in New York",

she whispered, not thinking Amanda had heard her.

Amanda looked up at her, tears forming spiderwebs across her cheeks,

"I know, Lupe."

she attempted a weak smile,

"I know."

Chapter 26

It was all great pomp and circumstance for the next week as Ed paraded the baby around the house as if a proud mother himself, with the baby in the finest silk gowns and bonnets. Amanda was slow to recover this time around. She kept to her bed mostly that first week and relied heavily on her staff.

She kept the room dark, curtains drawn, barely moving at times.

Amanda had balked when Amparo had asked if she was to bury the placenta in the garden. Lupe shook her head no, as Amanda had startled at the thought. When they disposed of the placenta that first night, Amparo was sure to quietly bury it in the garden as an offering to her Aztec Gods to protect mother and baby. She chose to place it in the dirt in front of the hydrangeas, to watch them later change colour. She could not understand why her mistress found this so odd. After all, what did they do with organs that were no longer needed where she came from? What better way to return us to the earth than with the blanketing of dirt? Amparo tried not to worry about it, as she knew something in her mistress was off. She would never tell her where she buried it, but if questioned, she would say the nurse had disposed of it.

Amanda found she had little appetite but was being cajoled at every turn by someone in the household to eat more and more. She was incredibly thirsty; her pitchers of water never remained full for long, and the servants would bring up different types of water, each pitcher with different fruits in it. Lupe insisted that she get her the nutrients she needed and that her waters be in a rotation. One pitcher would be mango water, Amanda would drain it dry with a thirst that frightened her. The next one sent up would be lime, or lemon or cucumber, agua de Jamaica, the hibiscus cold tea with sugar that she and the children had grown to love. Agua de guyaba, agua de fresa, another favourite, the strawberry water, the list went on. Amanda had to stay close to the bathroom, often needing assistance as she found herself too weak for the most basic of human necessities, and the urination of the first few days was scream-inducing. As thirsty as she was, Lupe agreed that simply drinking was the most important task if she could not bear to eat. Amanda had swelled up like an elephant the week before birth and she was still puffy- her face, fingers, ankles, everything on her had swelled, even her nose. Amanda noted her urine smelled slightly sweet and thought it must be the fruit.

"You are retaining water",

Lupe assured her. The only cure for which, oddly, was to drink more water. Every night Lupe would make her a tapestry of teas - banana tea or chamomile, rose and lavender tea to help her sleep, but Amanda had no trouble sleeping. She felt guilty spending so little time with the children, who were brought in twice daily to see her and chat. They were informed that the mother had just had the baby and, so, she was not well and needed her rest more than anything. Her two older children, so agreeable, seemed to understand instinctively that she must rest. They were quite fascinated with their new sibling but very respectful of the baby needing her sleep as well. They seemed quite pleased with the new addition, which was one of the only things that truly comforted Amanda. Her babies loved their new baby, even as she felt oddly reserved.

She needed bathing daily with help from Lupe to throw warm, soapy water and then salt water onto her delicate parts. Lupe brought her all kinds of remedies and poultices, with complicated names and strange aromas that proved more effective than anything she had encountered in New York. They were much more soothing than bread in milk poultices. Lupe brought in a large green cactus that did not have spines on it, and she proceeded to slice and scrape the jelly like insides out to apply to the delicate skin. It stung badly and then cooled the skin. Lupe insisted she drink chamomile tea and the leaves would also go into poultices with this clear plant jelly. Amanda let her help, as she figured refusing would lead to an even more determined Lupe, but through it all, she still remained weak and unresponsive at times. Despite all her rest, all her forced eating and drinking, and all the novel soothers brought to her round the clock, she did not perk up. She had no energy for anything. Her body felt different. Every part of her, though she dared not explore anything of her womanhood, lest she find something frightening. She was already fearful all the time since the birth. Her very skin felt strange. Her hair on her head, her teeth in her mouth, even her tongue and lips felt strange, bloated, changed.

"Señora",

Lupe groaned on the fifth day,

"You must get up and walk. It is not good for you to stay on your back like a dead little cucaracha.

Amanda shrugged,

"It's what we did in New York. All the mothers, we were meant to stay supine for thirty days, a month of as little movement as possible."

Lupe could not understand the gentry and their silly ways. Women had been birthing babies on the side of the road from time immemorial and walking, hiking or horse riding their ways back home or straight back to another kind of labour- the labour that kept their mouths fed. She could not understand why some people were so certain women, mothers especially, were so fragile. Lupe knew there was no metal as strong as a mother.

Yes, rest was needed after such an ordeal as labour, but to curl up like a dried flower was nonsense.

"Señora, perdona me but I am concerned. I have never seen you so low in espirits. Please, to think maybe you would allow me to dress you and we take a little walk in the garden? You love your garden. Stretch your legs. Maybe a butterfly comes to say hello again. Pretend you are one of the roses and turn towards the sun. It is good for you. You must let the sun see your face, so he knows you are still here."

Lupe felt tears climbing up her throat, threatening to make it to her eyes. This young woman was not so unlike her own daughter. She had watched Amanda wilt and wither as she neared the arrival of the baby, but this was not recovery or exhaustion. This was something else that Lupe had seen and heard of, that sometimes happened to mother's right after they give birth.

It seems right to grieve, she thought. That we women spend so long growing and becoming one with the miracle inside of us, only to then have it removed painfully and suddenly. Then, our baby is vulnerable to the horrors of the outside. Surely, every mother mourns the coming heartache she knows will beset her child. That is a pain that eclipses the pain of the birth- knowing that now, once in the world- you can never really protect them again. Their pain will be theirs alone. Their life and their struggles are theirs alone- so too their death.

The very consequence of their birth is their death written

somewhere in time. That is the saddest song, the darkest lullaby a mother will sing.

This realization of their vulnerability often left some mothers feeling low, but sometimes, Guadalupe knew there were the forgotten mothers. The ones left there in that strange, liminal place after birth. Some would never find their way out of that dark, small cave.

"We are born into this world to suffer",

she muttered under her breath, crossing herself, determined to say yet another prayer for this young mother.

"Bueno- Señora, you think about my offer to walk the garden. I will bring you some pozole-"

"I can't eat Lupe."

"Well, you think you are not hungry, but when you smell my pozole you change your mind Señora, I promise you."

"Lupe- thank you, but no, my stitches are still very sore, and they're itchy; I do not want to walk now. Maybe another bath later, but I'm not in the mood for a walk, nor do I want to run into any visitors downstairs. Diego has been here all morning- you'd think they'd never seen a baby before."

"Si Señora, el Señor Diego has been asking about you. Todos- everyone has."

"Just let me know when Señora Vanin-Goya gets here, please- she can come up. Everyone else downstairs can wait. They're not really here to see me anyway but to go on and on how much the new baby looks like Ed's mother. Another thing I had no say in", she grumbled before turning onto her side and closing her eyes.

La Señora kept calling the baby "the new baby" instead of her name Agatha. Guadalupe felt it very odd and part of Amanda's malaise. La Señora Tappan's only source of pride seemed to be when she told everyone how she had named her new daughter after her little baby sister who had passed. Yet, Lupe feared la Señora was not particularly interested in the baby.

She fed her when she had to but left everything else to the nanny Marta, Lupe, and Amparo. She would lie next to her on the bed while the child slept but Amanda always had a far-off look in her eyes, as if she was not in the room but really wandering lost in the mountains seen from the bedroom window. Lupe tried not to jump to conclusions. She was kind and understanding. But sometimes she wanted to go shake the lump of a woman curled up on the sapphire blue velvet bedspread, shake the sadness right out of her, shake her right onto her feet, back to the old Amanda, the lovely one that had arrived at this house full of smiles and wonder.

She wanted to remind her of the riches surrounding her in her beautiful home, in a stunning part of the city that most people in Mexico would love to have.

"Look at your beautiful children, your beautiful life!" was always on the tip of her tongue, but she saw that there was something broken in the young woman. Her soul had fallen somewhere that left her unable to see the good and beautiful right in front of her.

She wanted to find a way to get the old Amanda back, the silly one she had nearly been forced to drag out of the fruit and vegetable market. She wanted her funny and charming jefa, who had bought too many chamote and jicama that day in her childlike excitement. The grown woman who had eaten too many candied fruits which had sent her scurrying for the water closet.

Not even her two dearest friends could rouse her from her bed or what Ed called "Her pitiful malingering".

Amanda fell into a strange place where she would not allow Diego up to her bedroom to see her and only Raquel was to come up.

"You look terrible", Raquel told her one morning.

"I feel terrible but thank you."

"I must be cruel to be kind. How is the baby, little Agatha?

"Fine, eating, putting on weight…she seems fine, so that is a blessing, I know."

"And how is her mother….really?"

Amanda waited until Lupe had left the room to fetch the ladies a light snack.

"I can't explain it, Raquel."

She could not meet her friend's concerned eyes.

She sat in front of the baby's cot, staring out the window at the mountains. A light dusting of snow could be seen, sparkling in the sunlight.

"I don't understand why, but I feel like this baby ended my life. I am not alive. I am here; I take up space. I exist exhaustingly, but I am not here."

"What a bizarre statement", Raquel said, almost crossly.

"Of course, you are here!"

"I am not the same. I had felt a bit of melancholy for about ten days after Arthur was born. But not right away- it was two or three days after I had him, my milk had finally come in; I was so relieved. But I had an easy enough birth the first time around, and in comparison, to this time, I was elated. Ed and I were so in love and so besotted with our son. Then, out of nowhere, I felt overwhelming grief and sadness. I rushed to Edward, a physician, with my concerns, and he threatened me with the nut house and told me to snap out of it. I did when Arthur was exactly three weeks old and kind of magically came out of it one day all by myself. I woke up, and the dark clouds and feeling of not existing, it was all gone. Ed said that was further proof there wasn't a damn thing wrong with me. Amelia followed, and again, this one went even better than the first time. And after her, I waited for it; there was nothing, no upset, no…depressive episode. I was fine. Every once in a while, only ever in the years since I met Edward, actually, I feel panicky or very like my nerves are not right. Then it goes away, usually. And the times it lingers I can hide it from Ed, from everybody. But I started to really struggle this last time, with this last pregnancy. I thought it was the move, all the travel, but I was much sicker, much more tired than ever before, so I did, naturally, wonder if the melancholy would return."

"And now it has?" Raquel asked quietly.

"Yes, worse than ever. The baby is over four weeks old now; we are heading into Christmas; I should be over the moon. I have a full staff to help me, so I should not even be tired all the time, but I am – all the time Raquel I am exhausted, and it doesn't matter how much I sleep. I could sleep all day and night, and it wouldn't be enough. Tell me you have heard of something like this before, and I am not totally insane."

She turned to her friend, her face covered in tears.

Raquel nodded, "I don't think what you are feeling is all that uncommon or strange, my dear. I heard of this growing up in Russia, and my own mother warned me I might become unwell after having Jaime. I never did but I think my mother went through something very like what you have described. I know someone who might have answers….

"No, oh no, don't you dare say his name."

"Amanda, why on earth would you not turn to your friend who studies this very subject and works in this field? If I had heart palpitations, I would ask Eddie for help; if I was having a …psychosis or whatever this is, I would talk to Diego."

"No, I can't; he can't seem me like this."

"He hasn't seen you at all since you gave birth, as many times as he has called to this house to see the baby in hopes of seeing you. He has been very hurt that you won't receive him.

"He would know- he would see right through me."

Raquel was confused,

"And is that such a terrible thing? Maybe you don't have to even say anything. If you are so embarrassed, he can just read you like a book. He already knows you are not well-"

"How does he know?"

"Well, aside from your husband's big mouth and him complaining to Diego and myself about your state, do you really think a man as astute as Diego would not notice one of his dearest friends suddenly shutting him out and not seeing him for a month?

Right after giving birth? Who did you think this act would fool? Certainly not Diego. You're fooling no one Amanda; my God, I sell fur coats for a living, and I saw right away what was going on. I am no doctor. Even your maids seem worried about you."

Amanda balked at that, and Raquel laughed, although not unkindly,

"Love- did you really think they wouldn't pick up on it, as they spend their entire lives revolving around you? Listen to me, kid- this happens to women. Nobody ever speaks of it, or it is whispered about, but wise women know what this is or have an idea, and modern medicine is catching up to – well, sometimes, the workings of our minds and our hearts- maybe they can go awry just like our ageing bodies can? I mean, it makes perfect sense when you think about it.

Edward's own resistance, I think, just stems from ignorance and his jealousy towards Diego. They are the oldest of friends, but my God, he has always been so obviously jealous and threatened by Diego. Now, in case you are wondering, now you know one of the many reasons that I refuted a courtship with Edward all those years ago- I saw him. Edward, for all his greatness, all his medical expertise, he is – fallible- and he knows it, and it eats at him. He is angry and thinks he knows everything. Pay no mind to anything he has said to you on this or anything about the study of the mind, which, frankly, I think rather noble! And my darling, as much as I am fond of him if I had ended up marrying Eddie, I'd still be a widow today because I would have murdered him."

She said with a rueful smile that sent a laugh exploding out of Amanda- her first laugh in weeks.

"I would have taken a pillow and held it down in his sleep", Raquel continued, now attempting to stifle laughter, "Que Dios me perdona- God forgive me".

Chapter 27

More days and nights had passed since that first appearance of laughter out of Amanda, and Raquel was steadfast in her rallying of the younger woman from her depression and her bed.

Raquel laid out a beautiful dress, lavender silk, onto the foot of the bed in front of her friend.

"It will do you some good to have some much-needed adult time without babies and this sadness. You must start taking steps in the direction of where you want to end up, my darling. So, let's get you dressed, a lovey dinner into you- far too much booze.", She teased Amanda with a smile.

"Now, will I leave you to dress, with the understanding that you won't make me come back up here to get you?"

"Yes, yes, I promise. I will even wash my face and teeth for you." Amanda nodded shyly.

As she sauntered out of the room, Raquel threw a look over her shoulder to her friend,

"Darling, I assure you that washing up is really for you. Don't forget some rouge." She winked.

Amanda sat alone for a quiet moment, staring at the dress. Not so long ago, she had adored dresses. Now, she felt dressing gowns were much nicer. She had always enjoyed a bit of paint on her face, her hair done- either up or curled with rollers. These days if she managed to wash it more than once a week, she felt that was enough. She needed to snap out of this humour- it was more than a month since the baby was born. There were people waiting downstairs…the Christmas dinner would be on the table within the hour. She should have been eagerly awaiting her first Mexican Christmas, with its new customs and foods laid out before her.

Yes, she would get up and enjoy her time with family and friends as soon as she poured herself a little brandy first. She decanted a large sum into the glass on her bedroom table and drank it down with a thirst. She would have another before going to wash. Yes, tonight would be fine, and for the first time in weeks, she found herself genuinely hungry.

After dressing and preening and primping she decided that she looked sort of lovely despite her weight loss. The brightness of the purple in the dress brought a bit of warmth to her face- or was that the brandy? She felt a confidence she had not known for months.

Downstairs in the foyer awaited a small gathering made up of Ed speaking to a couple of gentlemen in military dress who she did not know, their wives, Raquel with Jaime and Diego. And, of course, there was Ed's sister.

Leonor had shown up the week before, unannounced without so much as a telegram. She had arrived in time for Christmas, she explained, and to meet her new Mexican niece. Amanda had met Leonor only twice before. She had missed, Ed always said deliberately, their wedding but travelled from Merida to New York after the birth of each child.

Leonor was cold and viewed Amanda through heavy lidded eyes that glared at her as if she found Amanda insipid. Her dark hair was always in the most severe of updos, pulled so tight you could see her skin pulled taught. Her husband never came with her, something to do with a falling out he had with Ed. They were childless, with

Leonor always announcing a pregnancy but then always being greeted with tragedy. At thirty-five, she was starting to age rapidly. She was usually as thin as a twig, with none of the soft roundness found on her own mother, but as the years added up, her shape was changing. Amanda was surprised to see Leonor looked rather lovely. Her dark olive eyes and a mouth like a trout made her look harsh and judgemental. She thought herself a great beauty but nobody else seemed to opine the same, not for the lack of appeal, but rather a personality that detracted from her good looks.

Amanda never felt comfortable in her presence, and she had let out a low groan of misery when Lupe had informed her she was downstairs. With Ed always gone, Amanda would be stuck having to make nice with a sister-in-law as friendly and loving as a bear trap. Amanda was frustrated with herself; she should have expected her to show up, especially now that they were much closer in Mexico, but she was genuinely taken by surprise.

Leonor wasted no time in moving into one of the large bedrooms down the hall and barely greeted Amanda before taking the baby out of Marta's arms to inspect the child like a prize pig at the market.

Despite how low she had been feeling Amanda had been hoping to have her spirits lifted with a lovely Christmas dinner, yet now she had this awful woman to contend with. Leonor was hard work.

Lupe remembered Leonor from her time with them as children and had much the same reaction as Amanda.

Lupe was determined to make the best of things for her jefa and the children.

The house smelled of cinnamon and anise and cloves and, of course, oranges. Lupe loved this time of year and wanted to make the first Christmas in the house a very special one. Lupe loved God and Jesu Christo, and so for her, the birth of her lord was more than just a holiday; it was a divine moment in time. It was holy, and she would not allow anything to disrupt it for the household. So, from December third all the way to January sixth, known as "dia de los tres reyes magos", or Three Kings Day, she would work tirelessly to make everything perfect.

Lupe did not seek the Dr's approval so much as she wanted to see his wife start to come back to herself.

December third was secretly Lupe's favourite day. It was the start of the novenas to honour the Virgin of Guadalupe, her namesake to boot. She would begin to decorate the house this day. She had Marta teaching Amparo the prayers alongside the Tappan children, who were by now speaking Spanish as if their lives in New York had never happened.

On December twelfth, she would cook up the feast for the Virgin of Guadalupe, an event that Ed had been late home for, and Amanda had eaten quickly and then returned to her bed. Not exactly the beautiful family dinner Lupe had been hoping for when she spent nine hours cooking away. She had attempted earlier in the day to get her Señora to mass, but Amanda refused, allowing the children to go with the servants to the church.

Lupe had told the children the story in the carriage on the way to the church,

"There was un indio given a Spanish name, Juan Diego. He was born many centuries ago, in a year called 1474. He was devout and loved the lord. On this day, December twelfth, our Virgin de Guadalupe appeared to him for the fourth time, in 1531, on a hill here in Mexico City that used to be called Tepeyac." She told the babies.

Arthur was five, almost six now, and Amelia was nearing four. She hardly spoke but had been picking up more and more Spanish. She smiled up at Lupe and seemed to enjoy the church service, although she did ask where her mother was. Her older brother had explained to her that mother was not feeling well- again. This answer Arthur had learned by rote, and it seemed to appease little Amelia. Lupe had hurried the children home, hoping to catch Amanda in a mood for receiving her children.

Chapter 28

Christmas dinner was proving to be as lovely a night as Lupe had imagined she could make it, with la jefa out of bed and looking more beautiful than ever.

Leonor seemed to take a sort of delight in watching Amanda squirm over dinner with her little tales of families in different parts of Mexico being murdered. Finally, Raquel had had enough,

"I do not think this is an appropriate conversation for Christmas, nor for a woman who has just given birth."

As Ed was blitheringly drunk and it was getting late, more and more of the last-minute revellers began to depart home. Amanda did not feel well and soon was passed out on the sofa. There had been atole, ponche with rum, whiskey, tequila and spiced red wine. Amanda was old enough to know better than to mix so many different spirits, but over the course of the twenty-fourth, from breakfast through to dinner, there had been a steady parade of alcohol in every corner of the house. Once past a certain point of drunkenness, all caution was thrown to the wind.

Raquel chastised Ed in the kitchen as he went searching for yet more alcohol.

"My coachman is here to take Jaime and me home. Your wife needs her bed- as do you, silly, old friend", she wagged her finger at him.

"Old, my old friend…what have we gotten into?" she muttered, disgusted with herself for a split moment before throwing her hands up in defeat.

"Jaime" she called to her son, "venga- vamanos lla!"

"Diego", she passed him on the way to the front door. "Feliz Navidad, buenas noches - get her to her bed will you please? Ed is too drunk, as usual."

Diego hugged his friend and clapped the back of the boy before he made his way over to scoop up Amanda like a baby herself and to take her carefully up the stairs, never knowing her husband and Leonor, watched stoically from the kitchen entrance.

Diego deposited Amanda onto her bed and instructed Lupe to give them two minutes.

Amanda's eyes opened, "Diego"

"Shhh, go to sleep now Amandita."

Instead of closing her eyes, she opened them more, drinking him in, smiling.

"We should have never brought you here.", Diego said suddenly.

"I don't know what he was thinking. I'm not sure I could have stopped him….but look at me."

His voice dropped to a low-toned, comforting whisper,

"I will get you and the children to somewhere safe if ever the time comes where you need to leave Mexico- you will not go alone, I will escort you all out maybe even old Ed too, while we are at it. Ok? Nothing for you to worry about, all the talk of bandoleros, you are safe. I will make sure of it.

I will always make sure that you are safe."

He left her without the kiss on the forehead he wanted to give, afraid to be that close to her lips.

The following day found a very hung-over Amanda sitting bundled up in the warmth of the early afternoon sun in her favourite spot in the garden. A mug of atole from Lupe, promising that it would revive her, along with a platter of fried plantains covered in cinnamon sugar, left a comforting fragrance in the air as Amanda nursed her head and kept a hopeful eye out for a return visit from her butterflies.

Her peaceful morning was erased as Leonor arrived and sat across from her, looking about, annoyed she may have to go looking for a maid to bring her coffee.

"Quite the celebrations last night, weren't they?" she purred in perfect English.

She held in her hand a paper.

Amanda said nothing, hoping she would go away, and her stomach would settle.

"You don't like me very much, do you?" Leonor asked suddenly.

Amanda finally made eye contact,

"I would have thought it was the other way around Leonor, if I'm being honest. You never seemed pleased with Ed marrying me; for some reason, I have yet to figure it out."

Leonor smiled, impressed.

"You're blunt. I like that. Not so shy and retiring after all, not so delicate as Ed would have made you out to be. I never had a problem with you; I didn't know you. I still don't, but you make pretty babies, and I like my nieces and nephews. They are all I have left of the Tappans. My parents have been long gone, and our only other sister living in Brazil. No children of my own- yet. You and those kids are all I've got, sadly."

Leonor was annoyed to admit that.

"Well…and Edward, of course.", Amanda offered.

"Little secret Amanda. I don't like my brother. I don't care for him, haven't since he skipped out on our father's funeral and then went up and down the eastern seaboard of both the U.S. and Mexico bad-mouthing our famous father, all in a desperate attempt to eclipse him. Our father was everything to us, to our mother, to me, to the entire Yucatan peninsula. He is the reason we are so wealthy and admired as a family. Most importantly, he was the kindest man God ever graced this earth with. Sadly, none of my siblings nor I can hold a candle to him. We are all ill-tempered and difficult, where our father was a delight. And Ed treated his memory like an inconvenience, like dried mud he needed to kick off his heel."

Her voice stopped short, choking on emotion, and she glanced away furiously.

Amanda was stunned into silence by this diatribe. She saw the hatred, not aimed towards her after all, but towards Ed. She silently agreed that Edward had become unbearable in recent years.

Amanda sat dumbfounded, as she could not imagine what Leonor was accomplishing by telling her all this. It felt like a trick for her to admit to the same feeling and then have Leonor go running to Edward with a secret.

"I….." Leonor started slowly and with great effort, "Apologise…if over the years I have been less than friendly. I could never get a read for who you were, and you married Ed, so I had to assume the worst about you."

"You didn't come to our wedding. He said it was a deliberate slight."

"Amanda- I didn't know. I got the telegram a month after you'd been married. He ignored my invitations for the two of you to visit me in Merida. Not wanting to overstep, I only ever came to visit after you had your babies. I always sent telegrams to let Ed know I was coming. I wanted to become close, but I saw Edward would never allow it. "

"I had no idea.", Amanda stuttered.

"I thought maybe you didn't. I know how manipulative Edward can be-; I should have seen it sooner.

But this conversation isn't why I came out here to talk to you" she held up the sheet in her hand as she shakily lit a long cigarette on her red lips.

"A few weeks ago, after I had telegrammed letting Ed know I was coming up to see you all in the new house and with the new baby- it had been years after all since I visited my dear brother- I was going through some old paperwork of my parents. I was looking for the deed on a house and some land the family owns out near Aguas Calientes, when I found this."

She put on the table next to the now cold plantains a rectangular piece of white paper with writing in Spanish, the state seal of Merida and the Mexican Flag embossed on it. It had Edwards' full name and date of birth next to the name of one Magdalena Inez Heredia

Boudreaux and a date of birth.

“I have no idea how or why this ended up in my mother’s papers, but there you have it.”

After a moment of silence where she could see the cogs of Amanda’s mind turning,

“You have no idea what you’re looking at, do you?

Amanda knew. She thought she knew but shook her head no, wanting it to be spelt out for her.

“Jesus”, Leonor huffed,

“Haven’t you learned *any* Spanish? This is a marriage certificate from Edward’s marriage to a Mexican girl in Merida in 1894. He was twenty and at Harvard, but he came home every summer. I remember him seeing this, Magdalena. I mean, I was only a girl, preoccupied with my own life, so I didn’t pay attention at the time, but it seems he married this girl behind the back of our mother and, for whatever reason, told no one. I thought you needed to know, seeing as how, if this marriage was not annulled, then yours in the United States, the one I wasn’t even invited to, well, I don’t think it could be considered legally binding. I put myself in your shoes. I would want to know if my children were bastards.”

Amanda felt as if ice water had been thrown over her, chilled to the bone. ‘Helada’, they called it in Spanish. She felt inside out, her mouth dry and hanging open, feeling she could burst into tears if only she had any water in her body. Her stomach threatened to empty its contents; she vaguely tasted gin in her mouth. She felt as see through as air and as light. She felt she could float away. Then it was all black.

When she woke in her bed, she had no idea how she had gotten there or how long she had been unconscious.

There was a fire going, the curtains drawn. It could have been two in the morning, for all she knew. She thought she was alone but then saw the two figures off to the side of the fire, heads together, conversation low. Her dearest friends in the world stopped whispering and looked at her.

"There you are, amor" Raquel smiled weakly.

Amanda sat up in her bed, rattled, with her stomach on her feet.

"How did you not know? You're his oldest friends, weren't you at the wedding?"

Diego looked at Raquel, who had daggers in her eyes.

"No, Amanda, I did not. Ed returned to Merida one summer when we were at Harvard, and it seems this was when he married this Magdalena woman. She couldn't have been very important to him as he never once mentioned her to me."

"He married her Diego!"

Amanda shouted while Raquel quickly brought her a whiskey.

"Amanda, I rarely saw Ed in those days; I spent my summers travelling," he assured her.

"There was no wedding. His mother never said a word to anyone. Gossip, like a wedding, travels fast. It would have been known; she would have attended – if she gave her blessing or even knew- but I am certain now more than ever that our dear old Eddie has been keeping secrets from every one of us."

Raquel scoffed,

"I was stupid to think he was only helping me import my coats to his doctor friends in the U.S.", she muttered, knocking her own drink back.

"He was smuggling cash in to get guns out to help who in Mexico exactly? To do what, exactly? He should have kept to what he knows: medicine. I was a fool to take him up on his 'kind offer'….I knew it was not genuine."

Amanda recoiled, "What?"

Raquel shut her mouth and shook her head. "I am sorry, I should have said nothing. You can't take much more. Ed is lying to all of us about everything", she spat furiously.

"One thing at a time please, and we must go with what we have proof of.", Diego sighed.

"Where is Leonor?"

"She had the driver take her to the hospital. Ed was called away to an emergency, a patient having a heart attack, and Leonor left to find him. After you fainted, she and Lupe put you to bed, and Diego and I each called to the house independently. I wasn't going to stay long, but then Leonor showed us what she had discovered, showed us the paper – she and Diego argued. I might have joined in, and then she left in a fury to go find her brother. Mostly, we have stayed to make sure you are alright. She said you fainted and got a nasty smack on the head."

Amanda's embarrassment at her friend's knowing the full extent of Ed and his shameful secrets was almost as unbearable as the thought of Ed having another secret wife.

"Does your head hurt?"

Amanda's head was throbbing.

"No. I feel nothing."

Chapter 29

February, 1913

Amanda stood behind the study door, not understanding why she had stopped to listen but knowing instinctively that she needed to.

"A fine Irish whiskey for my fine Irish friend", Edward winked as he handed Diego his drink, and they sat.

Diego did not drink. He did not feel he had the stomach for it on this night.

He sat upright and tense as he prepared to deliver news to his old friend that he knew would not be welcomed. Diego was not one to ever get nervous, but he felt positively ill with anxiety at the next words and a sweat had broken out on the back of his neck.

"I have news Eddie, and it is not - it is rather troubling. Things in Mexico are getting complicated, as you know. The American President has unknowingly caused a problem for many Americans in Mexico and for many Mexicans as well."

He said this earnestly, slowly, his usual jovial manner in everything nowhere to be seen.

Edward studied his face; he had never seen Diego so serious, not even at the funerals of his parents.

Diego changed his mind and took a swig of his drink, and after a deep breath, he said,

"Madero is dead. He And Pino Suarez were killed yesterday. Huerta is in – for now. The Mexican presidency is in danger.

"The Mexican presidency has been in danger", quipped Edward dryly as he put his whiskey to his nose, only half listening to his friend.

The news of the president's murder elicited almost no response from Edward, which chilled Diego.

Diego eyed Edward,

"Did you hear me? There was a coup- Madero, our Madero, the president was deposed and then assassinated, and you act as if you already knew?"

"I'm not surprised by much Diego, and it was in all the papers yesterday that Madero was deposed; what do you think they would do – invite him to a tea party? It was a matter of days until he and Juarez were dead. So, Huerta has taken over; these things happen in times of war and trouble.

"It is not just Madero and Juares being executed that is frightening news…. Your American President Wilson believes that supporting Carranza will be the best way to expedite the establishment of a lasting Mexican government. A stable Mexican government. His involvement is only exacerbating the tensions!"

"He is backing Carranza? Why, that is extraordinary.", Edward mused as he sipped, ever calm.

Edward's placid demeanour was turning the screw in Diego, winding him up. Diego took his fine silk handkerchief and patted the back of his neck. Ed often blew his top for no reason, so for him to remain calm was extraordinary.

"Of course, we knew the Americans would not be long in getting involved. It is understandable as our closest neighbours and some of the Revolution spilling into their streets in Texas would not go ignored. Seems logical." Ed shrugged.

"However, Pancho Villa is the issue now. He feels betrayed by the Americans, and he is out for blood. American blood!" Diego spat.

Diego sat back with relief, having said it. Now, to gauge his best friend's reaction. Diego was amazed there was no sign of Ed's explosive temper at hearing these things that should have him outraged and concerned. His small stature never stood in the way of his being an absolute fighting dog- ferocious and quick to bite. He was known to get rough at school, throwing schoolbooks and punches. Diego was fully sure of how Ed would take this news and yet his old friend surprised him once more.

Edward smiled and nodded in agreement,

"Yes, I can see that. Old Pancho is a hothead for sure; at least, he is portrayed that way in all the papers. I wouldn't know, I don't know him. He certainly seems to have a big mouth on him too."

Diego took another nervous sip before he continued,

"Amigo…Villa is more than that, I'm afraid. He's a very powerful crusader and has become a hero to many of our countrymen. He is rallying support among the peons and paupers of this nation. There is a word on the streets, and my sources are investigating, of course, but I believe this to be 100% accurate- Pancho Villla has made a declaration. That all foreigners- but especially all Americans are no longer welcome in Mexico, especially in the capital. That if he or any of his army find Americans – they will execute them on the spot. Van a matar a todos los gringos."

Edward simply laughed, "What an idiotic thing for him to say.

That ungrateful little pig. After everything the United States has done for Mexico?"

"The United States President should never have gotten involved." Diego shook his head.

"Of course, he should have!" argued Edward,

"These two nations- We are two brothers, bound by our histories of European invasion. Our ancestors came, taking these lands from the natives too stupid to know what to do with them. These sun-baked fools, with their many gods. Like animals, too stupid to come out of their mud huts or grow anything other than maize. My God, the Aztecs built an entire city on a lake, only to have it start sinking!

Pancho is one of those backward natives; I put no credence in what he spouts. He should be thanking one of his gods that the white man came to tame his people. He is simply angry with one man, one American. I'm sure this is showboating at its finest."

"Eduardo- We go back a long time, back to our Harvard days. You know, I would never tell you an untruth or exaggerate anything that I felt was vitally important for the safety and wellbeing of you and your family. They're my family as well. You are my brother. But- you and your children."

"What of me and my children?"

Ed asked him rather confused but now giving him his full attention.

"They are targets perhaps- "

"That is ridiculous. My mother was Mexican. Born in Merida."

"I know, may she rest in peace; I adored your mother- but she was one of those European invaders, or her family was -"

"I take it you're concerned Diego. You needn't be. My family have nothing to do with any revolution or anything with that crazy outlaw Villa."

"You are not hearing me- you are not the problem, not really; you are Mexican as well; your children, on the other hand, were born in New York; your wife-"

"I too, am from Merida even if I was born New York, or have you forgotten my roots in the Yucatan? Or can you not hear my Mexican accent when I speak Spanish, or for that matter, my American accent when I speak English?

"Eddie- your accent is not the problem here"

"My father was American of Irish and English background; what of it?"

Edward started in, defensive.

"He moved to Mexico, he married a Mexican of European blood, and here we are. I have nothing to apologize for. I'm not apologizing for being a European in a land of heathens. I am just as entitled to Mexico as any indio. I also am an American, and I do not apologise to anyone for that. I'm not sure I'm following what the problem is supposed to be. Never mind my father birthed half of the peons in this country."

He laughed tightly.

"Your children are small; they are picking up and speaking Spanish quickly; they will adapt."

"The baby was born here; she is Mexican too, by birth.", Ed

insisted.

"Ed- there is talk of all the big American companies closing their doors, of the staff being whisked away.

There is talk about closing the U.S. Embassy. I have heard rumours that the U.S. - that their own Ambassador, Henry Lane Wilson, was involved in the plot to oust Madero- if this is true, it will make things infinitely worse. "

"If the U.S. had anything to with Madero and Suarez being overthrown then Pancho Villa owes the United States a debt of gratitude, don't you think?"

Ed said matter of factly.

"There are not just two sides to this amigo- this is a trifecta of struggle. The enemy of my enemy is not my friend but still my enemy in this case, and Villa- has no loyalties to anyone, least of all the U.S."

Ed shrugged, trying to appear disinterested.

"I don't know what to tell you or why you think I need to be concerned about this. I am here to do a job. I'm just a doctor, not a fighter or politician.

"Perhaps you could take a sabbatical with your family back to the U.S. for a while until things calm down."

"Are you mad?"

At this point, Ed sat up straight, and his demeanour changed from relaxed to stoic and tense.

"You want me to go on a vacation because some fat little

blowhard, some pinche indio, makes threats?"

At this point, Amanda knew she needed to walk away back down the hall or to walk forward into the room and make her presence known, but she stayed behind the partition, her shoes glued to the floor. She didn't want her appearance to end the conversation, yet she couldn't leave them to talk in private.

She had to hear for herself. She had to know if her children were in danger, so she stayed hidden and immobilized.

'If Ed wasn't keeping secrets from me', she told herself, 'this wouldn't be necessary.'

She knew he was hiding things about his medical practice, finances, his reasons for wanting to come to Mexico, and perhaps even keeping secrets in regard to Raquel. She was tired of secrets, and she was tired of finding his breadcrumbs. She wanted the entire dish in one large serving. After moving her little ones so far from home, she felt she deserved answers she knew Ed would refuse to give her. She willed herself to stay quiet as a stone, her delicate little hand creeping up to cover her mouth, just in case.

"Please, Eddie- hear me out? Your wife- your wife is the problem, let's say."

"Pardon me?"

Diego stood and began to pace excitedly, and his speech matched his hurried pace.

"Her Spanish is very poor. She can barely speak or understand a word. She has a very strong, whatever that dialect is- Boston, Philadelphia, I don't know. But the five of you walking down los calles del centro, her walking with her creada to the market- with all of those blonde, blue-eyed babies- you all stick out! Normally, it wouldn't be a problem. Pancho Villa, for a long time, until recently, he had no real problem with whites if they were Mexican, born, raised Mexicanos, but he has changed his stance. He now only cares about the interests of the natives; anyone of European blood is seen as an interloper and not welcomed in Mexico, no matter how long ago their families came here.

He professes he is willing to work with some Mexicans despite their race. He has been known to toy with people before he decides to kill them if it suits his purpose. He has warned everyone of any importance: back him or else. Americans, however, infuriate him to another degree. He and his men are convinced that eventually, depending on how the revolution goes, the Americans are going to invade the country. Pancho has stated to this to his followers at his last three political gatherings. He is filling heads with the notion that the Gringos will come into Mexico and slaughter the entire native population just like they did in that country. Gringos in Mexico right now are not welcome, and this anger of his and his rhetoric is spreading like fire through the brush. From the politicians to the beggars in the street, more and more Mexicans are finding the U.S. involvement in our troubles as distasteful. Your family, as a group, stick out and draw attention. If they were confronted in the streets by the wrong person and they could answer in perfect Spanish with accentos de la ciudad I would not worry as much. If they could blend in as proper First Society Mexicans, at this point, it would still be a bit dangerous. However, los gringos…are very different from other whites. There is a strange arrogance among Americans; I don't know there is a tell. They are louder and more conspicuous. They often love to tell people they're from the U.S. I fear for Amanda here right at this moment. I know this is hard to hear but I'm suggesting if you don't flee the country within the month, you could possibly find some trouble at your door."

Edward stood up, snuffing out his pipe, his face red as if someone had slapped him.

The two men stood apart, both anxious, withdrawing to opposite corners of the room like two boxers ready to spar.

"This is outrageous.", He said quietly, calmly.

"This is the most ridiculous thing I have heard. It is the Europeans who run this country- not the peons. I'm supposed to fear what exactly, that my wife talks funny? I am in the prime of my career, I have all the hospitals in Mexico crying, begging for me. I cannot keep up with the universities showering me with money to go and even just speak to their students."

Diego could not help himself,

"Now, Ed, we both know that is not exactly the case."

"How dare you."

Edward hissed at him yet did not deny the statement. Instead, he began almost to tremble with rage.

"My father was a king in this country, an American king. If it wasn't for him and his introducing the use of ether in Mexico, half of your population that goes in for surgery would never make it out again. My father birthed half of Merida, he single-handedly saved the lives of thousands upon thousands of Mexicans, and I am well on my way to surpassing his success. I will go down in the history books, the medical texts, and I will do it richer than my wildest dreams, and you are suggesting because some little despot from the desert is in a foul temper that I should run away and leave all my work? Leave all my patients who need me behind, leave all my glory behind to steal away in the middle of the night with my babies and my ugly American wife-"

"Basta! Stop- Eduardo, I did not insult Amanda. She is a beautiful woman; I did not call her any such thing."

"It is an expression, the ugly Americans, due to their behaviour, and yes, sadly, her looks are fading fast after this last baby; let's not kid ourselves. She has become old and frumpy and stupider by the day."

"Ed, I won't hear this; she is an angel. She is a wonderful wife and mother, and this is not fair to her. It is not her fault nor yours that sometimes, during war, certain people are chosen to be the victims, chosen to be the losers. Many times, these tragic people get no warning- they simply have their throats slashed in their sleep. You are getting a warning. Pancho Villa is a villain; he is looking for someone like your wife to make an example of! He likes to throw his weight around; he enjoys the fame, but most of all, he enjoys the slaughter. He is out for blood! "

"Oh, Diego, you should have been a thespian; you are over dramatic to the last. Nobody is at war with Americans-

"Not yet- but it is headed that way. And if Mexico's most prominent new surgeon, an American with a Mexican mother no less -but with an American wife and kids- were to get caught up in these troubles in any way, The United States would retaliate. You could become targets of Pancho Villa, targets of the Mexican Revolution. They could take your family as hostages, they could kidnap your children, or they could simply murder them all to make a point to the United States. I'm not asking for you to give up your work. I am simply telling you what I know, what is coming, and that perhaps your wife and children would be better in New York for the time being. Or even in New Orleans, you stay here and send them away, perhaps."

"You're jealous of me and my work."

Ed shook his head, laughing now, a sneering smile creeping across his face.

"I have eclipsed you and your study of the brain; you are begrudging me and trying to invoke fear….of my own country, my own people -you forget I am Mexican too. I have just as much right to be in this land as that dirt Pancho Villa.

"Amigo, I am not celoso, I admire and respect your work immensely, but I am trying to be pragmatic and offer solutions to a coming problem. Let me, please add that you know I have turned my attention towards psychology not instead of but alongside neurology because I think it has promising implications-"

"Oh yes"

Edward said mockingly, his eyes wide,

"The study of the mind, how very noble, what lives will you save, asking about people's little feelings. Perhaps I should start calling you Sigmund, yes?"

"Dr. Freud has done amazi-"

"He is a quack and a charlatan, and you are happily destroying your medical career to follow in his footsteps, analysing people's dreams and pecadillos. How are you not embarrassed? It is utterly infantile to sabotage your career in this manner, and now, after realizing your folly, you're out to destroy everyone around you…...because you felt drawn to work with lunatics, and think you are going to cure those people."

Ed laughed cruelly.

Diego felt himself heading towards rage and grabbed his coat abruptly and placed his hat on his head, never angrier with his compadre than in that moment.

"Eduardo, I do not have to listen to abuse from you. I only am trying to warn a friend. I don't have a wife or a family to think about.

"And it shows, Diego."

"The study of the mind is vastly important in understanding human behaviours and can give glimpses into every part of the body. I will not have you attack my work nor my character."

"Yes, well, I am a surgeon, a real doctor, a cardiac surgeon who has held many a beating heart, the very life force in my hands. I get more than just glimpses into the bodies of my patients; I get lasting visions of the lives I save, and if I abandon my work to hide in New York or New Orleans like a coward, where there are many more doctors just like me- I fail the people of Mexico, and people will die because of such cowardice. I will not even hear another word; this most absurd conversation is over. This is a stupidity. We will go nowhere. "

He then paused for a moment to finish his drink while he concocted something spiteful for his friend.

"And I've seen how you look at my wife-," he spat.

"Perhaps you wish I would lose Amanda, send her away, so you can swoop in to save that pathetic, little dying butterfly."

"Eduardo, you go too far. Please do not say anything you might regret. I will also remind you that whatever inappropriateness you want to imply, whatever affections I may have for your Amanda, simply pales in comparison to your fawning all over Raquel and whatever else you're doing and with whomever– even as your wife has just given birth."

He felt his voice quaver as he admonished his old friend's nasty streak,

"Now, I am going to leave you, amigo, and I hope to one day be back, but before I leave here today, let me also assure you of this- you need to be very careful about what you are doing here in Mexico, your part in the Revolution."

"What did you say to me-?"

"Be very, very careful in whatever you might ..take an interest in. Who you meet with or speak to or have business dealings with could make you guilty by assoc-"

"I don't need your advice Mr. Psychoanalysis."

Ed said in a cold yet threatening manner. Suddenly, he went from blazing, white-hot rage to an anger so powerful he appeared utterly calm. The most dangerous kind of anger, like a snake before it strikes, is quiet, deadly.

"Perhaps you have something important to do right now - you should go and see to it, and you can call next week. Or perhaps whenever you are next free. I'm sure you will remain very busy with pontificating to all your patients. I will have Amparo show you out."

Diego stood fixed in his spot for a moment, full of potential rebuttals, unsure whether to punch his friend or fall down defeated, slumped in the armchair, begging him to listen to reason. The Tappan family, every one of them was in danger. He gave a sigh of capitulation as he realized Ed wouldn't listen.

"Hasta luego Edward",

Diego shook no hand nor approached Edward as he turned to leave the room.

"Adios Diego...... vaya con dios",

Ed snarked at his back, pouring himself another whiskey.

From where Amanda was hidden, she could hear Diego's fine shoes stomp angrily down the hall from Ed's office towards the front door. From the office, she could hear what sounded like Ed slamming things about, papers rushing to the floor, heavy objects meeting the thick Persian rugs, their arrival on the floor muffled. Then, the distinct timbre of glass breaking. She didn't need to enter the room to know he was destroying his office in an oddly silent rage.

Amanda turned to flee and nearly ran straight into Guadalupe, who stood frozen with a tray meant for Ed's office. Her rigid posture and the stunned look on her face told Amanda the housekeeper had heard a good bit of the conversation turned argument between the two friends.

"Perdona me Señora",

she whispered and stepped around her to enter Ed's office, briskly as if nothing were the matter.

"Doctor, aqui tengo tu café." Lupe said with a forced cheer meant to imply she had not been eavesdropping.

"Salga de mi oficina, con un carajo!"

Ed screamed, his face the colour of many of his patients during a cardiac event.

Lupe turned right around to head back to the kitchen to find the hallway empty with no sign of la Señora. She wondered how much her American jefa had heard but knew that it was enough.

Chapter 30

It had been a tremendously exhausting day, cold with a grey sky overhead and the fat, black clouds of a storm rolling in. Ed's temper matched the day, and he had stormed out just after he left his dinner untouched, without a word to his wife or anyone as to where he was going.

Everyone in the house seemed to sigh a breath of relief as he slammed the giant oak door shut behind him.

Amanda had decided to put down her worry for the night, like a pair of shoes by the bedside.

It could be picked up again in the morning. Her young body ached with tension; she was tired.

Guadalupe seemed agitated when she and Marta appeared to Amanda in her bedroom to inform her that a police man was downstairs, wanting to speak to her.

"The police?" Amanda asked,

"What does he want, Lupe?"

"No se Señora- a constable, eh Cervantes, he said his name was. Said he must speak to the lady of the house."

"Tell him I will be with him at once."

Lupe rushed back downstairs as Amanda put a thick cotton robe over her dressing gown and put on slippers. It was proving to be a very chilly February, and the mountain air had a bite to it at night that rivalled that of the coldest New York winters. She tied her hair back into a quick bun, slightly miffed and finding it inappropriate that this policeman, like so many in this city, deemed it their right to just show up in her home without warning. If it wasn't an emergency, then what was it? She glanced at Agatha in her cot, small and warm, sleeping in that magical place babies slumbered in.

"Marta, mind her for me while I run downstairs, please."

"Of course, Señora, not to worry, please."

The young nanny's dark eyes, puzzled, followed her out of the room.

Upon entering her own living room, two policemen, one impossibly thin, the other impossibly round, stood to greet her, shushing their conversation.

"Señora Tappan,"

the larger, older of the two began with his hand outstretched.

"Please, forgive this intrusion. I am Constable Armando Cervantes Guzman, and this is my First Deputy Ignacio Baz. You have a most lovely home."

This constable knew enough about Amanda to address her in English, which she found annoying.

"Gracias Señor.",

Amanda smiled tightly,

"Is everything all right? Is there some emergency?"

"No, no, we are simply checking round to all the houses of the neighbourhood to, how do I say this without causing alarm, but to ensure everyone has enough security personnel, you know, armed protection and if not, how we, la policia could help the families. Estas colonias house some of the most important people in all of Mexico City, and as you may know by now, there is a revolution gripping the country."

He nodded solemnly.

"Yes. But hasn't it been ongoing for quite some time now, Officer- excuse me, Constable Cervantes?

"True, but the violence and uprisings have now made it to the capital in much greater numbers than in years previous. Our president Madero was murdered two nights ago along with the Vice President Pino Suarez. "

"Yes, horrible news, but-

Are you an American?"

he asked as he helped himself to her favourite sofa.

Amanda hesitated. She had not invited him to sit, and she had begun to really resent that question, always being asked where she was from, if she was American, if she was foreign, and what she was doing in Mexico?

"Yes, seeing as how you knew to address me in English, I thought you knew. I am from New York. Well, Philadelphia, but my husband, Doctor Tappan, as I'm sure you know, is from Merida."

"Ah, yes, I thought this house seemed familiar! Now I know why," he grinned and looked to his second in command. Amanda could not fathom why he was pretending as if he didn't know who lived in that house.

"Yes, Dr. Tappan is the second buyer of this house- there was, I think, a politician in it for a short time after it was built three years ago…I remember watching it go up, an extraordinary mansion, to be sure. Yes, I am familiar with Dr. Tappan. I have even had it suggested I might go and see him myself. You know, the heart sometimes gives us older men a bit of trouble. I hear your husband is a very talented man."

He said with an almost genuine smile.

"Yes, he is, from what I've gathered. I've never been able to see him in action, of course, although I have heard of his many triumphs over the years."

"No, of course not", the constable said dismissively with a grin,

"The daily work of a doctor is no place for a woman".

There was an undercurrent with this man, like a stream that looked inviting, but the bottom was covered in a layer of slippery, green slime. He attempted to smile and lure her in, but she knew she would quickly fall. He wanted information, but of what sort, Amanda was unsure. She wanted them out of her house.

Amanda had been standing but decided to sit. The pair now sat opposite each other, blankly smiling and staring, while Ignacio Baz continued to pretend like he was supremely interested in the paintings of fruit hanging in gold frames on the wall. The younger man, or possibly boy, appeared to be on edge, wiping the back of his neck every minute or so, although it was not warm in the house. His eyes would peer out of their corners to watch Amanda until she glanced at him, and his eyes would focus once again on the paintings, his long dark lashes hiding any hint of expression. It was obvious to Amanda that the reason given was not the truth about an unsolicited visit at nine o'clock at night.

"Well, Señor, to answer your question, I believe we have a good amount of personnel for the house that would be classified as security guards; however, you would really need to verify that with my husband, of course, and he is, *even at such a late hour as this*," she said those words slowly to drop a heavy hint, " still not home yet from the hospital."

"Yes, of course, I will speak to him, perhaps tomorrow. Pardon the intrusion at this hour. We were in the area, and we saw the outside lamps were still lit, so we thought we might stop by. I will have to finish speaking with your neighbours tomorrow. I'm afraid it's getting very late, and I don't want to keep you with a new baby and all- felicidades on your new little Mexican."

"Muchas gracias", Amanda smiled,

"Your Spanish is beautiful Señora, bienvenido a Mexico."

"Oh, before we go- should you need anything at all, please do not hesitate to contact myself or my first deputy here. The station is only three roads up from this estate- on La Calle Granada. The large, black building, opposite the square. If you have one of those telephones, please ask the operator to connect you to Numero catorce- that is fourteen in Spanish, that is our station. And I want to assure you that if there is ever any trouble, we will call out to this house immediately- any trouble at all."

His words wore the mask of reassurance, but underneath it was a warning.

"We wouldn't want you living in fear in your own home."

"No, of course not. Thank you."

"Buenas noches Señora",

Amanda forced just one more tight, furious smile, hoping her eyes didn't betray her thoughts.

"Buenas noches, Officers."

Lupe shut the door and shrugged at her mistress. After a few seconds of standing in silence, as if both the women were making sure the police had moved away from the opposite side of the door, Lupe said,

"That was odd, Señora."

"You thought so too, Lupe? I wasn't imagining it. What in the world- what did they want, why did they come here?"

"It's fine Señora Tappan, you let me find out. Mañana I will go to the neighbours to the left of us and speak with their housekeeper Esperanza. I will find out if they are going around to all the houses and what they want."

Lupe didn't like the intrusion. This was her home too, after all. She had looked after this family for a short time but knew Edward from a boy. She had an affection for her Señora and the family. This was their hogar, their home, and there was something threatening about the visit they had just had. She feared the reason for what felt like an invasion. She felt deep in her stomach that it must have something to do with the revolution- the officers had said as much. But there was something else they didn't say that annoyed her. She would not make too much of a fuss because she didn't want to alarm Señora Tappan, so she changed the subject.

"Señora, I will make you a bolio con queso y frijoles refritos, like you like. A little merienda to help you sleep, perhaps with some hot cocoa?"

"Yes, please."

Amanda nodded in confusion and followed her to the kitchen.

The Orange Blossom House had a large kitchen with glass doors along one side that led out to the garden. Far from the fountain and main attractions of the garden, it was a darker, lusher, almost overgrown corner that seemed to disguise the kitchen from the rest of the house. This sleepy and forgotten area made it so that people could look out from the kitchen and spy on the unsuspecting inhabitants of the garden through the leaves of palms and ferns. On this night, the garden was cloaked in a swallowing darkness, lit only by the moon as Amanda peered out at the mermaid fountain in the distance. In the grey, cold light, la sirena looked almost like a menacing figure waiting to jump out at anyone who crossed her path. Amanda was trembling ever so slightly.

Lupe set about to lighting the stove and gathering her favourite copper pot for hot chocolate making.

"Señora, go rest; I will bring you to your room."

"No", Amanda sat down at the round oak table,

"No, if you don't mind, I will have it here. I'm in no rush….you can join me if you'd like a bite as well", she told the maid, sounding hopeful.

Lupe gave a funny smile,

"Gracias Señora, but I had my dinner. Nothing more for me until tomorrow's breakfast. I must work hard in my old age to maintain the shape of a younger lady."

She was so fond of her employer but didn't want to eat with her. It was too intimate an act for her, even though she had seen Amanda naked almost every day.

Amanda sat puzzled, staring at her long white fingers, cold and too thin looking.

"Lupe", she began, in a tone that told the housekeeper an important question was following.

"Do you think Dr. Tappan is- is involved in something – to do with this-"

She was cut off by the sound in the distance of the front door of the house closing hard, and both she and Lupe scurried to the large open foyer to see Edward in the door, black leather medical bag in hand, what looked like a large bloodstain on his shirt. It took a moment to register exactly what that was, like a giant orchid blooming across the front of him. The two women stood frozen, silent, eyes and mouths too wide for his liking.

"What is everyone looking at? A welcoming party, is it?"

he said tersely before he seemed to remember looking down, that he had a curious stain on his person.

"I will be in my study. Not to be disturbed, I'm working."

He ordered before he bounded down the stairs into his wing of the house.

"Good night", Amanda called after him, only half expecting an answer.

She wondered if he'd come to bed that night or if she'd find him passed out drunk on the settee in his study again, as she had several nights since the beginning of the month.

The women returned to the kitchen in silence. Lupe set about making her employer a light meal. Amanda, knowing it was not a good time to resume her question to the older woman, sat defeated at the table, staring out into the garden, silently pleading the answers would just open up before her like the flowers.

Chapter 31

Ed strolled into the grey, quiet dining room as the children were finishing their breakfast. The floor to ceiling windows that met the west side of the garden were wet, with sheets of rain washing down them. Amparo had a fire going, and it looked more as if it were ten o'clock at night than ten in the morning.

The children ate happily but quietly, the lashing of the rain and the crackling of the fire were the only sounds on this winter morning.

Amanda had decided to dress and come down for breakfast for the first time since giving birth three months prior. She had pin rolled her hair into glorious spirals, her face done up – powder, rouge, dab of lipstick, eyelashes darkened. She needed to look like she was in control, not nervous or exhausted. She sat in a beautiful navy blue and cream pinafore, her breakfast and coffee growing cold before her. Arthur and Amelia had devoured their eggs and fruit plates. It was a beautiful family scene from the outside looking in. Amanda never took her eyes off him as he elegantly pulled out his chair and sat at the far end of the table, face ashen, eyes downcast. Immediately he was brought a coffee by Amparo.

He flashed an insincere smile at his wife.

"Good morning my love."

Amanda looked around at the many pairs of eyes and ears in the room, some far too innocent for what was to come.

"Good morning, Edward; I take it you slept well?"

He answered with another tiny, quick smile that was all lips and cheeks moving but daggers in the eyes.

"Marta, now that the children have had their –

she paused, trying to remember the word for breakfast-

"desayuno, please take them to get ready for the tutor. Ms. Mayer will be calling to the house in about an hour for our lessons."

Marta took the children by the hands,

"Of course Señora, venga ninos, vamos a cambiar tu ropa y lavar las caras! Ya viene la maestra!", she told them excitedly.

Amparo brought Ed a plate full of scrambled eggs, refried beans, avocado, queso Oaxaca and bolios with a bowl of his butter that he loved.

"Gracias Amparo, please go see what Lupe might need in the kitchen."

Amanda dismissed her.

Amparo looked from la Señora to the Señor and then quickly left.

Ed began to eat in silence, stuffing it in as though he had not eaten for days, his usual manners out the window.

"You may just call her back in; I'm going to need more coff-"

"Where were you all yesterday and last night, Ed?"

He swallowed his food and finally looked up to meet the gaze of his wife, and she did not look like her old happy, pleasant self, or even her pitiful sullen look of late, but instead, her gaze was fire, her face stone.

“The hospital, of course. Where-”

“We had visitors last night Ed. The police. They left fifteen minutes before you showed up covered in blood.”

“The police? Came to this house? What did they want?”

“I was hoping you might know- why were you covered in blood, Ed? Whose blood was on your shirt?”

“I wasn’t covered in blood, Amanda.”

He chuckled, “There was a good bit on my shirt yes, these things do happen, you know. I’m a doctor. A surgeon? There’s going to be blood.”

He was talking down to her. He only ever did that when they were fighting, or he was hiding something.

“You perform surgery at nine pm now?”

She glared down the long table at him, feeling braver, angrier with every word. The zero sleep she had gotten the entire night only served as fuel for her fire. Her exhaustion meant she was running on pure adrenaline and bile.

Ed let out a giant sigh,

“What in the world is wrong with you, woman?”

“What is wrong with me? I’ve just had a baby!”

“It’s been months-”

“I’ve just had a baby, and I need my husband!”

She had to stop because she was suddenly choking on tears,

"I need my husband not to be gone all the time, all day, and all night and when you are here, you barely see me or the children. We barely had a Christmas and barely saw you for it. Our first holiday in this house-

"We had a lovely party on the twenty-second, or were you too drunk to remember?"

"That was not for our family; that was for you and your cronies. You have some strangers in this house every waking minute when you are actually here- when you don't, you are in a foul humour, or acting odd, or you're drunk."

"You have lost your sanity".

Ed said each word slowly as if reading them off the paper before he threw his napkin down in disgust.

"How dare you speak to the man of the house this way? You don't question me on who I have dealings with or who I have in this house. I'm a very important man here in Mexico, my dear, lest you forget it. Very important, very busy, hard-working to keep you in luxury.

You don't question me- ever."

"That's not how marriage works, Edward or how it's supposed to work. You brought me here promising me you would take care of me and the children, and you brought us here for what- into a revolution? You knowingly bought me and my little babies to a war? People being murdered in the streets? Bandeleros taking over haciendas and executing the white families they find there? These whites are actual Mexicans, not foreigners like me-"

"You stupid woman. Who has been feeding you this nonsense? You can't read Spanish and there are no English papers around here.

Who have you been speaking to?"

She would not admit to how much Spanish she had learned to read, not yet.

"Why, the police, Edward. La policia came knocking at our very door to remind me of the war we were sitting in the middle of. To tell me of our dead president – Madero was shot like a dog.

"You need not concern yourself with-

"Why on earth did we leave New York? Almost a year, and I've been in your presence for more than an hour, maybe ten times. The children hardly recognize you.

"I have a stringent, busy work schedule. My career-"

"You had that in New York, but we at least got to see you every day, at least for a bit. Here, it's been three and four days since you have seen your kids. Other than today's breakfast, when was the last time before the five minutes you just spent with them, that you even saw your children?"

"You sent them out of the room, darling wife."

"I needed to speak with you. What are you doing at the hospital when there are rumours you don't even have a secured position there anymore?

Edward folded his arms and leaned back to glare.

"Well, last night I repaired a man's aorta, not that you even know what that is or that I should have to answer to you."

"What of your place as a lecturer at the university? What of that? What happened there?"

At the mention of that which he did not think she had any knowledge of, his face froze in a mask of guilt.

"Did they tire of your ego?"

Edward shot up from the table, knocking the chair back and over and with a great surge of rage he cleared the table, sending dishes and food flying across the room.

Guadalupe came running into the room with Amparo right behind her, but both women halted upon seeing the look on their master's face and quickly walked backwards through the double doors into the kitchen without a word.

Amanda shook her head,

"Why are you acting like this Ed? Are you trying to frighten me? I am already frightened of what is happening all around us that you seem to be blind to."

She looked so hurt and vulnerable at that moment. Ed calmed just a bit.

He owed her no answers; she was his wife. She answered to him, that is how it was meant to be and always had been. His own parents popped into his head suddenly, his mother stern and foreboding, her regal Spanish forehead and nose, her dark blue eyes demanding, always demanding. She had run that ship, been the queen of the castle. His father, the Old Dr. Tappan, had been larger than life but soft, placid, and good-natured. He did not bow down to his wife, but she was most certainly in charge. Edward shook their ghosts away. He was not his father and would not be henpecked by any woman. His wife was not the steel pedagogue his mother had been. Amanda had become weak, proving herself unfit in many ways. She couldn't even do her wifely duty of being a mother without falling to pieces it seemed. This move abroad had proven that. He would not allow such insubordination from his little weeping willow. He pondered whether to slap the face off her or send her to her room like a petulant and punished child.

He took four long steps towards her and glared,

"If I come any closer, daring wife, I shall mop the floor with your face. Now do be a good little girl and return to your bed, where you have been most of these last ninety post-partum days, and you can stay there until you find your senses once again. And for your information, we barely had a Christmas because my wife was too hysterical from the traumas of childbirth to act like a normal person. We had a lovely get-together with our friends where my wife proceeded to get as drunk as a penny whore and had to be carried to her bed. If I was away on Christmas Day, it was because I was called away to do God's work. Now I will take leave of you, and when I return home, you had better be behaving correctly and our children well cared for, as is your sole duty in this life, to be a good mother. It is a shame my own mother is not here to teach you what it is you lack."

Amanda was stunned Ed spoke to her like that. He had never in eight years said such vile things to her. He could be difficult at times, even, yes, awful, but never had he been so cruel as to threaten her. He had never attacked her ability to mother.

"And it is a shame my father is not here to teach you what it is that you lack, Edward."

He grabbed his medical bag and froze, his back to her. He willed himself not to set upon her like a cat about to devour a mouse. His rage had him breathing so that his teeth were bared, but instead of throttling her, he grabbed his briefcase and coat, throwing his hat on his head, stomping all the way down the front hall like a petulant child.

"Where are you going, Edward?" Amanda yelled after him, so furious she felt as if her whole body was on fire.

"We need to talk!"

He stopped for a second and sneered at his wife,

"I am going to the hospital, as usual, you little idiot. I believe I sent you up to your bed ."

He moved towards her now swiftly, long strides taking him to within striking distance,

"And God help you if, upon my return to this house, I do not find you in it."

Chapter 32

Edward did not return to The Orange Blossom House for four days and four nights. He had left in a rage on a Thursday morning. While Amanda was at first concerned, that night nearly maniacal with worry, the following morning, found her calm. She decided if he had not returned from the hospital, something terrible must have happened, and so, obviously, Edward was dead. She attempted to seem upset at this thought, out of marital obligation, but instead felt only minute guilt at the strange relief that filled her body. For the first time since they had arrived in Mexico, she felt no fear, grief, or panic, only a wonderful peace.

The staff tried to appear as if they were also genuinely worried about the man of the house, but all, in fact, silently clutched their rosaries with prayers that he would not return. Every slight, every terse word and unkind gesture he had bestowed on the servants went remembered. Every time he was disgusting and cruel to his wife, the women all saw and stored away those memories in layers, each one added as if a coat of paint to the walls of the house. His own small children did not ask about him, not even Arthur or Arturo, as he had insisted he be called. The boy was oddly silent in the absence of his father. Marta wondered while she tended to the children if the little boy was not also relieved to have the doctor away.

His return on the fifth day found the staff crestfallen, but his wife felt a terror inside. If he had been away for that amount of time and had the gall to then waltz in without a word of explanation, that told Amanda there were very big secrets in the world of her husband.

His appearance was shocking, and she knew it must be painted on her face, but she could not remove the stunned look in her eyes. She was unsure if she was more upset at the abject state he presented himself in or if she simply was disappointed he had returned. She knew in this moment, as she should have shown him great tenderness and pity, that she hated him. She could not summon even a drop of affection for this man she had given her entire life to.

His hair appeared to be missing in places, as if handfuls had been ripped from his scalp. Both eyes were nearly swollen shut, his nose and lips having taken the brunt of the fat end of a rifle. He appeared to still have his teeth, but as Amanda followed him from their bedroom to the bathroom, he kept his left hand to his jaw as if holding something in place.

He accepted her one olive branch in the form of a cloth for his face as he approached the marble sink. He stood before it without a sound, staring at the water from the tap.

"Will we not speak of this? I should not ask questions then?" she asked him calmly.

"Leave me.", he whispered before spitting blood and a tooth into the sink.

"All too happy to do so", Amanda obliged.

As she headed downstairs, she thought she would use the telephone to call Diego. He would have the answers she knew Edward would never give. Thoughts began to whisper to Amanda that perhaps she needed to do something else.

Chapter 33

Her lovely auburn hair was tucked up neatly under her hat; only a fallen tendril in the back, which she was unaware of, gave her away. She looked around at the other people on the train platform. No one seemed to be paying attention to her which is exactly what she had hoped for. The news of Pancho Villa's edict was everywhere it seemed. People were fleeing Mexico. She knew leaving was the right thing to do. She found her car at the back of the train, relieved to see it was empty and she would have privacy. She removed her gloves but left her hat on and sat down with a sigh. This was only temporary; she thought and a wise decision. It would be best for everyone if she went to the United States for a while. She thought of Diego suddenly, and longing hit her. Perhaps she should have at least let him know of her departure. She felt guilty, leaving everyone behind, but was certain she had no choice. As the train began to move, she felt instantly flooded with relief. No one had explicitly threatened her, but she knew she was the very people Pancho wanted gone.

She had not seen the man at the far end of the platform, hidden in the shadows. When she had lifted her head to look around, he had been sure to look down at his boots, as if studying them instead of her every move. He could not believe his good fortune to find her travelling alone. It seemed she always had a companion or two. This would be quite the feather in his cap and would curry massive favour with Pancho. This was going to be a legendary accomplishment, someone of such importance. He couldn't help but smile with glee as he fingered his gun in his vest and boarded the train, waiting for his moment to say hello.

Not an hour into the journey, the door to her car slid open, and a filth-covered bandit stopped to look at her, filled with lust. She had such a glorious figure, even after just recently having a baby. She looked so peaceful sleeping; he almost hated to wake her, but he was going to. He slid the door closed behind him and sat down next to her, very close, almost on top of her.

Her eyes fluttered open, and she muttered in her sleep, "Diego?"

Within seconds, her vision cleared, and she saw not Diego but a man she did not know, a brown face with brown teeth and the stench of rot clinging to him.

"Hola, Señora Tappan, it is nice to meet you finally." he grinned.

Graciela Mayer opened her mouth to scream, but he had his left hand over her mouth and nose so fast she didn't even realise his right arm was already around her neck with a gun at the end of it, pointed at her, the metal just behind her ear lobe.

"We gonna go take a little trip to visit some of my friends who want to meet a pretty girl like you.", he whispered.

"Such a pretty, pretty girl."

Chapter 34

Not two nights after Ed's return and less than two weeks after the coup and execution of the President and Vice president of Mexico, Guadalupe rushed into Amanda's bedroom with a strange look on her face. She had with her two confused and sleepy children in their dressing gowns.

"Lupe? What are the children doing out of bed?" she asked as she brushed her long hair.

Her smile faded as she took in the sight of the older woman, who appeared shaken.

"Is everything all right?"

Lupe shook her head only slightly, her eyes never leaving her those of her jefa.

Then Marta came in quickly, carefully shutting the door, and with Amparo, they cajoled the children to follow them to the back of the bedroom to the large closet without a word to Amanda.

"What on earth is going on?"

Lupe came close to Amanda's face and said in a low, hushed voice, as calm and even as still water,

"There are men here, Amanda."

Amanda froze as she felt something crawl across her entire body.

"What kind of men?"

"They are here, waiting for your husband."

“What kind of men? Are they military?”

“They are not, Señora, no. I told them he would be home shortly, but I also lied and told him and his men that you and the children were not here.”

“They asked about us?

“They asked about you. I told them you all are in Vera Cruz visiting family but that they were welcome to wait. I told them they were welcome to stay because I knew I could not tell them to leave, and if they thought I wanted them gone, they might search the house. They are in Dr. Tappan’s office right now.”

The Orange Blossom House was gigantic, spread over three floors and three different wings, and the master bedroom was in the very back of the house, far enough away and behind several closed and heavy doors that there was no fear of being heard, but there was a chance they could eventually be found if Edward took too long in arriving and the men decided boredom could be filled with a look around the estate.

Amanda felt dread climbing her legs and encircling her belly, moving to her breasts, but she kept remarkably calm.

“Lupe…. how many men are in my house?”

“Only three Señora, but it is Pablo’s night off.”

Pablo had been the extra security officer put in charge of watching Amanda and the children. Pablo, young and strapping, was also large and intimidating but, on this night, was drunk on the other side of the city. Guadalupe felt these men must have known this information; perhaps they had been watching the house, but she dared not speak this now a certainty to her fragile mistress.

"Joaquin is downstairs, but the men let him know they were coming in to wait whether he likes it or not. They were very forceful. And they are carrying weapons." The fifty-year-old year old security officer and driver would not be any match for the three young men.

Lupe relayed all of this information as calmly as if she was listing off the fruits she had purchased at the market that morning long ago. Listing out the details for Amanda as if she was giving her a recipe and then following these instructions,

"You will go to your large closet in the back and get in with the children."

Marta gently lifted the sleeping Agatha out of her cot and placed her in Amanda's arms.

"You four will lie down quietly in the closet and sleep there the whole night if necessary, and Amparo, Marta and I will stay where we can watch things. The men have told Joaquin he is to sit with them in Ed's office, and they dismissed me to my regular duties. We are going to move the large dresser in front of the closet to camouflage it. The girls and I will continue our work cleaning and attending to these men until they leave. I have pozole in the kitchen; if I must feed them to keep them busy, I will. But you must not come out, do you understand jefa?"

The irony of her giving her boss orders was not lost on the women but in that moment, no one cared.

Guadalupe was mothering her, her protective nature and affection for her young employer threatening to spring forth from her eyes as tears. Lupe was petrified but could not allow herself to cry lest it invoke panic in the younger woman.

Amanda nodded her head in agreement and allowed her and the

kids to be led into the closet, laying down on blankets and pillows underneath all her hanging clothing, the cold of her sequined gowns caressing her face. Little Amelia said nothing but simply yawned and lied down, instantly shutting her eyes, while Agatha never stirred in her mother's arms.

It was Arthur, about to be six years old, who knew the gravity of what was going on. He just knew it was banditos, the kind that stole horses and women and robbed trains with handkerchiefs and pistolas. Though his face searched his mother's for clues, he decided it best not to try and interrogate her as he laid down next to his sister and stayed silent, his face stern, convinced he would not sleep. His father would deal with these fools, and if forced to, he would fight them off as well.

Chapter 35

Downstairs, Edward arrived home to see Joaquin come out of his office, looking glum. He was immediately followed by three men, all different heights and builds, but all dressed the same. The one was tall and broad as a buffalo, red-skinned and angry-looking; the next was a younger man, smaller but all muscle, and then there was the one in the middle, the shortest in stature but surely the most dangerous. They were all filthy, dirt packed under every fingernail, the aroma of sweat and manure wafting off them onto Ed. All of them stood with six-shooters strapped to their belts, one for each hip, wearing their greasy and dirty hats, with an air of confrontation as if Ed had interrupted them in his own house.

He only recognized one of them, the one they called "El Ciego", the blind one. They called him that because he had one grey, milky, unseeing eye in sharp contrast to the other functioning eye, which was black as oil. The appearance this deformity gave the man was that of a snake. He was horrible to look at, not that his companions were much prettier.

"What is this?",

Ed asked calmly yet confused.

"Hola Señor. We need to have a little chat, you and me."

El Ciego smiled, rotted, blue-black teeth amid the good ones.

"Come to your office Eddie", he said casually. He made it a point to address Ed in English, heavily accented but fluent.

"Offer us a drink. I have been looking at your collection of whiskeys there, waiting for you to get home, wanting to wet my whistle. I didn't want to just help myself, you know, manners."

El Ciego smiled mockingly, both men knowing he could have polished off every bottle in Ed's office, and there wasn't a damn thing Ed could do about it.

"Certainly, of course, welcome, mi case es su casa", Ed said rigidly.

"Oh……I know that", El Ciego and his men chuckled.

"I hope you haven't been waiting long", Ed started nervously.

His nerves made anger blaze inside him- he did not ever get nervous, yet here he was, practically timid in front of these heathens from the desert.

The men all accepted a glass of whiskey in the Waterford Crystal Amanda loved so. They drank his best stuff down like it was nothing.

"Amigo", El Ciego started.

"There is a lot of confusion these days in the streets of Mexico.

"Oh? How so?"

"Well, you know…men from all walks of life thinking they are military men, or thinking they are rebels, or as important as…..involving themselves in things…..gun running for Madero….

In the early days, getting supplies and arms from the U.S. into Mexico for Madero, then turning around and doing the exact same for our beloved Pancho and then, if you can believe los cojones, then turning around and doing the same for Huerta…..makes you wonder. What risks do some fools will take for money? Where does loyalty lie? Certainly, this person would not be so stupid to continue to just sell and sell and arm everyone in this war? Like for example, Carranza. But then you know, after what Presidente Taft and then Presidente Wilson did and what the U.S. ambassador did- oddly enough, he was also called Wilson- is everyone in los Estados Unidos called Wilson?"

He asked his men and they all guffawed, while Ed managed a weak smile.

"The thing is, the problem, the reason for our visit with you tonight is that after the betrayals of the two Wilsons, it is hard for my chief to trust or even like Americans. They always want to involve themselves in the business of others, and they always seem to double-cross you."

"All right,"

Edward nodded,

"Let's stop beating around the bush; what are you trying to say without saying?"

"I am saying Señor, that Pancho Villa does not like Americans. He has made that very clear. He also doesn't like coming up against people who don't have his – our -the rightful owners of Mexico- our best interests at heart."

He helped himself to another large portion of whiskey, filling the glass so that it spilled over the top and sat down to light his cigar that he gleefully took out of Edward's lovely and ornate cigar box. Sitting back in his chair, getting comfortable, he threw his feet up on Ed's desk and gave him a nice view of the bottom of his muck-covered shoes.

"You know, I heard that when they shot Suarez, his brains

covered Madero- they shot Suarez first and made el presidente watch. They say Madero got a little brain in his eyes….but he didn't get the chance to wipe it away."

They sat in silence for a moment, the companions one on each side of El Ciego, a young man no more than twenty, stone-faced and filthy, glaring, the other, the one the size of a beast, older like El Ciego, grinning from ear to weathered ear, his face like a saddle, his eyes sparkling with excitement of what was to come next.

"You should not have gotten involved Señor- Doctor Tappan Santiago……you are playing a game you will lose by running after anyone and everyone in this revolution who will pay you money and attention. You simply have no loyalty."

"I think- I think there has been a misunderstanding here", Ed began to stutter.

"Pancho Villa only respects loyalty. Pancho Villa demands it. What are we going to do with the good doctor? Or the bad doctor, so I hear?"

The men laughed at this quietly, threateningly.

"He wanted me to send a message – Pancho Villa- because your involvement with others has come to his attention. You have been disloyal, you see, to my jefe."

"Yo soy Mexicano. I am not American", Ed sputtered with a disgusted tone for his nation.

"Yes, we know, Doctor Tappan Santiago- one minute you are American, when it suits you, the famous American doctor, the next you are Mexican, again – no loyalty Señor. Even you, as a Mexican man, you lack loyalty, and yes, sadly, even some Mexicans are still getting in the way of things. You must remember Madero and

Suarez were Mexico's own son's tambien. More Mexican than you."

With that, El Ciego stood, and The Beast stood and pulled out something from inside his vest and handed it to El Ciego. El Ciego chuckled and put a brown envelope on Ed's desk.

"Open it."

Ed hesitated.

"Go on -it is a little gift from Pancho, a reminder."

El Ciego poured himself a third whiskey, draining the bottle while Ed took his letter opener and sliced across the top of the wax sealed envelope.

It felt light, with something but not paper inside. He shook out the contents and out came a large swath of red auburn hair that caught Ed's breath. He was convinced the hair was Amanda's and was about to ask, when a most delicate and white finger rolled out of the envelope, twice over his desk; it rolled as if propelled, stopping in front of him. He was stunned and dazzled to the point where he thought for a split moment, he was looking at a cigar. Upon further examination, it had blood on it…skin… and a fingernail. He shot up from his seat and backwards. This surgeon, who rooted around in blood every day, recoiled in horror.

Ed began to sweat, his stomach churning and making a noise like an injured animal.

"My God- who?"

fearing the worst that the hair and finger belonged to his wife, his hand went to his mouth to stifle a sob.

"Oh, you know her Señor- your wife's little – Spanish tutor? Graciela Mayer?

That is just one finger we took; we have the others- you know, in case people need reminders of their place in this revolution."

"The Spanish tutor? What did that young lady ever do to deserve?

"Nothing senor, except ……..be mistaken for your wife. Have you never noticed these most beautiful women bare the most striking resemblance to each other?" he chuckled.

"But, Pancho and I agreed it was better this way. This shows you that, yes, mistakes can be made by anyone. You made some big ones; now we may have made one as well. Lucky for you and your wife, we got it wrong this time, eh?"

Then men laughed as if at a poker night where bawdy jokes and the subject of women were the only things on the table, instead of the dismembered finger of a lovely and innocent young woman.

"But next time, maybe we don't get the wrong little white girl with the red hair coming out of this house. Maybe we get the right one after all. There is something to be said for second chances doctor. Wouldn't you agree?"

Ed sat, pale, horrified.

"So, she, Graciela- is dead?" They had her other fingers, El Ciego had said. Ed had to assume they killed her.

"Oh, doctor," he said slowly, "you do not want to know what she is at this moment."

"Doctor, it is time you got back to working on hearts and let us in charge worry about the guns, eh?"

El Ciego's companions stood, and El Ciego came around to Ed and clapped him on the back like they were the best of pals.

"My regards to your wife."

Joaquin saw them out the front door and locked it with the bolt.

Ed stared at the finger that once belonged to the sweet German Mexican girl who had nearly been Diego's wife, and then he vomited into his wastepaper basket.

Chapter 36

Amanda was often quiet, but she did not miss much in the way of the minutiae of what went on around her. It was a quality Ed loved about her. She seemed so innocent and simple, but she had a great mind that she exercised and pushed. Fooling her with his lies and manipulations over the years had an aphrodisiac effect on him. He could own her totally in every way, when her reality, everything she thought, was invented by him. He didn't just own her time as her husband or her body as her lover, but he owned every fragmented, tiny piece of her- he had assembled her the way one would put together one of those wooden jigsaw puzzles from the toy shop.

It had been so simple after they met. She had no parents to guide her, and she was adrift in the world, alone and young. Rich and beautiful. He had fallen in love with her, yes, but only in the way that Edward could love something other than himself. He had to own her. Everything she knew – or thought she knew – was from him. He had constructed her world the way he wanted it to be and, in doing so, made himself God-like and omnipotent. His children and his wife, his home, career, social standing, his life, would be perfect because he had orchestrated them so. What more power could a man wield than that? He would not allow anyone or anything to stand in his way and God help those that tried.

After the children had been returned to their beds for the night and Amanda and the staff told the horrible news of the demise of Graciela Mayer, Ed sat shaken in his office. He had Joaquin dispose of the girl's finger and hair.

His grip was slipping on his world. His wife suspected him, she was not so stupid she could not be fooled forever.

He could hear the women of the house sobbing down the hall. It reverberated through like the moans of ghosts, wailing they called it. The women were wailing. Amanda came into his office, her face destroyed and puffy from the tears for the young woman.

“I want to know.”, she began timidly.

“You don’t.”, Ed shook his head.

“They are monsters, all of them, not men. We must keep our heads now, stay inside, and keep to ourselves. I will fix those bastards.”

“I am not talking about that Ed. I know what is going on now. I didn’t for months, but I had ideas and imagined things- you said I was imagining things, but I turned out to be right. I do not want to ever discuss Graciela again; may God have mercy on her poor soul. I can’t imagine how we will tell Diego. However, right now, I have another woman to ask you about. Edward, who is Magdalena?”

The pause was so large she thought he had not heard her and so she began to form the words again, but he stopped her with a hand.

“Just a girl. She is no one of consequence.”

“You knew her then, did you?”

“What do you want woman? Say it.”

“You married a woman in secret? Almost twenty years ago, a decade before you met me? How is this possible? That you have a wife here in Mexico?”

“You are my wife, here in Mexico and everywhere.”

"Not for long", Amanda laughed, daring him.

"I beg your pardon, wife?", his voice taking on a dangerous edge.

"Are…our children bastards? Are they illegitimate Edward? Is our marriage at all valid? In the eyes of government, in the eyes of God?"

Edward was exhausted from the fright he had received from the unexpected visit of El Ciego. He was not able to comprehend how things were now falling apart around him. Now, the wife is asking questions about something she should have never known.

"She was a girl that said I was the father of her son. I was not, but she knew she could make trouble for my father, who was ill at the time. I snuck down from Harvard one week after everyone thought I was gone for the year. I married her to quiet her. It was not real; it did not mean anything. I gave her money and the satisfaction of a piece of paper and went on my way back to Boston. I promised her I would return at Christmas, but I knew I was only kicking the can down the road, as they say. I was going to need to do something-speak to my father, speak to her, explain how we could not remain married. However, not long afterwards, my father passed away, and so too did Magdalena and her son. There was a fire. That is all I know."

"How can I know anything you tell me is the truth anymore Edward? Why not tell me the tragic story of your first wife and son?"

"Because he was not my son, nor was she meant to be my wife."

"Did you consummate the marriage, Edward? Did she know she wasn't really supposed to be your wife?"

"Amanda- go to bed.", he said not unkindly but more out of exasperation.

“Not everything in this life is my fault, you know. As far as this woman was concerned, the problem took care of itself.”

Amanda stood up and back, feeling as though she had been slapped. She looked down in disgust at her once handsome husband, who had the bad taste to utter such horrible words. A woman and child who claimed a connection to him had died, and he had never cared.

“You look like a creature worth pitying if it was not so venomous. I am fairly certain there is something in you that is not human but perhaps even demonic.”, she glared.

She would leave. Diego would get her and the children out of this place.

“Señora?” Guadalupe interrupted.

“Desculpe- but that Constable is back to see you, Señora Tappan.”

“To see me?”, Amanda was indignant.

“I telephoned them. I had to – to inform them about the break-in.”, Edward said as casually as if mentioning the weather.

Amanda started out to the hall but saw Ed did not get up from his desk, where he sat like a dejected schoolboy.

“Aren’t you coming?”

“No”, he shook his head,

"Just you. They just want to speak to you."

The heavy-set man came alone this time, no young boy of a police officer beside him. Amanda found herself in the foyer with this man. She did not ask him into the parlour as she was fed up with his impromptu visits.

He began talking to her with a big smile, his dark eyes glimmering. She was not listening; instead, she felt the heat of eyes on her back coming from the direction of Ed's office.

The constable continued, ".... and we don't want you to be in fear, but also to make sure you do not go anywhere."

Amanda digested this bit of information. Why was he telling her not to go?

"Go? Where would I go? I've been very ill, and my children... and with a new baby and my Spanish is not the best. I don't think I will be going to Cancun for a vacation."

"No, no of course, not; the streets are not safe at the moment with all the fighting going on. Best for everyone to stay put in their homes for the time being. We are investigating the disappearance of your tutor as well, so we need to make sure you are safe."

He turned on his heel as if he were ready to leave, but as an aside, added,

"And we know you would never want to take your children away from their father; that would be positively criminal. A woman of any standing in society who attempted such a thing would find herself in the bowels of a Mexican prison."

He then chuckled as if what he had just threatened her with was a totally normal, pleasant conversation among old pals.

Amanda felt ice slide up her spine as if a knife were about to be embedded in it. She could not see him out fast enough and willed Guadalupe to shut the door and lock it tight after he crossed the threshold.

"Señora?" Lupe, asked "You look as if you seen una fantasma – a ghost."

"No, not a ghost, but a monster. How dare he threaten me when hoards of men are doing God only knows in this city? Why doesn't he arrest – or threaten the ones burning down the houses of the innocent?"

Lupe shook her head and made the sign of the cross.

Amanda's eyes lifted to Edward's office door. He stood in the frame, expressionless.

The constable did not even ask to speak to Edward about the men who had been in their home, making threats and leaving pieces of the innocent behind. Amanda knew why the police had come that night, and it had nothing to do with protecting her or the children.

Chapter 37

The train to Vera Cruz was due in ten minutes. Raquel, stood vigilant, her hair in a tight bun, under her hat with black lace in the front, covering her scrubbed clean face, her cheek still stinging like hell as she peered up and down the almost empty platform.

Her teenage son Jaime stood with his two suitcases and ticket in hand, unsure of what to make of all of this.

“When will you join me again, mother, next week?

“As soon as I can mi amor.”

She took his large, warm hands into her tiny cold ones,

“Just remember until you get to the U.S., in fact until you get to California, your name is Andres Benevides Leon, ok? Ok?”

She pulled his sleeve to get him to answer her when he simply stared at her, confused.

“If they find me, mother, they find me; a fake name won’t change anything.

“You will use it and keep your head down and keep the spectacles on your face the whole time. I will send a telegram in the morning to my aunt. When you get to my aunt in San Francisco then you can be you, but in the meantime, do not ignore any of my instructions. Do you understand me?”

He had not been there. He had not seen how that man was acting, knocking her belongings over casually, breaking things just to break them, not in a rage, but calmly, making it all look accidental.

The things he threatened her with, for her and her boy, that it all would appear to the police as accidental.

"Señora", the man with horrible eye had said to her after knocking her vase to the floor in an almost friendly manner,

"They burn this house to the ground, with you and your boy in it, but first, certain things will be done to your son, that you would be made to watch....and then maybe these same bad men rape you while making your son watch....before the act of mercy – and it would be an act of mercy by the end of it."

"What do you want from me?"

Raquel had asked quietly, as this man had been waiting for her in her bedroom when she walked in. He came alone this time, but Raquel knew through rumour that he always had compañeros, two of them with him at all times. She had kept looking around her bedroom for them to jump out and grab her, inching closer and closer to putting the wall at her back for a bit of comfort.

"I am only a widow who sells fur coats."

"Ah, but you see, your partner ..in crime...business... whatever the two of you get up to behind his wife's back...he has made some enemies of the rebellion....of Pancho Villa. And since you are so closely connected, like family, you too are now an enemy, you see."

"But I am not American – yo soy Mexicana, my son is –"

"Shut your mouth and listen to me. Pancho – he is a hero of the people of Mexico- the first, original people who own this land by heritage and blood. We are the rightful kings of Mexico, not you Europeans, with your sickly-looking white skin and your blue veins showing through like plucked chickens about to be beheaded for dinner. What sort of people cannot even take the life-giving rays of the sun without being cooked, like chickens? Hmm? Weak people. You are weak, Señora, but oh so beautiful. Maybe you and I can come to an arrangement so that I can watch over you and keep you safe since you have kept such troubling company?"

He smiled, moving towards her slowly, like a cat approaching a mouse frozen with fear, hiding in the corner.

His voice lowered into a husky whisper full of the lust of men Raquel had known all her life.

"Because, believe it or not, I would not want anything bad to happen to you, preciosa."

"Thank you Señor,"

She said standing up straighter, and tightening her shawl around her as if it offered protection,

"But if you tell me the problem is the company I keep with the Doctor Tappan, then I shall no longer keep his company- simple. And I will do whatever I can to help Pancho Villa and his men to right the wrongs of Mexico- the Mexico that I too love and courses through my ugly blue veins- but I have no need for any extra security at the moment."

"You say this to the man who easily snuck into your bedroom under the noses of the fools you have at your front gate?"

"I will reprimand my workers, but I do not need any more and I thank you for this warning of what could happen if we were to anger Pancho Villa- I will be especially careful who I do business with in the future."

The man with the eye smiled.

"Yes, that will do it. This was your one and only warning, but before I go…"

He slowly lit a cigarette and threw the match onto her floor carelessly.

She looked down at where it met the floor, afraid it would ignite the thick rug in seconds. When she looked up, he was inching still closer, forcing her back against the wall.

"I think you should know Señora….",

He said, slowly dragging on the cigarette, "that you are not as smart as you think you are….or as pretty."

He spat and brought the cherry of the cigarette to her face and stamped it into her cheek in one smooth movement. It felt as if he had hit her with the force of a closed fist. She stood there taking the burn, refusing to scream, refusing to give him that, even though it was her eyes and the fear in them that gave him what he was after.

He laughed as he dropped the smoke and sauntered out of the room as if he had not just scarred her face.

Raquel knew better than to touch it and went running for the basin to wash her face in cold water.

After washing the small circular burn in soap made of honey, she applied aloe vera to it, knowing full well it would never truly heal completely. It was a deep burn, and her face throbbed from the pain as she sat crying on the edge of her bed.

She had known what Ed was up to because she had known Ed. She had lied to herself and warned him when he started to leave a trail, but she never put a stop to it. Now, her Jaime was in danger. Now, there were men breaking into her home and making threats.

Burning her. It was more than a warning; it was a taste of things to come.

Half an hour later, when Jaime returned home from his card game, smelling of drink, she was so relieved it wasn't a body being placed in front of her by those men of Pancho Villas that she grabbed him in the tightest hug and began to weep. Jaime was totally confused.

"Are you- mother – what is wrong- what has happened to your face?"

Jaime rarely saw his mother without a palette's worth of face paint, and she had a blood-red mark on her upper cheek that looked like a burn from a poker.

"Don't ask questions, just pack your bags."

The ensuing inquisition turned near argument from her son went on as she changed into all black and covered her face and hair. She could not take the chance of them being recognized if they were seen out in the street.

"I've told you all your life, I didn't want you getting involved in the military of this – or any country. I did not have you to offer you up as cannon fodder for bastards. Now, the war has come to our door, which means we will be leaving. You are going to my family in San Francisco, and I will follow you in a few days. I must stay to clear some accounts and wrap up the business in such a way that it doesn't look to anyone like we are going anywhere. So – I don't know how much you had to drink tonight, but you better sober the hell up right now. We must take you to the last train tonight. You cannot stay here. They threatened to kill us and-", she withheld the threat of her rape with her son forced to watch-

"Burn the house to the ground with us in it."

Her son had listened, and now they waited for the train, Raquel constantly checking behind them, on the lookout. She started to breathe when she saw the train in the distance, and as it slowed in front of them, her heart started to slow.

"How long will we be in California?"

"I don't know Jaime, does it really matter if it's six weeks or six months or six years- just let's get away from the revolution for a while before this scum comes back, which could be in ten minutes or tomorrow morning.

"Si mama",

Jaime had never seen his mother like this, trembling, in a place somewhere between abject fear and blinding rage. She expected he would put up more of a fight and insist on staying to defend their home or Mexico, but he was that drunk he was more compliant.

"But I don't want to leave you behind tonight; why can't I stay, and we go together? What kind of son- what kind of man leaves his mother behind?" he asked quietly.

"You are the target mijo; that is the way they want to get to me, not by killing me- they will go after you first, so you must disappear- I can take care of myself. My God, I'm Russian. These Mexican bandeleros think they can't be outsmarted but they can. Those simple, slack jawed, donkey fuckers. And we are going to be the ones to outsmart them."

Jaime had never heard his mother use vulgar language, and it was that one detail that sent actual fear through him to the point that he realized just how precarious a situation they now found themselves in.

He promised his mother he would follow her demands, hugged her tightly one last time and got on the train solemn and still confused, now California bound.

Chapter 38

"Diego, what does all of this mean, I'm not understanding any of it?"

Diego put the letter down, "When does Edward return from Merida?"

Diego and Amanda were in Ed's office, a place no one was ever allowed in if Ed was absent, not even the maids for cleaning.

"His telegraphed arrived yesterday, saying he would be in the day after tomorrow. That we should expect him Friday evening."

Ed had disappeared again, this time in the middle of the night. While happy to see him gone, Amanda also worried he would never return, abandoning her and the children.

"He has not telephoned you while on this trip, correct?"

"No. I wasn't sure that thing even worked. Ed said the telephone lines are dreadful and not reliable like in New York. I'm not used to it anyway. I only used one in New York a few times. I suppose unless it is to telephone the police in an emergency or perhaps the fire brigade, I have no use for it. Why?

"Because he is right- as it stands, the telephone lines in Mexico only work in the city- I can use the telephone at the hospital and make a call to this house or anywhere in Mexico City that has a telephone – but only in the same city. I cannot, for example, connect to someone in Acapulco or Merida or Veracruz, or any other city. The lines are only viable within the cities. Our infrastructure is far behind the United States, and that Bell has got a monopoly on the telephone service up there. We have nothing to so organized here –

yet. So that means if he were to call you on this telephone, it would mean he was not, in fact, anywhere else other than still in this same city.

He would presume you don't know this, of course.

I wanted to know how you heard from him- he is clever – of course, he would send a telegram- do you still have it- I want to see it?"

Amanda shook her head, confused, "I don't think so, Guadalupe might have already thrown it out; why is that so important Diego? You're – well, you're frightening me just a bit.

"Did you see the telegram with your own eyes- or were you told?"

"No Diego, I saw it, I read it, it was addressed to me. The staff would never keep my correspondence from me.

"Just like they would never hide the newspapers or follow orders not to discuss the revolution in front of you?

"Diego- I understand why Ed did that. He was trying to protect me, and the staff knew I was in a delicate condition..."

"When has ignorance ever saved anyone? When has being kept in the dark ever been a kindness? To keep secrets is the same as telling lies. Lies are an infection left untreated- they will fester and always become poisonous."

Amanda realised she had no retort for that. Diego was correct, once again.

"My head is spinning- I don't even feel like I know the man I married at all."

"Amanda, I want you to pack a small case for you and the children and hide it away, ready to go at a moment's notice. Can you do that?

"Yes, I- I could hide it in the kitchen cellar; he never looks or goes in there. But why would I do that? Am I going to take my children away? It's come to that?"

"No one knows what Edward is doing, where he has gone, or what kind of danger he has put you in. His abrupt disappearance does not make me feel confident that everything is smoothed over, especially after what happened the other night with the bandits coming to the house."

No one had mentioned Graciela or her finger to Diego. No one had been able to say it. Amanda didn't even know if Diego knew.

"Amanda- I need to explain something to you. With the way the revolution is growing ever more violent, I am in fear and have been for a while, for you and the children.

"I know."

"So, Edward did tell you I had spoken with him?"

"No, Diego- he never mentioned it. I heard you talking in his office the last time you were here. I heard every word."

Diego looked around Ed's office, at the spines of the medical texts, as if he was interested in what they said and not just trying to avoid her eyes.

"The day of your wedding, I was miserable and came very close to doing the unthinkable- stopping it. I was going to pull you aside and beg you not to marry him. I even had my chance. Thirty seconds where you were by yourself, just as you were coming in the side entrance of the church. You didn't see me, I reached out to touch your elbow, but I hesitated unsure. You went inside, and it was time….I was afraid you would be angry instead of impressed by my declaration of love. I feared…if you rejected me, I would have thrown away my friendship with Ed and lost you as well, maybe even – well, surely would have angered the both of you. So, you see, my plan only worked if you said yes, you wanted to be with me. I took an educated guess and looked at the information before me-that, ultimately you had already said yes to my best pal, and we were at your wedding. It was too late. I could not bare the thought of causing you any distress precisely because I loved you. So, I stood there in that church, dying inside. I stood there smiling but resentful and jealous and full of guilt for feeling all of these things. I felt I never got a chance. I mean, after all, Ed had already started courting you. It was he who introduced us; I would have been a snake in the grass, a total cad if I had gone through with it, my attempt to steal you away. I thought it, in the end, would not be gentlemanly behaviour, and I wanted to respect you. I thought I would regret it, but in reality, I know now that I would not have regretted it, even if it meant losing Ed. Hell, even if you said no and I lost you too… I would have at least known and could put the fire out. Instead of watching you all these years, watching how he treated you as you gave him a family. I have always loved you and wanted your happiness, even if it wasn't with me. Imagine my dismay to see you then unhappy with him."

Amanda was stunned into silence at Diego admitting what she secretly knew in her heart. All these years, the unease she could never name was that they both felt she had ended up with the wrong man.

"I went to him with my concerns regarding your safety and this revolution, and he dismissed them. And this latest affront- you are not legally wed Amanda. You can go whenever and wherever you like, and if you want me to get you back to the U.S. with your children, I swear on my life. I will. I should have stepped in on your wedding day when I knew this was all wrong. It is all wrong again, and now your life is in danger, and I will step in now and do what's right."

Amanda stood up, moved across the room as if she was flying and ended up in Diego's arms, the warmth of her tears mixing with the warmth of his lips and face and breath in a kiss that confirmed for both of them what they had always feared. Neither of them knew where Ed was at that moment. He could have walked in to find them embraced. It no longer mattered. Amanda was done; her marriage, her entrapment, was finally over.

Chapter 39

He watched her every movement but was not processing the words she was saying. She was nervous and pacing. She was smoking cigarettes, an unusual sight for her. She was having one after the other as if she was pulling some unseen power from them with every inhalation of their tobacco magic. She stopped abruptly in front of the fire. Was she done speaking? He watched her beautiful face with dried tears on her childlike, fat little cheeks. She was very animated. He watched her put the cigarette to her lovely rosebud mouth with shaking, milky hands. He watched her flick the cigarette ash casually as if they were having a normal conversation. He watched as the ash floated into the blazing, open fire, hesitating in the air as if it was deciding whether to jump before finally accepting its fate and falling into its fiery obliteration. What had she done? And what would he be forced to do to her?

"Edward?" she trembled.

Amanda could hardly believe she was still standing upright. The news of Graciela's fate had rocked the house and everyone who had known her. Diego's declaration of love had imbued her with bravery, and Ed's return once again left her cold. She knew she had to leave and needed to knock some sense into Ed.

Now, on this night, hours after Ed returned without an explanation of where he had gone, the bandeleros of Pancho Villa's army were not content with simply threatening the wealthy elite of this fine neighbourhood. They were now inside of it in an overt way. Gone were their sneaky tactics of paying visits to different households; now, they wanted to let everyone know they had arrived for the start of a reckoning. A house a few roads down was engulfed in flames.

Amanda's mouth and throat were dry, her eyes destroyed from hours of tears. Her eyes were angry and gritty and burned like the fire she stood in front of, shaking. She was absolutely freezing, unable to get warm. Every few moments, a gun would go off in the distance, and a rifle would split the night. She had tried to call the police after Lupe came shrieking up to the house with news of a murder on the end of the road. The telephone made no sound or connection.

The thugs were angry and had brought bombs. Amanda overheard Marta telling Lupe they were going after the motorcars. Anyone who had one would have it destroyed. Lupe was more concerned with finding out who had been killed.

"Edward, did you hear a word of what I just said to you?"

she garbled out, her voice thick with upset.

"I heard you....say...that you are taking my children."

"The guns...those awful men...they shot her Ed. The talk on the street is that they took Graciela's face off. We can't stay here. I arranged for us to take the train to Veracruz tomorrow- "

"You are not taking my children."

"We can all go together as a family, Ed. Or just myself and the kids for now- but we have to get out. It's not safe- Lupe said one of our neighbours has been killed-

"Perhaps I was not clear- you my wife, are not going anywhere. And if you were to decide to sneak off, you are certainly not taking the children anywhere. So, it might be best for you to change your mind and just go stay in your room and wait for all of this to be over."

She stood looking at him silently, in shock. How could anyone elect to remain as the very streets were beginning to burn? Her fists clenched, her nostrils flared in furious defiance, eyes felt about to burst out of her head with loathing. She ripped the cigarette from her mouth and, threw it into the fire, and turned on her heel out of his office,

"We are going!" she shouted over her shoulder.

Ed was still for a moment, confused at what he had just heard. The nerve of this fool, this woman. She was not going to ruin everything he had put into motion.

She made it to the top of the stairs almost instantaneously, and Ed had to run to catch her and catch her he did by the back of the hair. He pulled her maliciously towards him, back towards the top of the stairs. He twisted her hair and arm with so much torque she felt a large tear on her scalp, and her arm bent backwards at an alarming angle as he shoved her forward in such a way, she felt sure he was sending her down the stairs.

"Be careful; these stairs are dangerous." She had heard in a dream.

"I said," he hissed into her ear,

"That you go nowhere- and my children will go nowhere- over my dead body or, if you prefer, over yours."

He shook her like a rag doll dangling at the top of the stairs like a child taunting someone with a toy they were preparing to release to see how long it took for it to hit the marble floor below.

"Edward!" she cried, about to pass out from pain and shock.

Raquel arrived and was just at the front door and took in the scene in horror.

"Eduardo- stop! Basta!!Basta!"

Raquel soared to the top of the stairs where Ed now had Amanda on her knees, but still with fistfuls of hair and shoulder, a crazed look on his face.

"Eddie- my old amigo- let her go, darling; we are not going to hurt anyone tonight- let go of her." Raquel pleaded on her knees next to them.

Her voice was soothing at first, and then, as he ignored her to shake his wife again, she exploded,

"Let go of her!" Raquel shouted.

"I won't be told by another bloody woman what to do!"

He shoved his wife to the floor to wrap his hands around Raquel's throat, but she ripped her hair pin out of her chignon and, quick as a crow peck, stabbed him in both hands and even landed a hit in his cheek.

He let go and shrieked like a bird in pain.

"You- you drew blood!"

He said in disbelief.

Raquel helped Amanda to her feet and back into his office, "Just lie down kid, ok?"

She placed her on the sofa while Amanda was trying to steady her breathing after sobbing hysterically.

"We are going to talk like adults here, and everyone calm down."

Raquel told Ed as he followed them into his office, bleeding on the carpet. He was in such shock he had calmed considerably.

"I should just kill you both now", he glared.

"Well, Eddie, you won't do that because Diego is right behind me, and what do you think he will do to you when he finds us, eh? So, stop this carry on and start talking. It's time for you to tell her the truth- and me as well since you're hiding so much from your business partner. How many of my cases of coats have guns hidden in them because of you!" She spat.

"I had a visit, just like you did, a visit from THEM. You got us all into this. I barely got Jaime out of town. They threatened us both."

Instead of talking, Ed poured himself a scotch and stalked out of the room, a handkerchief against his face. He had another pistol in his bedroom that he was sure would knock sense into their heads.

Amanda held her face in her hands, out of embarrassment or comfort; she was not sure. She was appalled by Ed's actions, frightened of what she always knew he was capable of. Tears and mucus poured out of her, there were tears in her hair and behind her ears, and she was horrified Raquel was seeing her like this.

"Why?" she implored her friend.

"Why would he do this to me? To us- all I ever wanted was a

family. I never asked for any of this. I just wanted- I wanted children and not to be alone; I wanted my family. I was always so alone. Why did he bring us here?"

She was gasping for breath now.

Raquel tried to calm her down by rubbing her back and hushing her the way a mother calms a raging infant.

There was shouting coming from the foyer; then a loud thud, and suddenly, Diego appeared in the doorway.

"Amanda- "

"Where is he Diego?"

Raquel looked at the door with concern. Although she did not fear Edward, she had never seen him this furious, and she needed to calm everything down before dealing with him.

"Old Eddie is going to take a little siesta – I punched him out, totally, lights out. We might not have much time to figure out what is going on.

Raquel grabbed Amanda's face in her hands,

"I need you to take slow breaths. I need you to hear me. There is not much time. I have called in some favours from some friends. There is an old carriage going to be here in ten minutes to take you – and only you on the train and out of Mexico.

Amanda pulled her friends hands off her face and moved back.

"What- why only me?

"We fear you will be singled out before you get on the train if it is you and three children. That is also why we didn't send for a motorcar; they're stopping all the motorcars. There are packs of them all over the city. It's not just Americans; apparently a Frech ambassador and his wife have been shot by the Cathedral. Look, this way, we get you out and back into the United States; we tell Ed they took you. Then, in a few days, Diego and I will leave with your children. We think it is the only way Amanda that we will not all be killed. Ed got us all into some very big trouble.

"The days he said he was on a business trip to Merida? He was in jail, Amanda."

"How can that be- Edward in prison- a doctor – in prison?"

"I can't do this," she whispered.

"You must, because even if Ed doesn't understand what is going on here or what is at stake, those men they will be back in a week or in a year, but they will be back before this war is over. I have sent Jaime away; I am selling everything I have here through my lawyer- the house, the business, everything. We all must abandon Mexico for now. You don't have much time; the last train tonight leaves in less than half an hour, and when Ed wakes up, we will all have a huge problem on our hands. I thought he was going to send you flying down those stairs. Amanda, I have known him for a very long time, and I don't know who he is anymore. I think he is every bit as capable as Pancho Villa's men to kill you in a fit of rage.

"You wanted to get out of Mexico, this is the way to do it, that keeps you and your children safe. Put your hair up and tuck it under your hat; you need not to call attention to yourself. Wear a scarf.

"No, there has to be another way to do this." Amanda shook her head.

She stood and went to Ed's desk, where a sharp and very large pair of scissors sat.

"What are you doing?" Diego gasped.

She twisted her long hair into one long thick section of red silk and began cutting at just below her ear. With five snips across, she had the whole of hair in her hand. Diego and Raquel watched in silence.

"Maybe if he thinks I am dead, it will buy me some time, and he will drink himself into a stupor, allowing you to get the children out….. …I can't leave the baby. She needs her mother; she is not even a year old; I have to feed her."

"We can find a wet nurse…"

"No. No, I must take one of them with me, so that I don't lose them all. Arthur and Amelia will remember me; if it takes a long time to get them back, what if it takes a long time? The baby won't know me. Babies are vulnerable; I can't leave her."

Guadalupe had entered the room and stood in the corner, tears on her cheeks.

"Señora, take the baby. I will mind your children as if they were my own, until they can get them to you. Take the baby; it is the right thing to do. Follow your instinct as a mother. Marta and Amparo will take you to the train and take them to the United States with you. Let them carry the baby, and you keep your hat pulled down and a big overcoat over you. Clean your face, put spectacles on and try to speak only in Spanish."

Marta piped up, "I will grab a suitcase Señora and put diapers and clothing."

Amparo, who rarely spoke up unless she was addressed,

“Senora I will get baby.

“Here”, Diego handed Amanda a stack of cash.

“Where will you go?”

“I will arrive in New York and stay in a hotel and then go to Philadelphia to see an old friend and get the last of my inheritance. From there, I do not know. I suppose- New York.

“You will send me a telegram with the address of where you end up; if I have already left Mexico City, you will need my aunt’s address in San Francisco”,

Raquel scribbled an address and phone number on a piece of paper.

“You will need to let me, or Diego know as soon as possible where you are so we can get the children to you.”

Amanda felt as if she could faint. She hugged her beautiful friend.

“Thank you”,

She whispered to Raquel.

Raquel, who never cried, had tears cascading down her face and could not manage another word.

Diego took Amanda into his arms,

“I told you at Christmas I would protect you and your children. This is not the way I wanted this to happen, but Ed’s temper has left us no other choice and we are all running out of time. Please trust me; I will see this through. Vaya con Dios, mi amor.”

He kissed her forehead gently, almost an apology, born out of the purest love and affection a man ever had for a woman.

“Señora?”, Lupe called from the door. Amanda was called away, and in her brief distraction, Raquel whispered to Diego,

“What do we do about Edward? Would it not be easier to kill him than to try and reason with him?”

“Jesus Christ Raquel, there will be no more bloodshed. I took an oath to do no harm-

Raquel shrugged,

“It’s just a question.”

Amanda stood with Lupe, Amparo and Marta, who held the baby in the doorway and looked back at her only two friends in the world.

“I have to say goodbye to my children.”

“They’re sleeping Señora”, Lupe told her.

Amanda was nearing hysteria.

“I know, I know.”

Chapter 40

The bottom of the carriage was cold and metallic. A motorcar would have been way too conspicuous. The thin blanket thrown over Amanda only hid her from view but did not offer much in the way of insulation from the chill in the air. The horse-drawn mode of transport was so slow compared to their usual Model T, Amanda felt they would surely miss the train and have to go back. Her breath caught as she thought of her children back in her bed. She should have woken them; she should have told them, tried to explain, but there was no time. What sort of a mother doesn't say goodbye? She had not even touched them because she knew if she did her resolve would disappear and she would not be able to let go of them, but she also would get them all killed.

She shook her head to push out the anguish she felt. In a matter of days, her children would be back with her in the safety of New York. Lupe had said they could hide the children, as they had done that night, in the closet, but she had agreed Amanda had to take the baby with her- babies made noise at the most inopportune times. They had no way to hide the baby if the men returned as she would surely cry or coo or sigh and give away their hiding spot. Lupe had agreed Amanda leaving with the baby was the safest and wisest choice. Everyone knew Ed would not harm a hair on his children's heads; his sense of importance was far too wrapped up in his gorgeous offspring. No one in the household seemed to care if anything happened to Ed. Raquel and Diego knew, and Lupe suspected that the bandeleros wouldn't touch Ed, not until they were done getting what they wanted from him.

The carriage ride was bumpy, and Amanda thought her hiding unnecessary, but was reminded by Diego and Raquel that if the carriage stopped for any length of time and was opened by whomever, bandits or not, she would be exposed, so best to keep her on the floorboard tucked under the seat, until it was time to board the train. Marta sat on one side with a mercifully sleeping baby in her arms, Amparo sat across from her, the suitcase on her lap.

The instructions had been clear. Get her and the baby on the train at all costs. Do not attract attention. Do not speak English.

Amparo took the baby and her unsteady mistress by the arm to board the train. Marta walked slowly behind them on purpose, her instructions from Guadalupe and la Señora Vanin Goya clear. Get them on the train. Do not let them be stopped or questioned; make sure they have their tickets and watch them pull out of the station. Marta surreptitiously moved her head around the nighttime platform, taking in the scene. Her eyes moved over everything as if she had been taught how to watch for and evade wild, dangerous animals. Then her heart fell as she saw a man who looked sickeningly familiar approaching the cluster of women. She recognized him as one of the men who had entered the house. Amanda's back was turned to him, but he was focused on Amparo, as if he knew her.

Marta took two steps to the right, and in between her companions and the man walking towards them, she quickly looked down and jammed her middle finger down her throat and lifted her head just in time mid walk to vomit all down the front of the man's already muck covered boots.

The shock of this event stopped him dead. He barely moved or reacted, but the confusion held him, staring down at his feet while Marta muttered apologies and continued to sputter and spew on the ground before him. Amparo saw this and moved Amanda onto the train without a word.

"Desculpe Señor!", Marta offered, horrified,

"I must; I must be very sick; I am so sorry- let me clean your boots? I am such a disgrace Señor, I am so embarrassed!" she stammered, not turning around to see if the women were gone but just praying that this little diversion would buy them the cover they needed to walk onto the train as if they had not a care in the world.

The man, annoyed, but so caught off guard by this beautiful young woman vomiting on his feet that he was quite speechless, forgot what he had been told to look out for. The girl was busy pulling a long handkerchief from her small satchel, stammering, upset and offering to clean his boots.

"Señorita, there is no need- fue un accidente", he assured her. "My boots were already covered in horse manure," he laughed. He was not angry, but instead curious. He wanted to know this girl's name. What a strange encounter.

"Marta, Señor.", she told him as she batted her eyelashes at him and then watched the train pull away towards Vera Cruz, with the India, the American, and the baby safely on board.

Chapter 41

They walked out of the hotel into the bright morning sunshine of a New York that looked welcoming despite their circumstances. Amparo held the baby while Amanda held their one suitcase and adjusted her hat, trying not to panic, looking right and then left up the street, trying to decide where exactly they could go with $3 dollars in her purse. She had not anticipated losing money on arrival to New York, if that is even what happened, or if she had been pickpocketed. She was too upset to know. She needed to telephone Julia, as the telephone was certainly faster than sending a telegram, but she wasn't even sure if Julia had procured a telephone device. Their hotel didn't have one.

"Señora,"

Amparo began with a nervous biting of her lip,

"The baby….she need be change".

"Yes, of course."

Amanda remembered the public library. The head librarian would surely remember her, and they could sneak into the ladies public toilet, and change the baby in there, she supposed. Put the suitcase on the floor and lay the baby on top.

"Yes, Amparo, follow me.",

she said with a bravado she did not recognize.

And just as she turned right out of the doorway of the hotel and took off with some speed, she nearly flattened herself by careening into a tall and statuesque young woman who was herself hurriedly storming up the path.

Amanda was nearly knocked backwards and lost her footing, but her assailant grabbed her arm to steady her. As miracles would have it, Amanda found herself staring into the most beautiful face of skin like snow, eyes of the bluest sky with the most perfect, strawberry lips and darling nose. The lovely face of Orla Keogh, her nanny from Roscommon, Ireland, stared back at her, and that stunning face broke into the biggest smile Amanda had seen in a long time.

"My eyes deceive me? Mrs. Tappan, is that really you?"

She looked quickly from her to Amparo standing behind her holding the baby. She looked for the others and then back to her beloved former employer's face, which was the same despite her cropped hair.

Amanda was quite shocked,

"Orla?"

The young girl she had left behind was no more. In less than two years, she had gone from lass to refined lady.

Orla surmised the situation, seeing Mrs. Tappan was not looking herself and quickly insisted the women follow her up the block to her apartment, which happened to be the tiny lower studios of the Hammersmith Tower.

"You wouldn't believe it Mrs. Tappan- I'm a married lady now and living in your old building! In the cheap apartments on the first floor, of course, but I see that Mrs. Heatherington lady and her daughter all the time and we always ask the other one about you and… and Doctor Tappan.

She quickly ushered the women inside,

"Please make yourself comfortable. I will put on some tea.

She led Amparo to the bedroom for her to change the baby and she returned to the whistling of the kettle and the pained expression on Amanda's face.

"Mrs. Tappan, what are you doing here in New York?" Orla started carefully,

"Are you on a holiday?",

Orla knew something was dreadfully wrong even as she tried to fill the space between them with small talk. She did not want to pry, but the appearance of Mrs. Tappan looking flustered surely had to be investigated. Where were the children? Where was the Dr?

The kettle started to scream. It sounded like the train in Vera Cruz, pulling her away from her children.

Amanda burst into tears.

Orla managed to quiet both the kettle and her guest at the same time, giving her handkerchief without a word. She knew that Mrs. Tappan would say what the problem was as soon as she could quell her sobs.

In a torrent of words, unaware she could speak that fast, Amanda told her everything. She tripped over a few words and hiccupped her way through the telling, all while Orla remained silent, disbelief etched onto her lovely face.

Amanda's secrets spilt out of her as if from a broken bag of grain, the seed covering the floor.....the revolution Ed had hidden from her, or tried to, the threats from police, Ed disappearing.

The realization that he had been jailed was followed by the

discovery of his first wife. Amanda paused, in horrified embarrassment, to catch her breath as she continued to catalogue the offences.... the men that came to the house, the men who had killed Graciela because she bore a striking resemblance to her. Ed's refusal to let her leave, then his refusal to let her take the children, and then her and Amparo stealing away in the night with the baby, gunshots ringing out, the unforgettable smell of gunpowder in the air.

"Ed..... His lies, his deceit, his machinations, all of it, for more money and control. He wanted control of our children, me."

Oral shook her head.

"I can't understand how he could take you down there to a war."

"He involved us in the war, put us at risk and then threatened – he nearly pushed me down the stairs; I thought he was going to kill me."

Her lips trembled at the forming of the words.

"He was involved with something, with guns, and perhaps, I don't know, he made some dangerous deals with very bad men. I only left the children because Guadalupe promised me, she would protect them, and I had to go- the carriage that was sneaking me out was on the side of the house. We could not all go at once, or we would arouse suspicion, draw too much attention to ourselves."

Even as she said the truth, it sounded ugly and hollow in her ears, like a strange echo of desperation.

She couldn't bring herself to say it. She could not form the words. She had left her children behind like a coward, a disgrace.

"But Orla, you see, I couldn't get us all out at once. They were looking for us. We would have been seen, whereas I had Amparo wrap the baby up and hide her where no one would see her. She got on the train separately from me. I was in disguise."

"Your hair?"

Orla asked quietly, sad to see Amanda's long red auburn locks had been butchered. Tufts stuck out unevenly from beneath her grey hat.

"Yes, I cut it before I left the house. Left it on Edward's desk. He always loved my hair. I thought it fitting. By the time he found it, we would have been long gone. I had hoped he would assume the worst, or I'd be back in the U.S. before he would have thought to tell the police to look for me with a man's haircut."

Orla felt a sickness in her stomach the size of a balloon. Her poor Mrs. Tappan.

She made the tea and asked Amparo if she would like a cup when she emerged from the bedroom.

Amparo was confused. No one ever offered her anything.

"I'm so sorry," Orla could only shake her head and keep saying the same thing.

Amanda stopped crying.

This show of emotion was almost unthinkable but at the same time, she simply did not care anymore at all. Most of the time she felt nothing, so to feel even upset was a relief.

"I am sorry Orla, for my -

"No, please don't apologize. What you have been through, Mrs.

Tappan-"

"Please, you are no longer in my employment. Call me Amanda.

She looked around the small flat, beautifully decorated, suggesting a pay scale above that of a household servant.

"I take it you are no longer with the Morgan family?"

Orla smiled.

"I met a gentleman. I did get married; I am Mrs. Ross now. I didn't last but two months with the Morgans."

Amanda felt a strange pang of guilt, "Oh, I'm- what happened?"

"None of the women in that household liked me, not the wife, not the other staff, not the teenage daughters. I was spat on, finally, by their fourteen-year-old girl, and I left. I wandered New York, barely eating for three days. I was so scared to use up the last of my money. Then I read an advertisement in the paper for a primary school on the upper West side. They needed cleaning staff. I certainly know how to do that. The principal hired me on the spot. That is where I met George Ross."

She said his name in such a way that her entire face lit up as a match that had struck coarse surface.

"After a month of seeing each other in passing he worked up the nerve to ask me to dinner. I only had one nice dress- he took me to a swanky hotel, The St. Regis. It was unbelievable and my dress still wasn't fancy enough, but nobody cared or noticed. They treated us like royalty. He asked me to marry him on our second date a week later. I had never met a man so lovely and charming before, and I said yes, and so, by the time you all had been in Mexico about six months, I was married. Soon after I quit my job cleaning at the school and became a seamstress and am studying to become a milliner. My husband works at the school and teaches Sunday school as well."

"My, how your circumstances have changed Orla. That is wonderful."

"I'm sorry to see yours have changed as well Mrs.- Amanda. Tell me what I can do to help you. I will do anything.", she said as she moved towards her new yet old friend and embraced her. Amanda began once again to weep.

Orla did not feel the need to speak her mind, that Edward Tappan was a monster, that she knew he had always been a monster, his vile face burned into her memory. The look on his face when he had tried to lift her skirt that night. She did not feel the need to acknowledge him lest they invoke the wrath of the devil.

Chapter 42

The door to Number 8 Hammersmith Tower was opened by a housekeeper Amanda did not recognize, who made her wait without an invitation inside. She supposed she did look like something the cat had dragged in.

Mrs. Heatherington was now as sober as a Catholic nun and had lost a good amount of weight so that she was both unrecognizable and yet the same. Her shocked face and giant embrace told Amanda her old neighbour had a genuine affection for her after all.

"They say it is my liver, and so I had to give up the drink totally. I didn't think I would be able to do it, but you know- people can change", she said softly, with a smile over tea with Amanda in the sitting room.

"Orla- Mrs. Ross- told you of my troubles?" Amanda muttered.

"Not in a sewing circle sort of way dear- we take no delight from your misfortune. I am really stunned that Edward would have taken your beautiful little family into such circumstances. And your trip back with a baby must have been harrowing. Tell me, how are you for money?"

"Well, I'm sorry to say that is one reason why I am here – and for the good fortune of running into Orla. We left in the middle of the night, and I did have cash. A good amount of money for travel, but there were three of us, by train, then boat, then a night in a hotel and purchasing food, then we seemed to be missing some cash, so I am afraid I am nearly- well, broke for the first time in my life- that is however until I get to the bank in Philly. I must get to Philadelphia to access my inheritance. I cannot ask Orla for a loan of anything, although she has offered me her last ten dollars for the week, she is limited to her husband's teacher salary-"

"How much do you need kid? Will $100 do it or would you like more- any number, tell me any number and you can have it. $1,000? I've always liked that number.

Amanda felt a lump in her throat. She had misjudged this woman for years. There had always been kindness there, simply hidden behind drink.

"I can't thank you enough for that Mrs. Heatherington, really. Orla has offered to mind Agatha and Amparo while I travel to Philadelphia. I must arrange the removal of my funds to bring back to New York."

Amanda found herself lowering her voice to a whisper as if Ed had spies everywhere.

"This is money Edward never knew about- the money that was left. He thought I cleared that account in the months before we moved to Mexico. He thought there was nothing left."

She grinned, nearly on the verge of tears.

Mrs. Heatherington, sober yes, but ever inappropriate, cocked an eyebrow, unable to help herself.

"And…how much is left?"

Amanda was too tired and triumphant to care for social graces and announced with satisfaction,

"I have over $20,000 US dollars in that account. Ed was eager to burn through the first twenty once we were married but his name was never on that account, and so that is all he ever thought was in there. He was unaware all this time that there was indeed double."

"A tidy sum, to be sure, enough to live on for years in the style you have always been accustomed to. Good for you." Mrs. Heatherington smiled.

"Oh, bugger, how I wish I could toast you with a glass of champagne, kid. I am so very proud of you."

"Well, that money will help me to get my children back. I can send money to my friends who swore to get the kids here by now. I sent a telegram the minute we landed in New York. If there is something keeping them from being able to get my children out, I can hire an attorney who will send letters to Edward to send the children to be with me until that dreadful revolution is over. It is no place for children."

"And then what will you do?"

"Well. I suppose, yes, I have been left with no choice,"

Her voice wavered, and her breath shaking,

"I shall seek a divorce if I even really need one, and if Doctor Tappan wants to be in the lives of his children, he can make an effort to come to visit them in New York, where they will be safe. Or he can come to his senses and leave a country that does not want him there."

"Quite right!",

Mrs. Heatherington smacked the table.

"Damn right!"

she swore,

"Children should be with their mother. Ok, let's get you some cash and get you on the next train to Philly!"

Chapter 43

The First Bank of Philadelphia was one of the oldest and most respected institutions in all of the United States. Amanda and her family had their accounts with them since she was in diapers herself, and so nothing felt like quite a touchstone, such a rock of safety and comfort as her knowing there was money in that account. She would secretly smile to herself over the years that her money remained safe, away from Edward and his bad habits.

Mrs. Heatherington had seen to it that Amanda purchased a lovely new outfit with a hat and gloves for her trip to Philly and took her to her very own hairdresser to put what remained of Amanda's hair into what they called a "bob".

"They are all the rage suddenly. Ladies just hacking off all their hair. I'm sure it won't last.", Mrs. Heatherington assured her.

Mr. Lancaster ushered her into his large office at the back of the bank and had her sit in an oversized leather armchair that made her feel quite childlike in stature. His office smelled of ink and had daisies in the window. Mr. Lancaster knew Amanda well and was always such a delight to deal with.

"Well, it has been a long time Mrs. Tappan; so nice to see you once again and to welcome you to First Bank. My assistant says you would like to remove your funds, or the majority of your funds, via cashier's cheque in order to open an account in New York. Is that right?"

"Yes, Mr. Lancaster, that is exactly right. I am unsure exactly, but I was thinking to leave $5,000 here in Philly and to move the majority of my estate to New York."

"Looking at your ledger here- yes, I see. The last visit we had for this account… was not from you, in fact, but Dr. Tappan that's right."

Amanda froze. Her breath caught; surely that was a mistake.

"I'm sorry- when was this?"

"February 1912, as it were, yes, I have some footnotes here, uh. He came about a withdrawal, yes."

"But…but …this isn't his account. My parents opened this for me when I was a child; this has only ever been my bank account. How could he-?"

"Well, he is your husband, after all.",

Mr. Lancaster looked at her down his nose and over his glasses.

"Unfortunately, Doctor Tappan did not have in his possession the bank book, nor the account number, 824. He was unable to withdraw any money that day. "

He continued apologetically,

"You see the Feds- that's the Federal Government- have really stepped things up in the banking industry- government regulation, getting tighter all the time. They insist that identification papers are not enough; the person in this case, you or your spouse, would need the bank book with them in order to take out money. Doctor Tappan came so unprepared he did not even have the account number. I told him I could have made an exception that day as we know you so well, I could have looked the other way for a doctor and forgo with the formality of needing the bank book, but without an account number, we could not just go into Mrs. Amanda Tappan's account. I would then be breaking all kinds of national banking rules. Not the sort of pickle I could put myself in for anyone."

"But if he had my bank book, or even just my bank account number, an account his name has never been on, you are telling me he could have taken out – every last dollar?"

Amanda asked through clenched teeth. She willed herself not to burst into a fit of tears.

While relieved Edward had not been able to clean her out, she was still seething.

Mr Lancaster happily shrugged and repeated himself,

"Well.....he is your husband after all. Said he was here on your behalf. He never did return, so I assumed you all had changed your mind."

"Do you remember how much he had wanted to take out?"

"I do; I worked with him myself; yes, if I remember correctly, he was looking to clear the account and close it; another thing I told him would require your signature at least. He said something about you all heading down to Mexico?"

Amanda stood,

"Thank you, Mr Lancaster. I would like all of my funds put into two cashier's cheques, and I will be closing my account with First Bank of Philadelphia, today."

Mr. Lancaster smiled. This young lady, who he had been waving at him in the bank lobby since she was about eight years old, seemed upset. He couldn't understand why exactly, but he was a man who enjoyed an easy life, so he didn't really think he needed to pry. Women were such strange creatures, after all.

"Well, all right Mrs. Tappan, give me a few moments, and I will get the paperwork for you – and your cheques. I do hope you enjoyed your stay in Mexico."

Chapter 44

A rain shower greeted Amanda when she returned from the bank in Philadelphia. She stepped off the train with her cashier's cheques in her bag, clutched to her tightly and walked the four blocks from Grand Central to her old apartment building. She wandered slowly, refusing to let the rain rush her. She fought back tears on the train, afraid to start sobbing in public, but now allowed her tears to do as they liked in the camouflage of the storm. She was drenched when she arrived to Mrs. Heatherington's penthouse, greeted with a warm blanket around her shoulders and the news that she could stay for as long as she liked. Amanda came in so pale and dishevelled, that Mrs. Heatherington,

"Call me Vivian from now on, please", she had insisted, put her straight into a hot bath.

Amanda fell into bed in a dark and warm guest room, Amparo and the baby sleeping on the chaise in the corner.

Amanda slept for three days. When she woke, she repaid Vivian's loan and had a telegram waiting for her from Philadelphia. The answer to her question, from the granddaughter of her beloved nanny. Julia Newsome was dead. There was nothing and no one in Philadelphia for her now. It was a ghost town full of Amanda's dead. Amanda did not shed a tear but let the telegram fall to the floor and went back to bed.

Mrs. Heatherington attempted to chat with Amparo, who she noticed took excellent care of the child, while Amanda barely roused for bits of food and drink at the older woman's insistence.

"I should have taken my children – I shouldn't have separated them.", she muttered on the rainy morning she finally woke. She sat on the edge of the bed in her slip, away from Vivian. The wet and dim sunlight shining in on her showed the weight she had lost in the days since her return to New York. Vivian thought she looked like an angel, albeit a sick one, bones protruding through satin.

"Amanda, I'm not sure there was much more you could have done in that situation my dear."

She said softly. On the one hand, Vivian thought it right to escape however one could, especially to protect a baby; on the other hand….to leave any child behind was madness.

"Would you not have looked rather conspicuous with your blonde-haired children at midnight on a train? Would that not have possibly put you in a spot of trouble? Ed refusing to let any of you leave, and what with that lunatic man Pancho, what's his name, wanting to murder Americans? That heathen. I think you did the only thing you could. Now, you must wait for a bit, send for your children, or rather, maybe you will have to go back, but I think if Edward has any shred of sanity or decency left within him, he will bring the children back to New York to their mother."

Vivian's words made sense and provided some comfort to Amanda. Everything had happened in such a rush that she was never sure if she had done the right thing if she was a hero or a monster.

Amanda was able to rent the bottom floor apartment in her old building- right across the hallway from Orla.

The landlord had been delighted to have her back and assumed the good doctor was right behind her.

"I do so apologize that we don't have any available

accommodation more befitting your family.",

The moustached man had said with a smile.

"The Dr. is returning then soon?"

"Yes, of course," Amanda had lied with a smile to rival his.

"And while I understand this isn't our previous penthouse, this flat will work out just fine for now.", she assured him.

She knew in time, when Dr. Tappan did not return, that so long as she paid her rent, there would be no further intrusive questions.

Everything in her life was turning into a fabrication, a figment of her own imagination. Everything in her life had been a lie; only previously, she was not the one spinning those webs, but her husband. She felt she was constantly now brushing the cobwebs off her face, attempting to wipe away the lies. Everything, or nearly everything, he had ever told her had been false. Of this, she was now sure. Their entire life together, from courtship to marriage and even their children, all had been a staged manipulation by a man, older, smarter, and dangerous.

"Said the spider to the fly," she mused.

"I beg your pardon?" the landlord spun on his heel, thinking he had misheard something as he left her.

"Oh, just remembering some old prose." she again flashed the fake smile she was so adept at putting on.

Chapter 45

The weeks fell into months, and many telegrams to Edward went ignored. Diego had sent no word, had not answered his telegrams and there was similar silence from Raquel. Amanda was unsure if Raquel had even made it to San Francisco. If she had, why hadn't she been in touch? Amanda had sent telegrams to the aunt in California. What if the address was wrong and they never arrived to her? What if this silence meant they were all dead? Had Pancho Villa and his men found their blue blood hiding away in closets in their mountaintop mansions?

This silence drove Amanda to the edge of her abilities. Some nights, she did not sleep at all. She often would go forty-eight hours or more without a wink. Other times, she would crash like a windup toy whose momentum was gone. She could scarcely eat, and she found Orla and Vivian seemed to take turns pounding on her door to make sure she was still with them, kindly forcing and cajoling her into eating. During this time, Amparo began to pick up English as if in a hurry. She cared for the baby round the clock, began to venture out for groceries and handle affairs for Amanda. The only time Amanda left the house anymore was to go to the bank, but most days, she simply signed checks for what she could, and Amparo bought food with cash. If it was not for Amparo, Amanda would have stopped bathing and brushing her teeth. She would wear the same silk dresses until they began to reek, and Amparo would stand in front of her with her goofy grin, holding a new dress. Amanda would stand silently and let the woman undress her. Amparo occasionally was able to get her into the bath, and occasionally was greeted with the odd slap, but always got her mistress into a new, freshly laundered dress.

Amparo held no ill will towards this strange new Señora Tappan.

She understood instinctively that nothing about this was normal. She had watched Amanda fade, seemingly covering herself in layers, disappearing deep into her chrysalis. She knew Amanda was not well. Amparo could have quit and returned to Mexico, but she liked Amanda. She felt a loyalty she could not articulate, so she just kept chugging along. This woman needed her, and she felt, perhaps, she needed her as well. Working for the Tappans, and especially now with the baby, gave her life a purpose she had not known she needed. Amparo felt important for the first time in her life, needed, perhaps even loved, every time that baby's face would devour Amparo's with affection.

Amanda had met with an attorney who was trying to navigate the strange waters of a mother leaving her children in a foreign land with their father, bringing a baby without the permission of the father back to the United States and the added aggravation of verifying the validity of the marriage that was now in question. All of this was compounded by the stress of the actions having taken place during a revolution that was still ongoing.

Mr. Malcom Tate, attorney at law, explained to her that this whole process, "could take some time".

Some days, all Amanda could do was read the papers, scribbling furious notes about U.S. and Mexican relations alongside small little pieces of poems to the children in the margins of the newspapers. On other days, she could not rise from her bed. She often felt she did not know herself or her surroundings.

Amanda was fearful of not being able to be reunited with her older children and distraught at the thought of the children being apart from each other as well- what sort of favouritism would the older two think had taken place? She had decided, in haste, but also in the fervent belief she would be saving all of her children by doing what she did that night. She thought it would be days, a week, maybe a month at most until her children were brought to her by either Raquel or Diego or both. Now, it was more than two months, and she did not know if she should return or stay. She missed her children terribly. Not a night went by that she didn't find tears on her cheeks, so often they fell now that she didn't even notice until her face was soaking. She had started drinking every night to try and sleep. Some nights, she would have to get blackout drunk, and the very patient Amparo would roll her into her bed. Dragging her limp form from wherever she ended up to her bed was not a chore for Amparo, as there was very little of Amanda left to drag.

Another gin-soaked night found the following morning stormy, and Amparo opened the door to the unexpected sight of Leonor standing at the threshold.

"Donde esta la Señora- where is she?" she scowled at the maid, thrusting her fur and bag into the woman's hands and marching into the apartment, taking stock as if she was some sort of military commander.

"You look awful.", she tsked at her sister-in-law, who she found sprawled on the settee in the front room.

"Hair matted, shoes on, and half asleep. I suppose it makes sense. Well, tell that girl of yours to fetch me some coffee- we have much to discuss."

"My God, you really do look like a corpse- what has come over you?"

Amanda eyed her for a moment, weary of this apparition.

“How did you find me?” Amanda wondered. If Leonor had found her, Ed was sure to follow.

“Like it was difficult? Your old apartment building, for crying out loud Amanda it was the first place I looked. I asked your landlord if you were here and voila.

“I wonder if you could tell me where my children are, dear cuñada”, Amanda called her sister-in-law.

“You left them, dear hermana”, Leonor said slightly, softly mocking, calling her sister.

“I am not sure if I am happy to see you Leonor- why are you here?”

“Ed has no intention of letting the children go. He is prepared to fight you tooth and nail to get the baby back, but right now…well, right now, it appears he is enjoying his – freedom.”

“What do you mean?”

“Well, he is absolutely traipsing about the place como un “chino libre.”

Amanda looked at her sister-in-law, “Isn’t that just another way to say……I do not know the slang, but.”

“Yes, “Leonor interrupted.

“…yes, he is as good as a free Chinamen….seeing all kinds of women, now that his wife is gone and he has no baby in the house. He is acting as though he is a widower; he is all but stopping short of saying that he is a widower. Pancho Villa’s men have left him alone it seems. Whatever deal they brokered has kept your older children safe. Not sure about your absconding friends. The Russian broad fled for California; who knows where that lothario went."

"Why are you here Leonor?" she asked again.

"Well, Ed did send to me to try and talk some sense into you. Nobody understands what this stunt of yours was."

"They were going to kill me."

"Who angel? Who was trying to kill you?"

"Those bandits."

"So, you leave your first two children behind, do you then? It really is disgraceful carry on, especially by someone of your station. The children- your children have of course, been asking about you."

Amanda stared at her, "So they are still with him?"

Amanda was up and at the liquor cabinet despite it being eleven a.m.

"Well, yes, where did you expect them to be? Hand me a glass of something, would you? Do you have any scotch? Since we seem to be imbibing at this hour?"

Leonor smiled up at Amanda, who poured two glasses of the whiskey she had left. She handed one to Leonor, who stood beside her.

She took a soft and tender tone with her sister-in-law.

"Now, Amanda, maybe if you smartened up a bit and came back, Ed would forgive you, and we could put all this ugliness behind us." she touched Amanda's arm, a rare moment of affection.

Amanda flinched as if she had been scalded and glared at this woman she knew had never liked her.

"He treated me like I was stupid, then he treated me like I was crazy, and when I figured out my suspicions were correct, he treated me like a disobedient child. Then he threatened to kill me, almost did, and tried to throw me down the stairs. I will never go back to him or to Mexico, where they kill their own people to make a point and murder young women because they look like me.'"

Amanda started to tremble and steadied herself to bring the glass to her lips. She was unsure if she was still drunk from the night before or perhaps dreaming. Maybe Leonor wasn't even really there.

"Lupe promised me she would look after my kids until Diego or Raquel could get them out of the country; here to me- that should have only taken a week or two, and it has been, I don't know how many weeks!! And what, my children are just there this whole time, and no one thinks to move this along? You're telling me my friends left and left my babies with Ed?"

"This won't go well for you, Amanda. Edward is connected, in Mexico and here in the U.S."

The baby had started to fuss, so Amparo went to attend to her in the bedroom and did not hear the following exchange.

Leonor was calm, sipping her morning whiskey and lit a cigarette, without meeting Amanda's eyes, said as breezily as if she was discussing the weather,

"Look at you- bloodshot eyes, you look like some street tramp.", she purred.

"If it were not for that little India, you would not even be fit to mind the baby you stole. That child has a home with siblings and servants and a father. What are you going to do here? Alone? What will you do if Amparo disappears?" she finally looked at Amanda's pitiful face.

"Let me take the baby back to her family. The revolution is almost over; you can come back when things have calmed down, and tempers have cooled- Edward's most of all. Darling....this is absurd. I want what is best for you and your family. Eddie, you know, he has never met a stack of cash he didn't like; he got – swept away with his excitement at his many opportunities in Mexico."

"He was running guns for them."

"For whom, my dear?"

"I- I am not sure, who exactly, but he was involved-"

"And how do you know this?" Leonor smoked, ever relaxed, her face revealing nothing.

"I- I- that man – that man that killed Graciela, that broke into our house. Raquel said it as well; Edward was involved in things...he shouldn't have been, and the night he disappeared, it turned out he was in jail!"

"All of these things can be explained away Amanda. Did you ever stop to think that maybe you have gotten all of this wrong? That Raquel and Diego have, how do you say- motivos- motives, ulterior motives. Raquel is a failing businesswoman, needs cash and wants to cause trouble for Eddie because he didn't marry her. Diego has eyes for you- also would like to cause trouble, perhaps for Eddie and you. Most importantly of all, my dear, you have not been yourself since this last pregnancy."

Leonor now looked at Amanda with a kind of pity that turned Amanda inside out. The crack inside her was growing bigger. She did not know if she was angry or frightened, or despondent. She felt bile bubbling in her stomach. It had been too long since she had eaten and too soon since her last drink. Amanda began to sway. Her legs began to buckle, and Leonor simply stood up and put her strong arms around Amanda's now almost emaciated frame. She would take convincing, Leonor knew, but not much.

The next morning, the three women stood in the front hallway, all eyes downcast. Leonor stood stoically. She did not relish her duty.

"Well, now…," she stood ready to take the baby with her back to Edward.

"Amanda, hand me the girl."

Amparo felt the urgency of what felt like needing to urinate. Her stomach felt bad, and she was not happy. She watched her mistress as she held the baby. It was the right thing to do; they all knew it, and yet Amparo began to cry.

Leonor began again, "Mrs. Tappan, Señora Tappan, give me the baby."

Amanda handed the baby calmly to Amparo and suddenly launched upon Leonor with desperate violence, open hands quickly slapping her across the nose like a misbehaving dog.

"Get out", she growled lowly, almost softly.

Leonor did not defend herself, the shock of this aggression making her take unexpected steps backwards into the hallway.

"Do not ever come back here."

"Amanda, my God in heaven, you are making a mistake!"

Amanda slammed the door to her sister-in-law, shrieking at her to go to hell.

Amparo and the baby cried together. Amanda, for once, did not.

After a moment of silence, where Amparo quieted the baby and Amanda slid to the floor, listening to hear Leonor's footsteps fade down the hall, she looked up at her companion. Amparo had been so good, leaving everything behind to protect her and this child. Amanda knew her children needed to be together. She could not let her baby go with Leonor. There was something frightening about that, but Amparo, Amparo was like a guardian angel. Amanda didn't feel well.

Amanda knew what she had to do for her baby, and her children.

"She is going with you.", she told Amparo quietly.

"No entiendo Señora". She did not understand.

"Then let me explain."

1926

Arthur, tall and tan in the summer sun, joined his little sister in the garden. At eighteen, he was taller than their father, with a full head of now dark hair, slicked back, his face clean-shaven to reveal a deep dimple in his chin and thin, serious lips. He was a handsome young man, every bit both of his parents in appearance and demeanour.

"Keep your hands out of the fountain," he chastised Amelia.

"You are not a child."

At sixteen, Amelia was blossoming like the floral inhabitants in the garden. Every spring, she grew taller and more beautiful. She was ripening from a green bud and quiet infant into a woman. Her cherubic face was round and plain, yet beautiful. She styled her blonde hair and applied her lipstick like that Clara Bow, and her eyes were a blue reminiscent of the damask found on fine china.

"Mother won't recognize us", she beamed at him, dipping her fingers in once again and flicking the water off her fingertips towards her brother.

"This is a linen suit if you don't mind. Knock it off, kid."

He glanced at his pocket watch.

"She is due within the hour- do not get me wet. Where is Aggie?"

Amelia's face fell.

"She is still in her bedroom; she insists she is not coming downstairs to meet her."

"I am betting she will change her mind when she hears mother is here. If not, I will go and drag her down."

"Arthur- you mustn't force her. That is something he would do. You must understand, Agatha doesn't remember her. This whole situation has been so exceedingly difficult for her, and she is only a little girl."

"She's thirteen, not three. She could have gone with you and me two years ago when we went to visit Manhattan, but no, she wanted to stay here, angry. She wanted to sit in her temper, also like him. Not seeing one's mother for years isn't exactly what any of us wanted, but what could anyone do? That visit was invaluable to me, and I know you enjoyed being able to spend time with our mother as well."

"I couldn't believe that I remembered her. That visit was wonderful- I mean before she..''

"Yes, you need not mention it."

"Before she got sick again", she shrugged.

"If only Agatha would try to understand, mother isn't well. Diego says she suffers from-"

"I have no interest in what Diego says she suffers from, that old quack. He used to be a real doctor, at least that is according to father."

Amelia shrugged again, getting frustrated,

"He is still a real doctor", she insisted.

"If Agatha wouldn't go to her, well, that left mother no choice but to come to us. It is monumental she was able to overcome her fear and finally return to Mexico, after everything that happened. Her nerves are very bad; they impede her from travel."

"You don't know everything that happened- none of us do…" he grew quiet for a moment, then shook his head with a sort of disgust,

"I remember hiding with her and the two of you in a back closet one night. We were there for what felt like an eternity- then, days later, she was gone, and the baby was gone. Then, one day, Aggie was back with Amparo. Still, no one would explain where mother had gone or why, but I knew. I knew it had something to do with the revolution. Listen, kid, I'm not in the mood to regurgitate the same old information. Things happened, mistakes were made, and it is time to move on. If Agatha insists on being stubborn-"

"I'm here now, aren't I?" Agatha interrupted as she joined her older siblings in the garden.

Agatha had grown into a vision of loveliness in the strange pause between child and woman. She was a tall and very slender girl; her ginger-coloured hair long ago darkened to that almost blood red, emerald green eyes so large they were distracting and the beginnings of a chiselled face. She was sullen, anxious. She wanted her mother more than anything, but she hated the very thought of her. The telephone calls and letters over the years had never been enough. The trunks full of American goodies, Hershey's chocolate and Whitman's candies, periodicals in English, and clothing from New York, over the years, became painful reminders of her want to be with them, yet she remained absent.

The child yearned for a stranger, and she knew not to trust strangers.

"Aggie", Amelia smiled.

"You've changed your mind."

"I don't want to discuss it. Where is she then?"

As the afternoon moved on, and Amanda Tappan was now more than two hours late, Arthur excused himself.

"I will telephone father at his office and Diego and see if they have heard anything, as in who was to collect her at the train station, that sort of thing."

He had begun to pace nervously, and Arturo never got nervous.

Amparo brought out a pitcher of limonada to the children without a word. Still, after all these years, Amparo was a mostly silent entity, a detail in the background of a family portrait.

Agatha had an attachment to Amparo she dared not speak, for she knew it was not appropriate to love one's creada, but she always knew it was she that had kept her safe as a baby from Manhattan back down to Mexico City. The maid could have abandoned her at any point in the journey, sold her even, but instead brought her back safely to her father's home.

"A precious package", Amparo had always told Guadalupe and Marta, with her odd smile and lazy eye.

Aggie was reticent with her as well because there was a small, inconsolable part of her that knew she loved the Indian woman but at the same time hated her for not telling her mother no. For not insisting she come back with them, *for* them.

Guadalupe followed shortly and brought the young girls out cucumber water and tried to convince them to eat something, leaving a bowl of melon and mango on the table by the mermaid fountain. She saw the limonada left by Amparo and smiled. Everyone in the household was nervous with anticipation.

Guadalupe had been the only mother Agatha had ever known. Lupe the housekeeper, and Amelia, only three years older than her, but bossy and controlling, as demanding as any mother could get.

They had all patched their way through life after the baby was returned without la Señora.

As the afternoon went from bright and full of possibility, the sun moved over the mountains of Mexico City and began to throw long shadows on the mermaid fountain. The rest of the garden began to feel cold. Agatha returned upstairs, silently, to her room.

Amelia remained seated, stubborn, at the mermaid fountain; she and the mermaid stoned-faced companions.

She began to pick at her fingernails, nameless emotions rising into her small frame. She would not cry for a woman she could not remember for most of her life. She is sick; everyone told her all her life. Father had called her a lunatic. Whispers of a monster. Rumours of the sanitorium, the Institution, Diego had called it.

As Amelia sat shivering slightly, a single, weary, orange and black monarch butterfly flew down and perched upon her hair, unbeknownst to her human friend. They sat together to wait.

The slip of paper was yellow with age, as if she had written the letter long ago and had held onto it for years in hopes of changing her mind or the outcome. Hoping for a different way. Her once beautiful penmanship had morphed into something altogether reminiscent of who she was and telling of who she had become. Nearly unrecognizable, save for the familiar flick of a t, or swirl on an m, it stood on the page disjointed, halting, a very faint scrawl of an unnamed illness. Many words filled the area, but only very few were legible.

"My children,

Forgive me. Canta y no llores.

We should be together; however, I don't feel well. I have not felt healthy in some time.

Always remember, as I gave you life, you gave me mine.

I think I might like to sleep forever with you in my arms.

I miss you all so much and I will see you again soon, very soon.

You are etched into every hidden place of my heart.

I am sorry that I have not been in this life what you needed me to be.

-Mama"

Edward, grey in the temples now and with lines on his face to mirror those on the paper before him, viewed the words with a black fury raging like the choking smoke of an inferno. He crumpled the apology, meant for his children and thew it into the fire.

As the October winds swept through colder and leaving them yearning to find warmth again, huge blankets of orange and black butterflies lifted as one into the air. The shorter days had come, the temperature reminding them it was time. It was time to go to the mountain. It was time for winter and to follow the path to sleep now, to the Oyamels. To the Oyamels that called their name, to the fir trees of their sacred Mexico, to bask in the warmth of the Sun God one last time. It was time to stretch their filament wings in the rays of the sun and feel the heat in every fibre and membrane in the whole of their being. The sick and the dying would not make it back, but the rest, they remembered their journey home- the journey that they had never flown before but knew by instinct, as if there were compasses instead of hearts beating within them. They followed the calling of the mountains and the songs of the hummingbirds. They followed the maps made by the rivers and the whispers of the trees. They were following the ties that bound them together, back and back again, to their beloved Mexico. High into the trees they fell, blankets of orange and black movement, and into the rivers they appeared to be dancing, swirling, soft and silent landings of thirsty creatures ready to find their final resting place.

She closed her eyes, slowed her breath, and pulled in her wings.

Made in the USA
Monee, IL
19 November 2024

70525287R00193